Brass Eagle

Also by Margaret Duffy:

Death of a Raven

A Murder of Crows

Brass Eagle

Margaret Duffy

St. Martin's Press
New York

Library of Congress Cataloging-in-Publication Data

Duffy, Margaret.
     Brass eagle / Margaret Duffy.
        p.   cm.
     ISBN 0-312-02880-6
     I. Title.
   PR6054.U397B74   1989
   823'.914—dc19   89-4101
                                                 CIP

First published in Great Britain by Judy Piatkus (Publishers) Ltd.

First U.S. Edition

10 9 8 7 6 5 4 3 2 1

Justin

Even the most dedicated novelist hopes to avoid bringing her first child into the world within the four walls of a bookshop, no matter how illustrious the establishment. With this firmly in mind I had done my mental arithmetic very carefully. *Two for Joy* was being rushed into print in time to lure Christmas shoppers, publication date December 12th. The author's offspring was due to put in an appearance two or three days after this. Did one agree or not to the signing session at an Oxford Street bookshop?

Ingrid Langley decided not to disappoint her readers and I blithely handed over the responsibility for the arrangements to my agent. This gentleman sighed in long-suffering fashion and went away to devise a scheme the eventual complexity of which rivalled plans to storm a foreign embassy. That he is also the child's father, my husband and an army officer perhaps explains the diligence.

With this, as it were, quadruple care and protection, I arrived by taxi at a quarter past ten, fifteen minutes before the signing session was due to start. Snug in my shaggy fake fur I didn't really look pregnant. Careful perusal in the mirror before leaving Patrick's *pied à terre* had confirmed this and I was ignoring his remark that the coat made me resemble a well-groomed yak. I never seem to be quite quick enough to compose a suitable riposte to his well-aimed but good-natured derision in the time available.

In his rôles of husband and father he stood on the pavement outside my destination, the collar of his grey leather jacket turned up against the cold. At this particular moment a casting director seeking an unknown to play the part of a literary agent would have passed him by without a second glance. If, on the other hand, he had been looking for someone to portray an authoritative upholder of the Queen's peace he would have fallen upon Patrick's neck with tears in his eyes. This for Patrick – always careful never to look like a soldier when not in uniform – was an unusual slip and gave some indication as to his distracted state of mind at the prospect of being a father for the first time.

'Are you okay?' he asked when he had paid off the taxi and was helping me out as though I was constructed of spun glass.

'I only saw you half an hour ago,' I told him. 'Relax.'

'Are you sure you'll know when it starts to happen?'

I took a deep breath. Ye gods, how many times had he asked me this? 'Of course. Either I'll start to get pains or the waters will break. Please don't worry so much – you're making me nervous. Anyway, first babies are never in a hurry to arrive.'

He gazed down at me. 'I'll stay with you – all the way through.'

He had said this before too and I was sure now that he was addressing the part of Patrick Gillard which quailed from seeing his child born. Every time he said it he knew he was committing himself more deeply to the promise and each time my eyes misted a little. I could picture him in mask and gown in the delivery room, whiter than the bleached linen around him, a man afraid of nothing on this planet but the prospect of his wife suffering agonies or worse.

I squeezed his arm. 'You won't be able to if I have to have a Caesarean.' There was the beginnings of a wish that this would be the case. Giving birth is messy and painful but it would be far worse if I knew he was going through hell every time I yelled.

The bookshop is large, inhabiting several floors of an old building. The ground floor, as might be expected, is devoted to both fiction and non-fiction, paperbacks nearest the entrance doors. Beneath this is a vast basement piled with textbooks of all kinds and everything concerning computer studies. The other floors contain stationery and map departments, a room with HMSO publications and an antiquarian bookshop in the attic. It is a treasure house and I was looking forward to a browse when the signing session was over.

I made a detour through the children's department taking more notice than usual of the brightly coloured mobiles and little seats and tables. A huge glittering cardboard dragon with red eyes that flashed on and off promoted a reissue of the Tolkien stories. Perhaps, in the not too distant future, I would be reading them to someone small sitting on my knee.

The manager and I are old friends, one of the reasons I had agreed to come. He advanced and smiling broadly flourished his handkerchief over the chair by the antique desk that was kept for such occasions. I removed my coat and everyone within earshot smiled too when I requested that they move both desk and chair away from the wall a little to enable me to squeeze in my larger than usual self.

'You're an angel, Hugh,' I said. 'And doubly so if you ask someone to make us some coffee.' There was no need for me to introduce Patrick as the two men had met several times. They shook hands, confirming my guess that Patrick hadn't entered the bookshop before my arrival but had carried out a surveillance to the rear of it. Quite a few terrorist and other organisations of that ilk would like to put a bullet in Major Gillard and his wife.

'Anything untoward?' I enquired when Hugh had gone away to arrange refreshments. The query was really to take Patrick's mind off everything else.

'Dustbins,' he replied absent-mindedly. 'A broken ladder. Someone's bike. A drunk.'

'It's a bit early in the day for a drunk.'

'That's what I told him. He pointed out that he was a meths drinker — they're stoned all the time.'

'Oh, you mean Terry.' Terry Meadows is the third member of our small MI5 team.

'So I poured some of the stuff all over him,' Patrick went on as though I hadn't spoken. 'To make him smell right. Never really seems to get to grips with his cover, does young Terry.'

My heart went out to Terry but I knew precisely what Patrick meant. Terry revels in living rough if it means he can be in the hills with a gun in one hand and a grenade in the other. Ask him to be a tramp or down-and-out for a few hours — and Patrick always insists that this entails giving clean clothing to such a person and donning their garments — and he is apt to fall

3

short. This has sometimes forced Patrick to take on the more unsavoury rôles himself, more often than not revolting his immediate subordinate.

The desk was situated between the travel section and a large stand where the fiction department commenced. This had been nearly emptied of other books and filled with copies of *Two for Joy*. I always have an absolute horror of not one copy being sold.

'Terry asked me to tell you that there's a stray kitten in the alley,' Patrick said.

Everyone knows about my weakness when confronted by small lost animals of any kind, even worms drowning in puddles. I said, 'Maggie wants a kitten. She had to get rid of that Irish Wolfhound after it started to chew up her flat.'

'I know.'

'Well?' I said impatiently.

'Now who's fretting?' he teased.

Nine months minus a few days pregnant my tolerance was not all it should have been. 'Patrick...' I began warningly.

He took a tin opener from his pocket and dangled it beneath my nose. 'It scoffed almost the whole of a small can of giraffe and porcupine. Or was it stingray and anchovy? I can't remember. Terry's going to pop it under his coat when he goes home. Satisfied?'

'That's if he can find it,' I remarked grimly, convinced that he wouldn't look very far.

'Short of chaining it to a dustbin...' Patrick said on a sigh.

In all probability any members of the KGB listening to this conversation would have overheard in open mouthed disbelief or would have assumed us to be talking in code. The fact that two of MI5's operatives were really concerning themselves over the fate of one kitten would not have occurred to them. They find equally confusing the English ability to spy hunt, smiling, over cucumber sandwiches and against a background of the muted footfalls of servants and the clink of expensive bone china tea ware.

'It's snowing,' said Patrick, breaking into my thoughts. 'That'll keep them away.'

'On the contrary,' I told him. 'It'll drive people in for shelter.'

Half an hour later I was wishing that the snow would cease such was the inrush of people into the shop. It became impossible to discern the genuine bookbuyers from those merely wishing a roof over their heads. They shoved, jostled and stared and I began to feel like an exhibit in a zoo. Two copies of *Two for Joy* were sold.

'Just say the word,' Patrick said, getting restless.

'Give it another half hour?' I suggested.

'You don't look too good.'

'Indigestion,' I replied. 'I've had it for the best part of two days. So would you if someone was kicking you in the ribs all the time.'

As I spoke it occurred to me that in actual fact I had been given a respite from the energetic feet of our offspring and wondered fleetingly if the infant had turned round. Not a breech birth, dear God, please don't let it be a breech birth.

Patrick acquired a chair and sat down. 'Seen the papers this morning?'

'I didn't have time to buy one,' I said. We didn't have one delivered to the flat.

'Another scientist has killed himself.'

'Surely that's the fourth!'

He nodded. 'First Jones, then Peterson and Cook. Now Alex Haywood. And like the three others he worked at a Research Establishment. Daws says that Whitehall's echoing with tom-toms but no one is sure whether to call in us, Special Branch or let the various police authorities sort it out until something turns up that offers strong leads.'

Colonel Richard Daws is our boss. Head of D12, the small department set up within M15 to counter foreign interference with the Security Services, he is not renowned for succumbing to hysterics in public. But I knew that he was very worried indeed by this spate of quite inexplicable suicides by government scientists.

'It's not *quite* in our field,' I said, aware that Colonel Richard saw enemies of his country beneath every bed, behind every tree killed by Dutch Elm disease, and holding the hands of every gangster in the land.

'It is if harassment is involved. We're concerned with interference to people who have signed the Official Secrets Act,'

5

Patrick said under his breath, taking a copy of *Two for Joy* from a woman for me to sign. 'You know that.'

Of course I did. I also thought the possibility of this being the case and it coming within our field of enquiry to be such a long shot as to be right over the horizon. I could envisage long, tedious and emotionally draining interviews with next of kin, women no doubt of such virulence that one would have to look no further for the reason their husbands decided to leave this world.

'Ingrid, you're unhappy,' said Patrick, wrapping the book while an assistant dealt with the money.

'It's hot in here,' I grumbled.

Perhaps at this point my real fans arrived for we became very busy. An hour later, and slightly fortified by more coffee and biscuits, I was still signing, the cash register bleeping ceaselessly. Any energy provided by the refreshments, however, had been more than cancelled out by the sheer discomfort resulting from their consumption. Surprised, and pausing for a moment in what I was doing, I discovered that my forehead was moist with sweat and I was quite literally writhing in my seat. Moreover, a glance in that direction revealed that the bulge of our firstborn was no longer just below my ribs but much lower, right in my lap.

Langleys never really panic.

I took a proffered book, opened it and wrote. Then, despite everything, giggled.

'Are you?' asked the customer, an attractive young woman, reading over my shoulder.

'Looks like it,' I muttered, reaching for another copy.

'Oh, please let me have that one. Just sign underneath,' she cried, and everyone crowded round the desk.

'Are you?' demanded a dozen voices at once but I wasn't in a position to answer them, squirming to a spasm so strong that I grabbed Patrick's hand and hung on. It was quite unnecessary for him to read what I had inadvertently written; he just took one look at me and knew.

'Is this a red alert?' he asked, with only the slightest tremor in his voice.

The shattering realization that I had been in labour for the best part of two days, and another appalling contraction, again robbed me of speech.

6

'Ingrid, answer me!' he said, louder, almost his army bark.

'Yes,' I gasped and he was gone, running with his slightly limping gait to find Terry and the two-way radio.

I continued to sign copies and everyone wanted me to add those magic words, 'I'm in labour.' It gave me something to think about until the ambulance came but even the five minutes or so it took was too long and Hugh was holding my hands by the time it did. I stood up and discovered that walking was out of the question. Pain scythed through me and the world revolved like a multi-coloured merry-go-round.

Then I was borne aloft in a cloud of methylated spirit fumes and proceeded thus to the ambulance. Laid down carefully within I kept hold of Terry. At that moment he was the strength I needed and he grinned down at me; brown eyes, thick glossy light brown hair, just a few freckles on his nose. I think I laughed when the doors were closed and I knew he was coming as well for I'm very fond of Terry. But the sound slithered up into a kind of strange shriek as a pain like a white hot sword thrust shafted through me.

'Organisation,' said Patrick, appearing in my line of vision and handing a tabby kitten to the ambulance man who popped it in a cardboard box. He took both my hands in his, his pallor giving the clue as to why he hadn't carried me.

'No,' I panted, pain making me like a fractious child. 'I must hold *yours.*' Agony again exploded within me and I tried to keep quiet but was never sure afterwards whether the noise was me or the siren of the ambulance. The spasms peaked, merged into something that simply couldn't be borne — when I know I did shriek — and then transformed themselves into something else that I could put to use. Was one really supposed to push?

One was. The ambulance man, a kindly soul surely near retirement age, examined me gently, offered gas which I declined, and then told me to go for gold.

We were all in it together; never have four people worked as such a team. I'm prepared to swear under oath that it was Terry who had pulled my pants down. It must have been, the ambulance man was donning plastic gloves at the time and I was still holding Patrick's hands. A while later, the vehicle seemingly at rest in a traffic jam, he rescued his wrung fingers, wincing, and I gripped his wrists instead, no longer in extremis.

'There's been an accident!' yelled the driver. 'I'll try and get round another way.' The siren blared into the whirling snow.

Labour means exactly what it says but I was fitter than average, and in between the strong, fierce surges there were moments of rest when I gazed up at Patrick and he kissed my eyes and lips. Then it seemed that it was just me in conflict with my own heaving body and I drew up my knees and groaned.

'Don't push!' ordered the ambulance man and I opened my eyes to see Terry watching, utterly fascinated, as a tiny pair of scissors were utilised at the business end. The ambulance lurched around a bend just as the baby's head was born and then there was a slithering slippery sensation and a warmth that felt like a spurt of blood on my thigh.

Another sound came into existence, emanating from a furious small person with a mop of sticky black hair. I told myself that I wasn't dreaming all this, our son really had arrived somewhere in a backstreet of London, and in a hell of a hurry.

I looked down at him and blue eyes looked back at me. They would almost certainly soon change colour to grey, I decided immediately, like his father's. Therefore he would be called Justin, Patrick's second name. Our lighthearted reference to him as Siegfried throughout the pregnancy no longer made any sense now he had put in an appearance.

The tiny face crumpled like a handful of red velvet and he started to wail again. Even someone new to the game could tell that he was hungry.

Chapter One

Alex Haywood had killed himself very thoroughly by driving over the high chalk cliffs of Beachy Head in Sussex. Even though the tide had been in at the time the vehicle had exploded after hitting rocks. Subsequent investigation of the wreckage washed ashore had resulted in the discovery that several plastic containers filled with petrol had been loaded into the boot. Of Haywood himself little was found; a shoe, his wallet with money still in it, and a piece of scorched cloth from his Harris tweed jacket. No one had expected there to be recognisable remains for the force of the huge blast had broken several windows in nearby holiday chalets. Then, a fortnight later and after heavy gales, a badly decomposed arm was washed up on Brighton Beach.

'It's pretty conclusive,' said Patrick, looking out of the window for once and not at his baby son.

'You don't sound quite sure,' I commented.

He smiled at me and then the grey eyes drifted irresistibly down for another fleeting gloat. In the wake of Patrick's appalling injuries sustained during the Falklands War, Justin's existence is something of a miracle. 'Let me do that,' he begged.

I handed over bottle and baby, the two parting company with a sound akin to a sucker fish sundering from its whale. Justin's mouth immediately re-adjusted for a bellow but his father deftly reunited him with his passion in life before he had time to draw the necessary breath.

Patrick said, 'There was nothing to identify positively except that the hand was wearing a wedding ring that Haywood's wife thinks was his. So we might have to accept that it was all that remained of him and hadn't been pinched from the anatomy

11

lecture room of some teaching hospital. It had been in the water too long for fingerprints to have survived – not that government employees are yet required to provide them.'

'Surely,' I said, 'an arm taken from a hospital lab would look different from one torn from a man's body in an explosion.'

He regarded me solemnly. 'Sorry. My idea of black comedy. I wasn't serious.'

'You were,' I insisted. 'You have a devious mind and it works like that. I've a feeling you were trying to spare me the more revolting details of what someone might do with an anatomy specimen to make it look as though it had been severed in a serious accident.'

'You were feeling queasy yesterday,' he reminded me, a quirk to his mouth.

Perhaps it *was* unusual to be suffering from morning sickness after the event. 'I'm all right now,' I assured him. 'Was there positive identification in the other three cases?'

After a moment's thought Patrick said, 'They didn't go in for high drama. Jones shot himself with his uncle's shotgun, Peterson put a length of hose into his car connected to the exhaust, and Cook slashed his wrists.'

'It's usually women who slash their wrists,' I remarked.

'Too right,' he agreed meaningfully.

'Oh,' I said. 'Like that was it?'

'A lover's tiff. The other guy works in a night club. I really think we can leave Cook out of the case. He was a very unimportant scientific officer. The others were much bigger fish.'

'But *is* there a case?' I queried. 'A real connection?'

'There might be.'

'I have signed the Official Secrets Act,' I pointed out.

My husband laughed softly and took advantage of Justin's eyelids drooping sleepily to sit him up for burping purposes. Justin is a most rewarding burper.

'What's so funny?' I asked.

'You're a mite prickly.'

I prepared to explode with justifiable wrath, somehow choked it all back and said instead, 'You saw our Richard yesterday and I've yet to hear what his views are on my carrying on. I want to continue working with you more than anything and I also want to write. Any suggestions as to how I can cut myself into two or has the decision been made for me?'

Justin belched resoundingly and was rewarded with the rest of his 10 a.m. feed. The three of us had been at home in our Devon cottage for just over a week and I was doing as instructed by taking life very quietly. The system in the maternity unit had not been geared up to fit thirty six year olds who produce their first in the ambulance. The staff had not been able to decide whether to keep me in for a fortnight or send me back into the world with all the other mothers after forty-eight hours, beds being at a premium. So a compromise had been reached and I had stayed in for three days and was then discharged on condition that Patrick took time off to look after me. Childless colonels being shy of having to write down the word 'maternity' we were both officially taking two weeks' compassionate leave, actually slightly more because of Christmas. Patrick's summons to London the previous day had come as a surprise.

Patrick was lost in thought, twirling a tendril of Justin's hair around a finger. Then he said, 'The nanny's due to arrive on March 22nd − just as you'd planned it, to give yourself three months' recovery time. Right?'

'Right,' I said, omitting to mention that the actual date of her coming had not been my choice for the simple reason that she was still working for someone else and had pleaded to be permitted to take a holiday as she hadn't had one for two years. When I had made the arrangements I had been in a state of panic, convinced that I couldn't cope with a young baby for such a time, but could hardly refuse the request.

'You'll have to get fit again.'

'I'll start jogging as soon as my insides settle down,' I promised. The silence remained unhelpful so I added, 'What did Daws *say?*'

'He seemed to think that you'd prefer your maternal duties from now on − understandable really.'

'What did *you* say?'

There was another agonising silence before Patrick spoke again. 'I told him that initially you were terrified at the prospect of looking after a young baby but as with everything else

13

you do, were coping splendidly. I said that a nanny was booked for Justin and would be arriving in three months − about the right time for you to bond yourself with the baby as his mother and recover from the birth. I also mentioned that I didn't think the department could do without your flair, energy and intellect. He agreed with me.'

I had been forced to swallow hard before he was a quarter of the way through this and by the time he finished my eyes were swimming.

'About Haywood,' Patrick said.

'Yes?' I croaked, blinking rapidly.

'I *was* keeping back some of the grimmer details. Daws asked the forensic people to have another look at the arm but their findings are still pretty inconclusive. There's a difference of opinion between the two senior men. One says that it's highly likely that the limb had been sawn off and then sort of worried with an instrument like a craft knife to make it look as though it had been ripped away, and the other insists that the condition is a result of long immersion in salt water. They're going for a second opinion.'

'But the wedding ring −'

'Very worn,' he interrupted. 'It could be anyone's ring. It might be wishful thinking on Haywood's wife's part, too. They've lived apart for a couple of years and she has boyfriends.'

'It still might be his ring,' I said. 'The whole thing − the suicide − might have been staged.'

'I was coming to that. Daws doesn't believe that a man would go to such trouble and expense to disappear − it was an almost brand new Mercedes. And as he pointed out, you don't trip over dead bodies on the way to the station every morning. No, either Haywood *is* dead or something really big's going on.'

'Or the arm has absolutely nothing to do with it.'

Patrick actually looked disappointed for a moment. 'Yes, you're right. I suppose one must bear in mind things like students' rag weeks.' He gazed down at the sleeping baby in his arms and I wondered if the novelty would soon wear off.

'Where did Haywood work?' I asked, busy on another train of thought.

14

'On the outskirts of Bristol.'

'Then why drive all the way to Sussex? What was wrong with the Avon Gorge?'

He frowned. 'That's a very good question. There's a road running through the Gorge though, perhaps he didn't want to kill anyone else.'

'Those bent on suicide are usually in a state of mind that doesn't even consider that. Tell me about the others.'

He counted off on his fingers. 'Cook slashed his wrists on broken glass in the greenhouse at home in Potter's Bar. Peterson inhaled carbon monoxide in a lonely country lane not far from where he lived in Blandford, Dorset, and Jones killed himself on his uncle's farm near Chester.'

'But where did Jones live and work?'

'Chepstow.'

'That's only just over the Severn Bridge.'

'I do follow your line of thinking. All these incidents – with the exception of Cook and Haywood – took place in the South West. And if we eliminate Cook altogether and throw all the accepted detection methods to the four winds then – ' He laughed. 'What?'

'Haywood driving several hundred miles in order to kill himself looks even more suspicious.'

'Jones travelled a fair distance.'

'Jones shot himself,' I countered. 'Perhaps that was the only way he could face going and his uncle was the only person he knew who had a gun. I think it's worth investigating.'

Patrick nodded slowly. 'You might be right. At the moment Daws has given the problem to John Brinkley at the Yard. He'll co-ordinate info from the various police authorities and keep us posted.'

Inspector John Brinkley was D12's Liaison Officer at the Yard, an arrangement recently set up following a suggestion by Daws himself. He was provided with the movements of all D12 operatives so that, where possible, they received back-up. More prosaically, it prevented our people who were watching someone from being arrested for loitering with intent.

I rose and put Justin in his pram. I was still glowing from the approbation from Daws, a man slow both to damn and praise. This was nothing to do with any womanly inferiority complex.

D12 *is* a man's world and entails taking risks; for my own safety, and that of those working with me, I had undergone the same training. I was a better than average shot, could read maps, knew how to abseil and could defend myself quite adequately from assault. Training had been definitely hair raising and thankfully I had not had to utilise many of these skills since.

'Where's the christening to be?' I said, brought back to reality with a jerk. 'Here or at Hinton Littlemore?' Patrick's father is rector of Hinton Littlemoor, a village a few miles east of Bath.

Patrick didn't reply for a moment but reached up for a road atlas on the bookshelf. 'Bath,' he murmured after finding the page he wanted. 'Right in the middle of your South West of England Bermuda Triangle.' He jabbed a forefinger at the map. 'Yes, and come to think of it the place has five Ministry of Defence establishments which amongst other things are engaged on several secret defence projects for the Navy. I'll ask Dad when he can break the ice and dip young fella-my-lad in the Avon. When we've fished him out and dried him, I'll do some unofficial sleuthing.'

'Scientists apart,' I said, 'I'd much rather your dad officiated. His other two grandchildren haven't been christened because Larry and Shirley say they're going to let them make up their own minds when they're older.'

Unconsciously perhaps, Patrick grimaced at the mention of his brother's name. 'Zen Buddhism, Christianity, Paganism, they say it's all the same to them. I wouldn't mind so much if that were true. The fact is they're too bone idle to get up on Sunday mornings.'

I never argue with this kind of pronouncement for deciding when people are lying and when they are telling the truth is part of Patrick's job and it is nearly always he who interrogates suspected spies. But as far as Larry is concerned he might be just a little biased. The two brothers have not seen eye to eye for as long as anyone can remember.

16

Chapter Two

I should have known better than to make plans. Picturing a family weekend in the near future for Justin's christening I rushed out and bought clothes – ecstatic at finding myself still a size 12 – and phoned Elspeth, Patrick's mother, to ask if there were family christening robes. They were fit only for a museum now, she informed me, but she had fine cambric and Honiton lace left over from the underskirt of her mother's wedding dress that she had been saving specially for such an occasion, and if she made it up would that do? I stammered out my gratitude and gave her Justin's measurements.

At six a.m. on Boxing Day the phone rang. Still half asleep I heard Patrick answer it and then there was a long silence but for Justin snuffling softly as he fed, Patrick having changed him and put him into bed with me. My feelings upon realizing that Nature had somewhat belatedly provided me with milk to give him had been mixed; after all, he was quite happy with his bottles.

'That was Daws,' Patrick said upon returning with the tea. 'He wants me there pronto. Wouldn't say why – not over the open line.'

I squinted at the clock. 'The train's at ten past eight.'

'No, we've a bit longer than that – a chopper's collecting me at Plymouth airport at nine.'

I glanced up and surprised an odd look on his face: tenderness perhaps, longing, and then, like a flash deep in his eyes, a spark of something hard, even ruthless.

Probing carefully I said, 'It *is* a bit sexy. The womb contracts and you get your figure back more quickly.'

'Well done the Oink,' said he, purloining Terry's term for young children.

'In military parlance,' I continued, determined to sort this out once and for all, 'my weapons handling annex is not yet in operational mode.'

'I know that,' Patrick said quickly.

'But there's absolutely no reason why you shouldn't. . . .' For once the writer had to pause and ransack her brain for the right word.

'What?' he demanded.

'Come closer,' I finished, sticking to basics.

He carefully set down his tea.

'Take everything off,' I said.

Women really could rule the universe if they wanted to, I thought idly as the strong man whom I had seen reduce other strong men to tears with his voice alone hauled off his bath robe and judo style pyjamas. We could, I reasoned, embroidering my idea — between the washing up and putting the finishing touches to our novels — take the universal chair, decide a few fates, bestow largesse on lovers and followers.

Justin, finally replete, was laid down in his crib by the bed, perhaps a little more perfunctorily than usual. Then there were other lips where his had been, just as hungry but in another way. Unlike many woman and most so-called feminists I do not find it demeaning for my body to be host to both baby and husband, it provides a heady form of power for those subtle enough to perceive it. Perhaps on the other hand I am merely earthy and enjoy the perks.

No, it was power. I touched Patrick in ways that I knew turned his bones to water. Supine, he abandoned himself utterly to my ministrations and this, oddly, instigated delicious sensations in my own body. But I did not want power and it was sufficient for a short while to have this man of mine as pliant under my hands as grass in a meadow, bending before a breeze. He might have been a girl with her first lover, yearning and finally begging for what he wanted. It didn't matter that we weren't paired; the moment, when it came, we enjoyed together.

When he looked up at me through half closed lashes I said, 'I've never really thought about our relationship like that before.'

18

He still couldn't speak, breathing hard.

'Did you mind?'

'Oh brother,' was all he said.

It was just as well that I had plenty of work to do. In the spring of the previous year Patrick had taken the rough draft of a novel titled *A Man called Céleste* out of a drawer of my desk and thence to the States where he had sold the film rights. Nothing had happened for a long time and then one day a large parcel with a London postmark had been delivered, containing two copies of a film script for my approval. It was unbelievably bulky, with endless camera instructions and about three words of dialogue on each page, and had been sitting on my desk ever since. I decided to tackle it now.

Fully two minutes after my bottom touched the chair the phone rang and I had to tuck Justin under my arm and carefully negotiate the narrow staircase. Clearly, a telephone extension would have to be put in if I was going to live on my own for a while.

It was Sue from my publishers, Thorpe and Gittenburg.

'Just wondered how you were, Ingrid,' she said guardedly. Sue is a guarded sort of person, ready to retreat like a tortoise into its shell at the first sign of aggression. Some authors must be incredibly nasty to her.

I swallowed my irritation at the interruption. 'Lovely to hear from you, Sue,' I cried, and then went on to give her an up to the minute account of my life. She always seems to expect it.

'How are you getting on with *Ghosts Never Lie?*' she enquired.

My brain reeled. 'That's not one of mine,' I told her when I could think straight.

'Sorry! Oh God. Sorry. No, it's *Echoes of Murder,* isn't it?'

I could imagine her going red and then white and then red again on the other end of the line. 'I'm feeling my way into it,' I lied, cursing Patrick and my own big mouth. Ye gods, I hadn't even started it. The title was one I had mentioned to him as a possible choice for the next book.

'I think you're really wonderful, being able to write *and* look after a baby,' Sue said, obviously trying to make up for her gaffe.

19

'It's a question of organisation,' I told her, and after a little more chat we rang off.

'Organisation,' I muttered, going back upstairs, half the morning gone already. I put Justin back on his rug on the floor, cleared the film script out of the way with a sweep of my arm and fed a new sheet of paper into the typewriter. I tapped out the words *Echoes of Murder* and sat looking at them for rather a long time.

Nothing.

Not a trace of an idea.

Ingrid who?

In the end I bloody-mindedly typed – *tea, bread, cat food, toilet rolls* – ripped the paper out of the machine, gathered up a by now grizzling Justin and went downstairs. I was putting his bottle to warm, only having enough of my own milk to feed him last thing at night and early morning, when the phone rang again.

'Yes?' I snarled.

'It's me,' said Patrick. 'Look, I might not be in circulation for a while. If anyone asks say. . . . No, on second thoughts you don't know where I am. You might have to postpone the visit to Somerset. Got that?'

His voice had that whip crack tone it assumes when he's really under pressure.

'Of course,' I said. 'Patrick –'

'Oh, and Haywood turned up,' he cut in, answering the un-spoken question. 'Down in Bude living with another woman. It was all going to be a big insurance fiddle and then he chickened out of seeing it through. We can forget that one.'

I stared at the receiver. He had rung off.

I gazed around the room at the Christmas decorations, the tree with fairy lights that had been put up specially for Justin, the Thomas the Tank Engine china set of mug, plate and bowl that Patrick had bought him, on the mantelpiece, and a tear trickled slowly down my cheek.

Without really meaning to I took down the road atlas, thumbed through until I found the page for Cornwall and located Bude on the northern coastline of that county. Scrubbing at my eyes with a sleeve I wondered how big an insurance fiddle would have to be before I would wreck an almost new Mercedes car.

During the next few weeks, virtually confined to the house by appalling weather that had not really abated since Justin was born, I was drawn several times to look at the map. Then, the last day of January dawning bright and cold, I shovelled the snow away from the front of the garage and went for a drive.

Snow was piled high at the sides of the road all the way to Lydford, two miles away, and I was grateful for front wheel drive. After this the going became easier as I dropped towards the Lyd valley. Dartmoor lay spread out before me, ice white, only the tors dark where high winds had stripped them of snow.

I had no clear idea of what I was going to do. Theoretically I could walk into the police station in Bude, show my D12 card and ask for everything they knew about Alex Haywood. I had no intention of doing that. The reason for this decision was simple. Patrick and I, unlike Terry, only work for the department part-time. Patrick's official duties since being invalided out of a special unit not far removed from the SAS is to supervise all security measures surrounding the Prime Minister's travels outside London but within UK. His family occasionally catch glimpses of him on the nine o'clock news but to everyone else watching he is no more than yet another ceaselessly vigilant security man. It suits MI5 if the KGB and other organisations file him in this slot and do not connect him with the tiny esoteric cadre to which, when required, he is called and given virtual *carte blanche*. I had no intention of jeopardising this mind-blowingly responsible job by throwing my weight about in North Cornwall.

I drove via Okehampton, Hatherleigh and Holsworthy, enjoying the freedom after weeks of confinement but for one quick trip to Plymouth. Bude was as quiet as a Sunday, the beach deserted but for a few dogs running wild, the sea sparkling in the thin winter sunshine.

I was not unrealistic enough to suppose that I would see Haywood walking the streets. But his description had stuck in my memory, the out of focus photograph printed in most of the newspapers at the time of his disappearance as easy to recall as though he was a member of my family. For he did not have the sort of face one would look at and immediately think of careful, painstaking research. Frankly, Alex Haywood looked like a thug. Patrick is always warning me that people aren't necessarily what their features suggest but when I had first beheld the picture I had thought the papers had got hold of the wrong one. Yes, he looked like a thug. Heavy brows, a sulky mouth, coarse dark badly cut hair, a thick neck set on powerful shoulders. I suddenly found myself very curious about the woman with whom he had started a new life.

Parking the car was not a problem. I stopped on the sea front and took Justin, asleep, for a long walk in his pram. Sheltered from the cold east wind the beach felt almost warm after the Siberian conditions at home. Not a flake of snow had fallen, it seemed, within ten miles of this coast.

A holiday town in deepest winter can be a depressing place. But Bude, it seemed, slept peacefully. All was tidy and still, nearly all of the souvenir shops closed up for the winter, the cheap tawdry goods in the windows faded and dusty, rejected things from almost forgotten seasons. One had to probe deeply for reminders that life went on but I found an excellent small café open where no one minded me giving Justin his bottle and taking an hour over lunch. Next door was a tiny boutique the inner recesses of which, a kind of shop within a shop, sold knitwear made locally and of such fashion flair and quality as to take my breath away. I bought a crimson sweater embroidered with huge crazy sequins and a white evening shawl made of hand spun wool.

In a kind of self-congratulatory haze after my finds I wandered down the High Street. Justin was awake and placidly watching the seagulls wheeling around the chimney pots even though his nappy was in dire need of attention. By now I had come to know what a certain preoccupied look on his face meant.

I took him back to the car, changed him on the back seat — not at all easy — and then had a brainwave. Carrying him in my arms I went back to Boots and bought a baby sling. Put into it there and then with the help of the young assistant, Justin promptly fell asleep and I set off to explore the town without having to worry about the pram wheels fitting the narrow pavements.

I found myself scrutinizing every woman I saw, wondering

with whom Haywood was now living. I let my imagination have its head for a few minutes, building up a mental Photofit picture of her; fortyish, bleached hair scraped up into a bun on the top of her head, a hard face with thin lips and high cheekbones. When she spoke her voice would be pure downtown Portsmouth or Devonport.

'Now why should a perfectly normal-looking woman walk about grinning all over her face?'

He was quite young, perhaps in his early thirties, and lounging behind the wheel of a car parked at the side of the road. His lunch, fish and chips eaten from newspaper, and a can of Coke, was spread before him on the top of the dashboard. He was most certainly CID; the car was unmarked but fitted with the right sort of two-way radio.

'Are you trying to pick me up?' I countered.

He laughed and nearly choked on a chip he had just put in his mouth.

I said, 'I was just having a bit of fun imagining the kind of trollop a man would fake suicide for.'

He stopped chewing for a moment and then took a drink of Coke, looking at me over the top of the can. Then he said, with just the right shade of disinterest to make me know I had hit the jackpot, 'Oh yes?'

I checked that the pseudo yak fur of my coat wasn't interfering with Justin's breathing. 'I came to the conclusion that she'd have to be loaded.'

He nodded slowly, still watching me. 'Think about that kind of thing a lot, do you?'

'Of course. I'm a writer.'

He relaxed, grinning, and purely on impulse I shot my question at him.

'Has Alex Haywood gone to earth in that house over the road?'

He flung open the passenger door. 'Get in.'

I stayed where I was. 'Anyone who read the *Western Morning News* and saw you parked opposite an opulent house would have come to the same conclusion. Those with eyes in their heads and an enquiring frame of mind, that is.'

He gestured to the wide open door. 'Would you care to join me for a friendly chat?'

23

'That's better,' I told him.

'Cute little chap,' said he when I had seated myself and closed the car door.

'They all are when they're asleep,' I said. 'How do you do? My name's Ingrid Langley.'

'Forbes,' he replied as we shook hands. 'Colin. I wasn't aware that Haywood was mentioned in the *Western Morning News.*'

'Yesterday,' I said, giving him a smile. 'There are a couple of news-hounds in that Allegro over there but they're too nervous of the guard dogs to go through the gates.'

'Just what is your interest in this, Mrs Langley? Other than the fact that you have eyes in your head and an enquiring frame of mind.'

'Miss,' I corrected. 'I write under my maiden name. Nothing, other than that real life drama interests me. After all, Haywood would have been the fourth scientist to have taken his own life. It also interests me why his movements are being monitored if it's a straightforward attempt at insurance fraud.'

'It never got that far,' Forbes said. 'He was recognised by an off-duty constable and when interviewed said he'd decided not to go through with it. You can't prosecute someone for a crime they haven't committed.'

'Then why the continued official interest, officer?' I murmured, and Forbes flushed.

'Hatemail,' he said after a short pause. 'Threats. Does that answer your question?'

'From novelists with twisted minds?' I said evenly, and for a moment we eyed one another in hostile fashion. Then Forbes smiled.

'I'm not trying to get rid of you or even criticising. He's had nasty letters and I'm keeping an eye on his front door. Okay?'

'Okay,' I said, getting out of the car.

He spoke through the open window. 'Haywood's a nice guy.'

'I have no intention of using the situation for the plot for my next book,' I said sarcastically. 'Don't worry, his reputation is quite safe with me.'

He rammed a chip in his mouth and chewed hard.

'Nothing makes me more angry than seeing someone with integrity slide into telling lies they hardly notice,' I continued. 'Nice guys don't go and live where there are slavering guard dogs and security cameras. You've been told that there might be something going on.'

He wound up the window and stared woodenly ahead through the windscreen. When I looked back after crossing the road he was talking into his radio, watching me. I waved and, getting safely out of sight of both him and the newspaper men by standing between the stone pillars of the entrance to a public park, took several photographs of the gates, walls and driveway of the house with the camera that I always carry with me. Three Dobermanns looked through the gates at me.

The house was called 'White Lodge' and could be glimpsed through the bare branches of the trees. In summer it would be completely hidden. I continued with my walk into the park, took the first turning left and came to another gateway in the park boundary. Again I turned left, walking more quickly along a suburban road. As I had expected I came to a cross roads, guessing, rightly as it happened, that 'White Lodge' with its extensive grounds was an 'island', so to speak, with roads all around it.

I walked all around it but there was nothing to see but high walls with two strands of barbed wire on the top plus another that looked as though it might be electrified. There was no rear entrance or even a side gate for those on foot. I could hear rustling on the other side of the wall. Were the dogs following me round?

Before I ran the risk of being spotted again by Colin Forbes I took another road to the right and finished up near the beach. I felt tired and was glad to reach the car and sit down. There was not a lot to show for my day. I hadn't even discovered the woman's name.

Over the next few days, perhaps revitalised by my trip to the seaside, I applied myself to the film script of *A Man Called Céleste*. There was no need to read it all the way through, the dialogue appeared to have escaped from the cutting room floor of an American film studio specialising in soap operas. Finally I lost patience with it and dumped both copies on the set of

shelves where Patrick keeps all his files. My agent could compose a sufficiently pungent letter.

I had other things on my mind. *Echoes of Murder* to be precise. A rather interesting tale was forming in my mind concerning a financier who faked his own death, ostensibly so that the woman with whom he was in partnership could claim the insurance. But she didn't claim. He made sure that he was discovered to be alive before there was danger of her being prosecuted for fraud and was thus exposed to the public gaze as a rather weak character who had not had the courage to see it through. For my financier had other, far more interesting, crimes planned, crimes for which he was being paid vast sums of money. . . .

The time went by and then the date originally planned for Justin's christening, February 8th, and still I hadn't heard from Patrick. Daws had rung me three times during these weeks to assure me that he was safe and well. I knew from his choice of certain code words that Patrick wasn't working for him and was grateful for his thoughtfulness. In situations like this messages from 'our Richard' — as we fondly refer to him — are my only way of knowing that my husband is still in one piece.

On Thursday 26th of February I sat down to watch the one o'clock news. The programme had already started and my sandwich went untasted back on to the plate as a shouted commentary burst into the room.

'. . . kept completely secret so that the police could investigate the threat. The Prince insisted on carrying on with his normal engagements but his bodyguard was augmented by the man who heads the Prime Minister's security team, Major Patrick Gillard. As we've already seen it was he who was in the car with His Royal Highness when the kidnap attempt was made.'

A London Street. A large black limousine slewed to a standstill across it and almost totally surrounded by police cars, ambulances and people. The camera zoomed right up to it. My ears roared and I couldn't hear what the commentator was saying as I beheld two inert forms lying face down in the road, ignored by those stepping over and around them. A thick rope of blood from one of them was finding its way into a

26

nearby grating. He had curling black hair and was tall and slim. Then I saw that the body was wearing red socks. Patrick never wears red socks.

The chauffeur of the car was being given first aid by an ambulance crew, his face being sluiced with water. The BBC man didn't know whether it was ammonia or acid that had been thrown into his eyes. The voice babbled on.

'A doctor's still in the car with the Major. We don't yet know how badly he was hurt when, after his accomplice was shot by Major Gillard, one of the attackers pulled open the door of the car and lunged at the Prince with a knife. Eye witnesses said that they heard another shot and the man fell dying but it appears that the Major was stabbed as he fended the man off before shooting him. One can only assume that he didn't fire straight away for fear of hitting. . . . '

He carried on talking but I didn't hear him. I was trying to make out details through the car window. But all I could see were the reflections of buildings opposite and a flock of pigeons circling in the sky. Then there was movement, a hand beckoning urgently. An ambulance man came forward and opened the car door.

Every cell in my body silently screamed.

When I looked again, peeping through my fingers, the previously still figure on the back seat had been resurrected and was leaving the car under his own steam, jacket off, left shirt sleeve rolled up redly to his elbow where there seemed to be a tourniquet affixed, his forearm host to a makeshift bandage through which blood was already seeping.

Patrick looked round when cheering broke out, realized his gun was still in his hand and slipped it back into the shoulder harness. There was then an argument, which he lost, as to whether or not he should enter the ambulance. That was all I saw before the camera panned away to the van abandoned by the would-be kidnappers and the commentator began to go through his account of what had happened all over again.

I poured myself a very unsteady double Scotch − breast feeding or no − and grabbed the phone.

Chapter Three

Larry, Patrick's brother and a chip off no one's block, said, 'You're slipping. There was a time when you'd never have let someone stick a knife in you first before you killed them.'

Patrick turned to face the speaker who was smiling good-naturedly. 'They've put me down for weapons training,' he said, smiling back and obviously determined not to cross swords with his brother on this occasion on account of the eleven stitches in his arm.

'Must be deadly driving a desk most of the time,' Larry continued. 'Although plodding round power stations and shopping precincts with the PM can't be a bundle of fun either.'

'Hell, no,' Patrick replied with feeling. 'Those places are a security man's nightmare − a million hideaways for bombs and assassins.'

I wasn't openly snorting even though not counting myself party to the amnesty. The Prince had been sitting nearest to the door when it had been wrenched open and, being young, fit and brave, had endeavoured to kick his attacker's legs from under him. It is difficult to kick someone when you are sitting in a car. Patrick had deflected the thrust of the would-be assassin's knife with his arm and then shot the man in the body when he was off balance. For these few seconds of quick thinking he was down neither for weapons training nor a medal, it being considered all part of his job. But today he was wearing a pair of solid gold cufflinks decorated with horses designed by Stubbs that so far no one had noticed.

Patrick's good-natured smile changed to a foxy grin when he

saw Shirley, Larry's wife, approaching. Hostilities are never in abeyance as far as she is concerned.

'I can't get over how right you look with that baby in your arms,' she said by way of a greeting, at the same time giving me a smirk that was quite indecipherable.

Patrick glanced down at Justin who had behaved admirably at his christening a little under two hours previously. The smiled-upon-by-angels demeanour could not be disassociated from John having warmed the jug of water on a radiator by the font before blessing and using it. This was just as well for the child had been well and truly baptised. Not for John Gillard a ponderous holy sprinkling. Justin's head had broken the surface of the water and he had received the contents of a scallop shell a couple of times for good measure. The now grey eyes had opened wide and he had actually spluttered. I had glanced sideways to see Patrick's shoulders shaking and then back to Justin who by then had decided not to cry. He seemed to be getting used to his family never doing anything by halves.

'I mean you were only interested in soldiering at one time,' Shirley elaborated quite unnecessarily. 'It's really amazing how people change as they get older.'

Her rather shrill voice had by now woken Justin, who, as it was at least an hour after the time for his feed, burrowed instinctively towards the warmth close by, his mouth fastening purposefully around a button on his father's shirt.

'Surely you don't feed him on demand!' cried Shirley in horror when Patrick had rescued the button and raised his eyebrows enquiringly at me.

'We change him when he's shit himself too,' said Patrick, his fuse as far as she was concerned short as ever. And with that he bore his son in the direction of the kitchen.

It was exactly a month since the date originally planned for the ceremony and was now March 8th. In the aftermath of the attempted kidnapping Patrick had been kept in hospital overnight because as well as inflicting a long deep slash, the knife had severed a small vein. The next day Daws had arranged for him to be brought home when it became apparent that otherwise he was going to be literally dumped on the doorstep of his London *pied à terre* just off Gower Street.

I had waved my thanks to the driver of the army staff car and firmly shut the door, locking it. Impetuous young neighbours might otherwise have been unwise enough to rush in with congratulations in mind. After a mug of tea, his son in his lap, Patrick had gradually ceased to shudder.

There was no sign of delayed reaction now and he had slipped with easy familiarity into the routines of his parents' country parsonage. This was not to say that he paid lip service to family conventions with a tolerant smile on his face. A soldier he might be with occasionally a soldier's turn of phrase but on the Saturday we arrived he did not have to have his arm twisted to don surplice and sing with a depleted choir for a marriage service, nor to help his father afterwards, as of old, as a server during the Nuptial Communion. Covertly watching him, lending my own presence to swell a tiny congregation, the bride a daughter of a friend of Elspeth's, I saw the same careful precise movements with carafes of water and wine as when he cleans his Smith and Wesson at home and was reminded of his intention one day to follow in his father's footsteps.

Certainly his family knows of this, and every time he returns home I am aware that discussions take place between priest and son that inexorably tugs Patrick in that direction. But his father does not disapprove of him working for MI5 even though he must know that killing is involved in situations far removed from war. In fact I get the impression that the chosen, present career receives his blessing, literally.

For a while I had tried not to think too deeply about this for the conclusions I reached did not tally with the milk and water Christianity I had been taught at Sunday School.

Elspeth, a slim, pretty, fashionable woman in her late fifties, paused in removing sausage rolls from the oven as her eldest son detonated into the kitchen.

'Shirley!' she announced, and then clapped an oven glove over her mouth. Then, more quietly she said, 'I can tell by your face. Oh, do let me feed the little angel – I shan't see him very often. That's if he doesn't mind.'

'Frankenstein, Ned Kelly, the Abominable Snowman – he doesn't care, I'm afraid, as long as it's milk,' I told her.

'Fancy John nearly drowning him like that,' she said, and then went on to ask Patrick and me to finish organising the buffet lunch.

A small family gathering had grown into a village event. The christening had taken place during the normal ten-fifteen morning service and the church had been full, mostly with older inhabitants of the parish. Presumably most of them remembered our first marriage in the village and some must have been present when prayers were said for Patrick when he was badly injured in the South Atlantic. The same people no doubt had heard of our divorce and were now curious to see us again after our remarriage and the birth of our first child.

Many of them had written to Patrick when he lay gravely ill in hospital on his return home from the South Atlantic, sending the letters via his father. Some had sent small keepsakes; medallions from Lourdes, Palm Sunday crosses, an exquisite miniature bible. He had gone round shaking hands after the service and I had kept right in the background.

'Go with him,' Elspeth had whispered. 'Take Justin.'

I am not yet a church person and had still been mentally reeling under the weighty vows I had made on behalf of my son.

'He depends on you,' she had said. 'Perhaps not before that grenade exploded, but now more than you'd ever imagine possible.'

So I had joined Patrick and we had ended up by inviting half the village back to the Rectory for a drink. There had been a sudden egress of ladies hurrying home to turn down the Sunday joint, with Terry amongst them, despatched to the Ring O' Bells next door for further supplies of beer and wine.

Later, when the village folk had gone home to their overdone dinners and close friends and family were collecting their coats or, having said their farewells, extricating cars from the traffic jam in the driveway at the front of the house, I sat down in the warm kitchen and took a break from collecting dirty glasses and crockery. Terry was feeding plates into the dishwasher one-handed, a pint tankard in the other; Patrick wandering around the room sipping from a glass of white wine. Anne Walker, a neighbour and the local GP, was sitting hugging her knees, staring into space, on an oak settle by the door.

'Last time I saw you. . .' Terry began, speaking to me and then breaking off and grinning provocatively.

'I shall never feel the same about you, Terry,' I said, an utterance from the depths of my heart. 'But then again, I saw your backside first.'

'When?' both Patrick and Terry said together.

'When you slid down the Forestry Commision fence, showing off, and got that splinter in yourself,' I replied urbanely. 'It was me who held the torch for the medic.'

'At night!' exclaimed Anne.

'One of those adventure weekends,' I explained, still able to recall the exercise for D12 in some detail. No doubt the incident was etched into Terry's memory too for the two-inch long sliver of wood had been forced under the skin in his groin.

'I didn't know it was you!' Terry exploded, still young enough to blush.

'I wouldn't normally have said a word,' I promised, straight-faced.

Elspeth and John came in, and when she had shut the door Elspeth put her arm around him. 'Well, wasn't that lovely? Despite the star of the show almost being full fathom five.'

When the laughter had ceased I said, 'John, who was that man in the dark suit who was on his own and looked miserable? We asked him over but he didn't come.'

'I know who you mean,' John said. 'His name's David Prescott. I think there's some kind of trouble but he hasn't been to church recently for me to make enquiries. I'm reluctant to knock on his door and ask him — that seems so nosey.'

'You must,' Elspeth said.

Patrick said, 'He kept looking at me. I felt that he was summing me up.'

'Wants you to shoot his nasty neighbours, I expect,' Terry said, and then in response to the frosty stare slammed shut the door of the dishwasher and switched on.

Out of the mouths of innocents and babes. . . .

It was the time of day called dimity by the country folk in Devon, deep dusk. Even though there was a large log fire in the sitting room, most members of the family had gravitated to the kitchen where a kettle sang a steamy song on the Rayburn and Elspeth had switched on the several small lamps with which she illuminated her domain when she didn't need the large strip

32

light in the ceiling. The sun being considered definitely over the yardarm Anne was helping Patrick 'tidy', as she put it, the contents of a bottle of white wine, Elspeth was enjoying a glass of her beloved sherry and Terry was initiating John, who usually just indulged himself in a pint of mild, into the joys of Wadworths 6X which came by the jugful from the pub.

Larry and Shirley and their two children had been invited to stay for supper. The children were watching television in the dining room, their parents side by side on one of the pine benches by the kitchen table, drinking gin and tonic. I have never been able to fathom why the two brothers are so dissimilar; Patrick is an attractive but not a handsome man, Larry easily described as good-looking. But for me, at least, there is something about him that is vaguely repellent. Both have the same black curling hair – only Patrick's is now greying rapidly – and grey eyes, and that is where the resemblance ends. Whereas Patrick is tall and wiry, his brother is shorter and goes in for weight training; broad shoulders and muscular arms not completely hiding the fact that he also measures too much around the middle. For a moment I imagined Patrick wearing the same chunky gold jewellery, open-necked shirt and tight trousers and had to hide a grin behind my hand.

'How's school?' Patrick said suddenly, coming out of a reverie.

Larry jumped when his wife nudged him. 'Oh – fine, fine,' he said vaguely.

'Still on strike?'

Elspeth and John sighed in unison and Elspeth gave Patrick a look that would have dropped an ox in its tracks. He chuckled, inclining his head in capitulation, and raised his glass.

'To Justin, who deserves a better father. Hello, we have a visitor.'

It was David Prescott who had burst in through the back door, utterly distraught.

'Why, David – ' John began.

'Help me, John,' the man blurted. 'I thought you might be in the church, locking up, but. . . . ' He stared around, seeming to see us all for the first time. 'I'm so sorry. Shouldn't have

33

butted in like this. Forgive me.' He turned as if to leave and then stopped, listening. 'Oh God, they're here! They must have followed me. Hide me, John, for God's sake.'

Larry half rose to his feet. 'Do sit down and tell us about it,' he said in the manner of one talking to someone not quite right in the head.

'No. No,' Prescott said. 'And now I've drawn all you good people into this mess. I'll go. I should have known better than to come here.'

Terry caught Patrick's eye and went outside into the gloom. Those who listened as a matter of habit rather than speaking had heard the sound of a motorbike. It sounded as if the machine was motionless nearby with its engine ticking over quietly.

'Is that them?' Patrick asked calmly.

'I – think so,' Prescott stammered. 'I'm not sure. I never quite know how. . . .' He stopped speaking and even from where I was sitting I could see that he was shaking. 'Nothing will stop them.' He made a dive for the door but Patrick got there first.

'He's quite mad,' Shirley hissed.

'I hardly think so,' John rebuked her angrily. 'David works for the Ministry of Defence in Bath. David, do tell us what this is all about. Shall we call the police?'

'No!' Prescott shouted. 'Whatever you do, don't do that!' He pushed against Patrick ineffectively and was taken by the arm, apparently quite gently but the grip, I knew, would be like a vice, compelling him to follow, and leading him away from the door. One-handed Patrick flipped open Terry's weekend bag, for some reason in a corner of the room, delved, removed gun and harness and shook the weapon free.

'Does that make you feel better?' he asked Prescott.

'You're gun happy, Patrick!' shouted Larry.

'Shut up!' he was told without ceremony. Then, again to Prescott, Patrick said, 'Let's start off on the right footing. You came here hoping to find me. Correct?'

'I'm taking the children and getting out of here!' Shirley shrilled.

'Sit down until I make sure it's safe,' Patrick said.

'To hell with you!' she snapped, and made for the door into the hall.

34

'Shirley.' He didn't shout, he didn't have to, the deadly cold voice said it all. And when she turned round to face him, for a fleeting moment the barrel of the gun twitched in her direction. She sat down.

Patrick's gaze returned to Prescott.

'Yes,' he said meekly. 'I was hoping to find you.'

All at once the bike's engine roared and headlights shone directly in the window. All of us, I think, wanted to run away for the sound was extraordinarily menacing. But then we saw Patrick, silhouetted against the brilliant light, open the kitchen window. At that moment Terry cried out, the sound clearly discernible above the noise of the bike. And in the next moment, Patrick fired.

The light went out like an eye that had been blinded. I blinked and Patrick had gone. Even with a right leg below the knee of man-made construction, he can still move like a cat when the adrenalin's flowing. There was a clatter that sounded like the bike falling over and then feet pounded gravel.

With less speed and a lot more noise Larry and Shirley rushed from the room. By the time Patrick had half carried in Terry, his head streaming with blood, children were protesting violently as they were hustled away and the family departed with screaming tyres.

'Bastards,' said Terry, adding 'Sorry' when he remembered the nature of the company. He slumped into the chair Anne had run forward to provide and for a few moments was out cold.

'Well!' Elspeth said. 'I never thought I'd see the day when shots were fired through my kitchen window.'

Chapter Four

The aftermath was very difficult.

Patrick made several telephone calls and some time later David Prescott was collected by car and taken away to a safe place where he could later be questioned about his predicament. In private, to John and Patrick, he had given assurances that he was not personally involved with crime or with criminals. Patrick did not think it necessary to inform him that he would be conducting the forthcoming interrogation himself.

Anne had insisted that Terry have X-Rays and no one was inclined to argue with her even though Patrick knew it would subsequently mean a visit from the police. The phone call from the hospital with the information that Terry had a hairline fracture of the skull and would be kept in for observation came when the police were taking statements. This was not a protracted procedure as Patrick had shown them his ID card and given them a detailed account of what had occurred, typed by me on the rector's typewriter and sealed in an envelope for the Chief Superintendent's eyes only. They took the motorbike away with them together with the weapon with which Terry had been attacked, a large spanner.

We were all of a mind to go to bed, even though too shocked and restless to feel like sleeping, when the phone rang yet again. It was Larry demanding explanations and apologies, the latter from Patrick. In vain did John explain that his actions had been justified. Larry's voice became a lot louder. He seemed to be under the impression that his wife and children's lives had been in danger from a man in need of psychiatric

36

help. He went on to call his brother quite a few things and I distinctly heard the words 'royal toady' yammered down the line.

Finally, Patrick also being present in the room and in possession of acute hearing, he went over to remove the receiver from his father's hand. Then, in language never heard before or since in that house, he made his feelings known. Heavily censored, the rebuttal started with the threat that if Larry bleated what had happened all over Bristol, Patrick would inform the police about his car's tax disc being out of date as well as the matter of two bald tyres. It ended with a promise that if that failed to deter him, he would be kicked all the way from Avon to Kent and back. Put in those terms the diatribe sounds childish; delivered as it was using quite the most breathtaking obscenities I had ever heard, it was formidable, enough to make a naval rating blench. When Patrick put down the phone it was to discover that I was the only one remaining with him in the room.

'You went too far,' I said, but only by way of an explanation for the general exodus, not a remonstrance, for by now he had wound himself up until he was speechless. I also prepared to leave the room for when he is like this he is not quite sane. I met Elspeth in the doorway.

'I was wrong,' she said cheerfully to Patrick. 'You once killed six rooks by shooting them from the kitchen window. D'you remember? It was when you came home from hospital and you hadn't slept for three nights because your legs hurt.'

A shudder went right through Patrick and he turned away from her and clutched at the back of a chair, knuckles white. I could almost hear the tendons in his fingers creaking. Then he made an odd sound, a kind of choked laugh, and faced her again, taking right on the chin her method of getting him to control his temper: making him sound like a small boy in a paddy because of a grazed knee.

'I came to ask if you'd put a couple of screws in that wonky bolt on the back door before we go to bed — you know what your father's like with tools.'

Patrick went over to her and kissed her cheek. 'For you ve kill ze bull,' he murmured.

'You're the only person in the world who can say things like

37

that to him,' I told Elspeth the next morning when we were clearing away after breakfast.

She laughed. 'I used to make him split logs when he was a teenager and got like that. You soon come off the boil when one slip with the axe will take your foot off.' She paused in wiping the draining board. 'Poor Patrick — he did lose his foot in the end. Isn't life cruel sometimes?'

'How well do you know David Prescott?' I asked when we had finished.

'Hardly at all,' she replied. 'He lives in one of those new bungalows at the other end of the village — I'm not sure which one. I think he moved in last year but you know how time flies. He comes to church nearly every week and is on the P.C.C. but does tend to keep himself to himself. You must ask John, he'll be able to tell you more.'

'Perhaps it *had* better be me,' I said. 'I don't think he's speaking to Patrick after the language he used.'

'Oh, John's all right,' she said gaily. 'It wasn't as if Patrick used blasphemy. Anyway, he's already apologised.'

There was a rather awkward pause which I broke by saying, 'I'm sure there's nothing for you to worry about. Those people were after David Prescott — they must know that he's not here now.'

She patted my arm. 'I understand that it's all arranged and we're going to be watched over for a short while. It won't be the first time I've given cups of tea to armed policemen in the garden.'

There was no need for me to be present at David Prescott's interrogation in order to be able to reconstruct an accurate account of what happened. I have attended others — that is on the other side of a one way mirror — and have in my possession a tape recording of the proceedings. I also made a note of Patrick's comments when he played me the tape afterwards.

It was plain from the start that the passage of two days, and being provided with a secure bolt hole, had done nothing to allay Prescott's fears. Rather, the extra time to think in peace and quiet, for Rawlston House in Bushey Park is a delightful place, had only served to prey on his nerves. Therefore, when Patrick entered the room where the questioning was to take place, a little lounge on the first floor, he renewed his acquaintance with a man who was in a similar frame of mind to his condition at their first meeting.

Patrick was in uniform, deliberately, and deposited hat and document case on a low table. Then he moved his armchair a little closer to Prescott's, rang for coffee to be brought, and sat down. Only after he had done these things did he look directly at Prescott and wish him good morning.

'Frankly, Major,' said the scientist, after greeting him warily, 'I'm surprised to see you.'

'Luckily or not, you stumbled on the right bloke to ask for help.'

The slightly obtuse reply, possibly an oblique threat, did nothing to soothe Prescott. This was deliberate too.

'I imagined you in an office somewhere in Whitehall.'

'Did you?'

'I should think the entire nation does after what happened in London.'

Patrick clicked open his document case and extracted a dossier from it before he replied. This is an old trick – allowing people to think that you have a fat file on their activities. 'I only ride shotgun some of the time. Now and then I'm let loose on government employees who –' a quick but penetrating stare – 'get themselves into trouble. My apologies for calling you Mister just now – it's Doctor Prescott, isn't it?'

All hopes of friendly informality on Prescott's part must have been dashed by now. He made an attempt to break through what was probably almost unbearable aloofness.

'Your young colleague...I hope he has recovered now.'

Patrick chuckled humourlessly. 'His head aches. Especially after the reprimand I gave him.'

'Surely not!' Prescott protested, and probably earned himself another stare.

'Operatives who have that much money spent on their training are presumed careless when hit over the head with a spanner,' Patrick said, and spent the next few moments perusing the dossier. During this time it was likely that Prescott abandoned any ideas of chummy half-truths and began to hate Patrick more than those threatening him. This could only be a

39

good thing. He also ceased trembling. But it didn't necessarily mean that he would tell the truth at the first time of asking.

'Right,' Patrick said with an air of finality. He tossed the folder back in his case. 'Who are they and what do they want?'

Prescott said, 'To answer the second question first — money. I've no idea who they are.'

Patrick didn't respond; at this stage he prefers those whom he is investigating to do most of the talking.

'It's a case of mistaken identity,' the scientist went on. 'They're working for someone who seems to think I owe him a lot of money.'

'And you don't.'

'Of course not. I owe no one money.'

'Sort of heavy debt collectors.'

'Yes.'

'Then why didn't you go to the police?'

'A note was pushed through my door saying that someone I loved would suffer if I did.'

'To whom might that refer?'

'Quite a few people. Although I'm not married I have nieces and nephews, and old friends. My mother's nearly a hundred and lives in a nursing home in East Grinstead. I've a brother in Scotland and a sister in Canada.'

'Do these people appear to know that?'

'They appear to know everything about me.'

'Ah,' said Patrick, slowly and softly.

Irritably, Prescott enquired, 'Is that of any significance?'

'If they know everything about you, it can hardly be a case of mistaken identity.'

'You simply don't understand! There must be someone with the same name as me and these thugs have done their home-work on the wrong person.'

'Are those the words they used?' Patrick said sharply.

'Which words?'

'Did they say they had done their homework on you?'

'They might have done,' Prescott said, confused now. 'But —'

'It's not an expression you would normally use.'

Prescott remained silent.

'What are you working on at the moment?'

'Surely if you've familiarized yourself with every smallest

40

detail of my career and private life, you know the answer to that already.'

'Please answer the question.'

'It's quite irrelevant. Besides, I have no intention of discussing my work with you.'

'I suggest to you that it's of the utmost relevance. I also suggest that your statement that these people appear to know everything about you, is the only thing you've said so far that's true.'

'I'm not interested in your suggestions, Major,' Prescott said furiously. 'Just tell me how to get rid of these thugs.'

'That kind of advice entails the presence of police officers, detailed descriptions, attending identity parades – all the rigmarole that comes with law and order. If on the other hand the threats do involve your work, we can go through the magic door to the place where all information will be confidential and the parties bothering you can be warned off if necessary in a very final manner.'

There was a knock at the door and a steward brought in the coffee.

When he had gone Patrick said, 'I'm astounded that you haven't asked anyone what, if anything, has been discovered about the bike. After all, they did leave it behind.'

'Perhaps it was stolen,' Prescott said.

'There were no fingerprints,' Patrick commented quietly. 'Nor, come to that, number plates. The police have it in their pound in Bath – I'm afraid the security services do have to co-operate with the police sometimes.'

Again Prescott made no response.

Patrick said, 'Why should two people on a motor bike reduce you to a state of incoherent terror?'

'I told you – they threatened me.'

'What with? Death?'

'Yes.'

'If you were dead, you couldn't pay.'

'You're trying to confuse me?'

'What the devil did you want me to do when you burst into my parents' home that evening?' The tone in which this question was uttered was not pleasant. 'I'm still trying to help you and you're fighting me all the way.'

Prescott's hands were shaking as he picked up his coffee

cup, rattling the china a little. 'I did say I regretted that. I was too scared to realize the consequences.'

'Lies!' Patrick spat out. 'You knew what you were doing. You saw me put a couple of bullets in those jokers on television and you thought I might just do the same for you if my family was threatened. What do you have to hide?'

'Nothing!' Prescott shouted.

Patrick slammed his palm down on the table, making all the crockery jangle. 'I saw you watching me all through the church service. You were eyeing me up — trying to decide if I was a trigger-happy moron who might just solve your problem. Let me tell you this. Officially, I'm not permitted to lay a finger on you, but when I think of the way you led that murderous pair right into the place where my parents, wife and baby son. . . .' He broke off and the way he was breathing hard comes over clearly on the tape. At this moment he was not acting. 'Drink your coffee,' he finished disgustedly.

Silently, Prescott began to sob, his coffee slopping out of the cup into the saucer. Patrick took it from him, set it back on the table and went over to stand by the window, hating himself.

'They won't trace them through the bike,' Prescott said some minutes later, after blowing his nose.

'What makes you think that?' Patrick asked gently, turning round.

'It belongs to a dead man.'

'You mean the real owner of it was killed.'

'Yes.'

'Was he killed to gain possession of the bike?'

Prescott was still dabbing at his face with his handkerchief.

'How did they kill him?'

The hands holding the square of linen were now shaking uncontrollably.

'Take your time,' Patrick told him, sitting down again.

'He was shot,' Prescott said, a pause between each word.

'Were you there?' Patrick whispered.

'Major,' Prescott said after another pause, 'I cannot live with my memories. If you force me to recount what happened, I think I shall die.'

Whereupon David Prescott collapsed.

Chapter Five

I played through the tape once more. At this point Patrick went to Prescott, knelt at his side and loosened his tie. He told me afterwards that the minute or two before the doctor arrived seemed like an eternity. The emergency was probably the reason for the recorder being left running during the ensuing conversation between Patrick and Colonel Daws after Prescott had been taken from the room.

'No need for recriminations,' Daws said.

'If there's one thing I hate doing it's shoving people like him over the edge,' Patrick replied savagely.

'He didn't take much of a push though, did he?'

'That doesn't make me feel any happier. I should have played it down a lot more, not let my feelings get the better of me like that.'

'Be honest — his memories would have put him inside a psychiatric hospital before much longer. Talk to him again when he's recovered — tomorrow or the day after. You know damn well that you're just as good at winching 'em up again.' Daws chuckled then, obviously well pleased, and I could imagine him standing, hands rammed into the trousers pockets of his Savile Row suit. Now and then he would remove his right hand from the pocket to rake his greying fair hair from off his forehead, a lifelong mannerism.

'What d'you reckon happened?' Daws asked.

Unhesitatingly, Patrick said, 'From the expression of deepest horror on his face I should imagine they made him kill this man. I'd like to take a look at Prescott's house. I take it the police haven't been over it already.'

'No, there was no real need.'

A short silence.

'But you'd rather I didn't,' Patrick observed politely.

'Major, is there really anything in this or has the poor fellow a few screws loose?'

'Meadows *was* hit on the head by one of two people on a motor bike,' Patrick reminded him.

'Could that have been a case of straightforward assault — those who did it high on drink or drugs?'

'No, I think that in the sudden glare of the headlight they thought Terry was Prescott. They're about the same height and build. Terry was quick enough to begin to duck but Prescott, being older, might just have had his brains knocked out.'

'Murder? If there's a connection with the other cases —'

Here Daws was interrupted by an orderly who knocked to tell him that Prescott had recovered slightly and that there was nothing seriously wrong with him.

Patrick said, 'I'm not a shrink but I'm sure he's sane. Sane but under tremendous pressure. Whatever he's witnessed or been forced to do, the purpose behind it is the same — to make him crack up. I did check on what he's working on — a new generation of submarines for the Royal Navy.'

Daws grunted. 'Peterson was engaged on design work for a fighter plane, Jones very highly thought of in research into defence against chemical weapons, and. . .what was the other chap's name?'

'Cook, sir. He was involved with the testing of ground to air missiles for the army, but not in an important rôle. I'm all for leaving him out of it.'

'And you're still convinced that this is a job for us?'

Patrick replied by asking another question. 'Where are they getting the list of names of top boffins from? If they've decided that Bath has rich pickings they might simply be going through the telephone directory for the Navy Contracts Department — which is also restricted information.'

'I'm fully aware of what is restricted information,' Daws growled, noticed that the recorder was still running and switched it off.

Patrick rang me that night, for I had returned home to

Devon, gave me a swift résumé of the day's events and asked if I'd like to bring baby, typewriter, film scripts and all back to Hinton Littlemoor as he intended using the village as the base for his investigations for a while. When I hesitated in replying he told me that Terry had been replaced by a tough individual by the name of Tom Holland, known to all as Dutchy. It was Dutchy who had been keeping an eye on the Rectory, not, as Elspeth had assumed, an armed policeman.

Although not looking forward to another long drive I agreed, admitting to myself that I would rather not be on my own. Also, Justin had the miseries and had successfully prevented me from getting on with writing. He seemed to have a slight temperature. It was arranged that I would travel down the next day.

I deliberately set out to meet Dutchy by driving much faster than I should have done through the village, and swinging into the Rectory drive scattering gravel. Level with Elspeth's prized clump of scented white narcissus, a wheelbarrow suddenly shot from behind the golden privet opposite, forcing me to brake hard. The barrow was followed by Dutchy. It immediately became clear that he was not the sort to take kindly to the boss's wife testing his security arrangements. Here was none of the childish glee with which Terry and I try to catch each other out, even to the extent of flour bombs and plastic bowls of water balanced on the tops of doors.

'Sackcloth and ashes,' I said, having checked that Justin hadn't been bounced right out of his carry-cot.

'Are you the Major's wife?'

I told him I was.

'Then you ought to have known better. That little kiddie might have been hurt.'

I swallowed all retorts concerning people who hurled garden equipment under the wheels of vehicles, smiled and parked the car. He watched me unload it for a short while and then sauntered away, leaving behind an impression of well-scrubbed lack of humour, the sort who would obey orders to the last dotted 'i' and crossed 't'.

The next person I clapped eyes on was Terry, supposed to be on a month's sick leave.

'I'm only allowed to peel potatoes and baby-sit,' was his

45

reaction to my amazed stare. He was lying with his feet up on the settee, several tins of beer nestled around him.

'Does Patrick know you're here?' I enquired, getting right to the point.

'Er − no. Elspeth says she'll fix it.'

'But he said he'd be here before me.'

'He is. Arrived about two hours ago and went out again. I kept my head down. Where's this nanny of yours then?'

Faintly, Justin could be heard proclaiming his disapproval of life.

'Skiing,' I told him. 'I'll have to be back home to greet her next Monday.'

At that moment the phone rang and Elspeth, who had put down the shopping and picked up Justin, answered it. 'Right,' I heard her say from the hall, 'I'll tell him. . . No, don't worry, dinner isn't until seven. What's what funny noise. . .? It's your son, for goodness' sake! I think Ingrid had forgotten she'd left him all on his own in the garden.'

Wrists slapped twice in so many minutes, I hastened to take him from her.

'That was Patrick, in case you didn't hear,' she called through to Terry. 'He said he's borrowing that bike from the police and doesn't want you to shoot him.'

Terry was sitting up slowly when I re-entered the room.

'It must be that rather aggressive aftershave you use,' Elspeth said comfortingly. 'Guide's honour I never told him you were here.'

'Thoughtful of him to warn me,' Terry muttered with a brave smile for both of us. 'Does this place have a priest's hole?'

Despite the warning my heart did miss a beat when I heard the big Kawasaki purr to a standstill outside. It missed another when the rider came in through the front door. He was all in black, even the helmet which was one of those with a tinted visor so you couldn't see through it.

Patrick removed the helmet and grinned at me, his face flushed with exhilaration.

'You've bought yourself some leathers,' I gasped. It was some years since he had possessed a bike of his own. There had been a short-lived experiment with one when he had been forced to give up driving for a while because of weakness in his legs but this had been destroyed when someone else was riding it.

'Thought I might give it another go,' Patrick said casually. 'I'm toying with the idea of taking up fencing again too,' he added, catching sight of Terry. He snatched up a walking stick from the umbrella stand in the hall. 'Young puppy! Defend yourself, sirrah!'

'Patrick! He's not supposed to...' I began, but it was hopeless, they were away.

Terry, whose grasp is total concerning these occasional no holds barred clowning fits that Patrick is given to, threw himself at the nearest weapon to hand. This just happened to be Great-great-great-uncle Bertram's sabre, hanging on the wall over the fireplace in the living room. It appeared to be just as sharp as the day it had been used alongside General Gordon at Khartoum. A short space of time proved this to be perfectly correct for two minutes later Patrick's walking stick was precisely six inches in length, and Elspeth and I were crying with laughter.

'Yield or die,' Terry said grittily, the sabre point firmly in the leather jacket a hand's breadth above Patrick's navel.

'Name your price, varlet,' said Patrick, also regressing a couple of centuries.

'That you kicketh not my arse for succumbing to that knave with the spanner.'

'Agreed.'

'And that you purchase the ale when we next repair to the hostelry.'

The vanquished one nodded meekly and was released to collect up the whittled away chips of his walking stick.

I said, 'I'm surprised the police let you loose on the bike.'

'With the piece of paper I had in my possession, they'd have had to let me set sail in the *S.S. Great Britain.*'

'Is dinner nearly ready?' enquired John, coming out of his study, a blare of Mahler following him out. 'Good gracious! You look just like one of those Hell's Angels in that outfit.'

Hands clasped around his small pile of firewood, Patrick said to me, 'Perhaps that's what the owner of the bike was. People like that aren't reported missing so quickly as ordinary folk.'

'Start your own Chapter,' Terry suggested. 'Okay, Heaven's Angels,' he corrected when John bent on him a black-browed gaze. 'Brass Eagles. How about that?'

'Like the one in the church heavily disguised as the lectern, you mean?' John remarked. 'I'll fix it on the handlebars if you like.'

Up until that moment I had always assumed that Patrick had inherited his odd sense of humour from his mother.

After dinner, Patrick, Terry and I borrowed John's study and listened to the tape of David Prescott's initial questioning which Patrick had brought with him from London.

'Poor guy,' commented Terry when Patrick switched off the recorder.

Patrick said, 'I saw him fleetingly before I left and he looked quite composed. But looks can be deceptive − the medics had probably filled him up with sedatives.'

'So we're going to give his house the once over?'

'Ingrid, Dutchy and I are going to take a short walk in that direction,' he was informed. 'I should like you to have an early night.'

'Yes, sir,' replied Terry after only the most infinitesimal pause.

'If you can't sleep,' Patrick continued, 'I've no objection to your whiling away the time by loading the cannon with grapeshot and being prepared to repel boarders from your bedroom window.'

'You'll have to count me out,' I said, hearing with a sinking heart Justin's roars of anguish in the distance. 'I can't dump him on your mother making that noise.'

'To the Oink,' announced Terry, heading for the door.

By the time Patrick and I had caught up with him, Terry had lifted the raging infant and put him on his shoulder where Justin continued to grizzle tiredly.

'He's sickening for something,' I said. 'D'you think I ought to ask Anne if she'll pop in and take a look at him?'

'He's too hot,' said Terry.

'Of course he's too hot,' I stormed. 'He's got a temperature.'

But Terry was undoing the snap fasteners on Justin's stretch sleep suit. 'Wool vest,' he said triumphantly. 'My sister said that wool next to the skin made her pair nigh-on parboil. In these days of central heating you don't need to dress them up so much. Look, the poor little sod's virtually glowing he's so hot.' He pulled off the offending garment.

'Well I'm damned,' Patrick whispered as our son faded before our eyes.

'Brushed cotton ones are the answer,' said Terry, adroitly slipping Justin back into his sleep suit. 'You go – I'll put him back to bed.'

I am only recording this little episode because it could so easily have been the last time Justin was in his parents' company.

Chapter Six

Elspeth had been quite correct when she had said that David Prescott lived in a new bungalow at the other end of the village. But Rannoch, for that was what it was called, did not form part of the small estate, having been built a few months earlier in the grounds of a large house next door.

We walked as it was only a few minutes away, the church clock striking eleven into thick chilling mist as we went through the Rectory gate. Dutchy brought up the rear. He was older than Terry by several years and, according to Patrick, was what the department regarded as an all-rounder. In other words could think for himself as well as supplying muscle. Terry, who was being coached eventually to take Patrick's place and displayed the occasional flash of pure brilliance as would be expected from someone of his high intelligence, still preferred to use violence to get himself out of trouble instead of his brain.

I found myself wishing that Terry was with us now and not his somewhat morose replacement.

'I really wonder if we ought to risk your parents' safety by using the Rectory like this,' I murmured, huddling into my thick sweater.

'I'm doing it deliberately,' Patrick said. 'Think: the people getting to Prescott must have been to the village several times. There's a chance that they were seen by locals. Besides, if they do return there are four of us forming the welcoming committee instead of possibly just one copper, at a guess unarmed.'

I gave myself a mental shake. Just a few weeks of baby

minding and I was making statements that would never have passed my lips before Justin was born.

'Basically, of course, I agree with you,' Patrick went on. 'But Prescott did start this by asking for our help instead of going to the police.'

'I'm glad you didn't give Terry hell,' I said when we had walked in silence for a short distance.

Patrick gave a harrumphing sort of chuckle. 'Waiting for it served just as well.' Then he halted so suddenly that Dutchy almost cannoned into him. 'This isn't going to be a raid — we're not even going to break in,' he said in a whisper. 'I have the keys. Prescott doesn't know that we're going to be snooping around his house so nothing must be moved. For his sake this is vital.'

We walked on, Patrick loudly wishing one of his father's parishioners good night as the old man staggered blind drunk out of the 'Marquis of Granby' on the other side of the road.

An ancient avenue of holm oaks led up to the Catholic Church, St Joseph's, the first pair — and seemingly the largest-looming right over the main street of the village. The rather feeble illumination from the street lights was quite unable to penetrate their thick evergreen foliage and for a few yards it was like walking through a tunnel. Along the lines of trees I could just discern a glimmer of light from the church windows.

'It's a bit late for anyone to be in the church,' I remarked.

'The lights are on a time switch,' Patrick said, mind obviously on other things. 'Father David had it put in after a couple of break-ins lately.'

'After the silver?' asked Dutchy.

'No — Communion wafers for use in black magic ceremonies.'

'Go on,' Dutchy whispered. 'I thought all that mumbo-jumbo was only in stories.'

'Has your father had any trouble at St Michael's?' I enquired.

'I put an alarm on both doors of the church after someone tampered with a grave one night.'

I repressed a shudder and hitched my arm through Patrick's.

'I try not to get involved with any of it,' said Dutchy. 'One side or the other. With all due respect to your father, that

51

kind of thing doesn't really seem relevant in today's modern world.'

'Quite,' said Patrick. 'It almost serves a lot of old fuddy-duddies right if people steal their sacred objects and do what they like with them.'

Dutchy didn't have to be telepathic to realize suddenly that he was on very dangerous ground. 'I wouldn't go so far as to say that, sir.'

'Why on earth not?'

'Everyone has a right to have their beliefs respected.'

Patrick gave a bored laugh. 'But you just said that black magic is a load of mumbo-jumbo.'

'But it's — it's evil. Good things twisted and defiled.'

I couldn't see his face but knew that Patrick was smiling gently. 'Don't let being an atheist worry you. D12 won't throw you out. But strange as it may seem you're in the minority. Even Daws, who insists that he's a lapsed Catholic, attends Mass occasionally in his lunch hour. It's strange how people are afraid of others laughing at them, isn't it?'

We reached our destination, a fleeting stab of light from Patrick's tiny flash lamp illuminating the name plate of the bungalow we were looking for. It was partly screened from the road by a high privet hedge and, one on each side of the gate, holly bushes had been clipped to form an archway.

'This was the original side gate of the house whose owners sold off the land,' Patrick said. 'Dutchy, be so good as to check around the back while Ingrid and I wait here.'

But Dutchy just stood there.

'What's the problem?' Patrick asked.

'Nothing, sir,' replied Dutchy. He snicked up the latch of the wrought iron gate and went from our sight into the darkness.

'Does he think I can't read what's written in his records?' Patrick muttered.

'What is he so scared of admitting to believing in?' I asked.

'He's a Baptist.'

'Blame today's modern world,' I told him. 'When keeping in with the pagan crowd is the thing.'

'But that's bloody cowardly,' Patrick burst out.

'Then cross your self-constructed barrier, priest to be, and

52

see the modern world before it's too late.' Into the ensuing silence I added, 'You're not like other people – you don't care what the world thinks of you.'

'You're really mad at me,' he said, sounding surprised.

'Only because your strong ideas of right and wrong are in danger of becoming bigotry. Go in the public bar for a change, listen to the profanity and ignorance. Slum it for a while – see how the real world lives.'

He didn't actually shrug or turn his back on me, just gave exaggerated attention to what Dutchy had to say when he returned. The most interesting piece of information in the short report was that the back door was unlocked.

'Did you go in?' Patrick asked.

'No, sir, I just flashed my torch around the kitchen to see if vandals had been in.'

'And have they?'

'Nothing seems to have been disturbed.'

'Any muddy footprints?'

'There's a bit of dirt on the mat where people have wiped their feet. I took that to be Prescott himself or the trio from the local CID who drove him to London.'

'Never presume,' Patrick said shortly.

'He *would* tend to use the back door rather than the front,' I said.

'Why?' asked Dutchy disbelievingly.

Patrick took the keys from his pocket and closely examined them in the light from his miniature torch. 'You're right – the one for the front door looks as though it's hardly ever been used. The other one's only a cheap alloy thing and is quite worn at the corners.'

'He lives on his own and does all the cleaning,' I said. 'He's also particular and slightly old-maidish. Going in the back saves wear and tear to the hall carpet.'

'So we'll go in the front,' Patrick said, 'in case anyone arranged a surprise for those using the back door.'

We went up the path. It was very dark, and from where I was walking in the rear the men's torches were useless to me. Faintly, the moon shone through the mist but any benefit from this was almost totally negated by a thick screen of trees. Mostly fir and pine, the majority of them in the garden next

53

door, they cast the blackest of shade. Already jittery from talk of black magic and the disturbance of graves, I was half expecting icy hands to grab me round the neck.

'Light!' Patrick snapped.

'Sorry, sir,' said Dutchy, hastening to shine his torch on the front door.

'The damn bulb's just failed in mine.'

The lock yielded but the door wouldn't open.

'Bolted from the inside,' Patrick said. 'I don't like the fact that the back door's open at all.'

'Why don't we come back in the morning?' I enquired, reasonably I thought.

'Because I've got to be in London in the morning, that's why,' he retorted, and plunged off around the side of the house, leaving me with no time to ask what on earth I had come all the way from Devon for.

David Prescott's home smelt fusty; stale cooking of the greasy variety and another odour redolent of blocked drains. We all, I think, were surprised for the scientist was undoubtedly a fastidious man, the sort you'd expect to have a penchant for fresh air and wholesome food rather than fry-ups.

Patrick clicked down the kitchen light switch and nothing happened.

'Don't tell me he turned it off at the mains,' Dutchy said. 'Shall I find the fuse box?'

'No, stay here,' he was ordered. And then, nerves making him give way to exasperation, 'How many times have you practised entering booby-trapped buildings? The last thing you do is blunder off opening cupboards. You two stay here while I have a look.'

I usually do as I'm told but this time I squeezed past Dutchy in the narrow kitchen doorway and stood where I could see Patrick as he made his way down the hall by the light of the borrowed torch. The fustiness and darkness of the house seemed to press against me and with a sense of mounting horror I realized what the smell was.

'There's a body,' I hissed, finding myself clutching Dutchy's lapels.

'The main fuse has been removed,' Patrick called back

down the hall. 'No sign of it. Probably all part of the plan to frighten Prescott silly.'

Glancing neither right nor left, even though it was dark, I went to him. 'Patrick. . . . ' I'm not very good, even now, when in the company of cobwebs or corpses in murky places.

'I thought I told you to stay in the kitchen.'

'There's a body in this house,' I managed to get out. 'I can smell it.'

He sniffed the air. 'I can't smell anything.'

'That and a kind of sweet smell. Like a woman's perfume.' When he didn't react I said, 'I've thought for ages that your sense of smell hasn't been right since you had that bad cold.'

'We'll look around,' he muttered after hesitating.

'Together,' I added. 'There's only the one torch.'

Patrick whistled for Dutchy. He does this when he's on edge, and no one minds.

'Sir?'

'Lock the kitchen door and come with us. Don't touch anything.'

The layout of the bungalow was decidedly odd. To our left as we stood facing the front door was a sitting room. One went through an archway in one wall of this into the dining room, the only other entrance to which led off from the kitchen. To our right was a double bedroom. Between this and a large open area to the rear of the hall with the bathroom off it was a passage at right angles. This ran the width of the bedroom and then again branched left and right. We started with the sitting room.

'You're right,' Dutchy said in my ear. 'Either that or something's gone off in the larder.' He seemed to be coming alive by the minute, relishing the tension, and was quite unlike the man I had met in the Rectory drive.

There was the same sort of three-piece suite, television set, bookcase and standard lamp as in a million other homes. The colour scheme was muted, the only real colour in the room provided by a large framed print of Constable's 'Haywain' over the fireplace. We went no further than the archway to examine the dining room. There was no need for it was very small; table, chairs, sideboard, another Constable print.

The bedroom bore all the signs of hasty packing, the most

poignant a single blue sock lying on the carpet by the door. In his hurry Prescott had not even closed the wardrobe doors.

'The curtains are all closed in this house,' I said. 'And yet he left in broad daylight.'

'And in that much of a rush he wouldn't have stopped to close them,' Dutchy added.

Self-preservation, commonsense, cowardice — all were screaming at me to leave and return in the daytime in the company of comfortingly large policemen. But I had to carry on walking around this nightmare dwelling with what I was convinced was the smell of decomposing flesh strong in my nostrils.

Through the open bathroom door the torch beam picked out an overturned talcum powder tin, some of its contents spilt on the floor; a bathtowel crooked on the rail where the one next to it had been snatched quickly away. I looked away when Patrick glanced in the shower cubicle.

'Nothing,' muttered Dutchy. 'But we're getting warmer, as the saying goes.'

In single file — for it was too narrow for it to be any other way — we went along the passage that led off at right angles to the hall. Patrick first, then me, then Dutchy. The ghastly smell was much stronger here and once or twice I had to swallow hard.

To the right and left at the end of the passage were doors, both closed.

'Suicide,' Patrick said thoughtfully. 'Fright, heart attack or electric shock?' He picked up a small rug, folded it in half, stood on it and touched both metal doorhandles with the toe of a shoe.

'No main fuse,' Dutchy pointed out.

'Quite possible to kill someone with portable equipment,' he was told. 'Both of you stand right by the wall — no, on second thoughts go back round the corner. I'm going to open the right hand door first.'

'Let me do it, sir,' said Dutchy. 'That's what I'm here for.'

'You most certainly aren't,' Patrick said savagely.

Just after he opened the door I knew I was going to be sick. Somehow, retching helplessly, I groped my way back to the bathroom and located the toilet with not a second to spare. Then

I heard Dutchy shout. But I couldn't go to help right then, I was totally incapacitated by nausea.

Suddenly, people ran down the hall and, a moment later, the lights came on. Sheer fright kept me where I was, stomach heaving.

'Where's the woman?' a man yelled.

'There wasn't a woman,' someone else called, a female voice.

'Stupid bitch! I heard her talking. Go and look for her.'

I wasn't armed. Not even a knife.

The next moment she was there, standing right in the doorway, pink jeans, black leather jacket, a black mask covering her face. I could see only her eyes which were blue and utterly, utterly terrified.

We stared at one another for several seconds and then she yanked on the pull switch to put the light out and slammed the door.

'The bathroom window's open,' I heard her shout. 'She's gone.'

I took the hint and opened the window. But I didn't climb through it, just hid inside the airing cupboard that switching on the light had revealed behind the door.

No one checked.

I made myself count up to fifty and then crept out. There was not a sound. The light was still on in the hall, I could see that by the narrow strip of brightness beneath the bathroom door. I opened it cautiously and a cold draught of air wafted on to my face. This was coming through the wide open front door, which still shivered slightly from the violence with which it had been wrenched open.

'Patrick?' I croaked.

Both of the doors facing each other at the end of the passage were now ajar. I pushed the left hand one wide and looked into another bedroom, the entire room a mess of crumpled covers, a litter of beer cans, fish and chip papers, and cigarette ash.

The other room was a study of sorts, a desk, chair, an armchair, bookcase, china cabinet. It is strange how my powers of observation are heightened at such times.

Patrick and Dutchy were sprawled on the floor. In the arm

chair, which had been placed so that it faced the door, was the body of what had probably been a man. Such was the advanced state of decomposition that it was difficult to guess age or sex.

The left arm of the corpse was missing.

Chapter Seven

I had the receiver of the phone actually in my hand when Terry strode in through the front door. He recoiled at the stench.

'You can't leave the Gillards,' I shouted at him.

'John sent me,' he said, setting off up the hall. 'I left him mounting guard with his twelve bore.'

'Terry. . . .' I ran after him and he turned.

'Correction to my last. John sent me by pointing his twelve bore in my direction *before* mounting guard. I never argue with anyone in this family when they get really upset. He seemed to think you ought to have been back ages ago.'

'We'll need a doctor.'

'Then fetch Anne.'

'And the police.'

'I'll call the police. You get Anne.'

I must have swayed for the wall suddenly hit me hard on my left side. All I could see, hear and smell was superimposed by rotting flesh, fingers with the bones showing through, eye sockets like. . . . No, don't think about it. In that direction lay madness.

'Get Anne,' Terry said again and quite gently.

Anne, by some miracle, was just swinging into her drive in her battered Fiat. The run in cold night air had restored me to virtual normality and I was able to make my request in what sounded to me like a calmly efficient manner. She threw open the passenger door for me.

Patrick was lying nearest the door of the study so she went to him first. I marvelled at the way she got on with the job after giving the body in the chair only the most cursory of glances.

With Terry's help she straightened him out on the floor, lifted an eyelid, smelt his breath and then pushed up his thick sweater to check pulse and heartbeat.

'He's in no danger,' she said with a quick look at me in between examining his arms. Even with my limited medical knowledge I knew she was looking for puncture marks for it was obvious the men hadn't been beaten unconscious. 'I'm not sure but I think they were given a whiff of something in an aerosol. Illegal in this country, of course, but quite easy to obtain if you know where to go.'

Dutchy groaned and rolled over.

I said, 'Patrick reacts very strongly to some substances. It's because he had so many drugs when he was in hospital.'

'We'll give him oxygen,' Anne said, and went out to her car.

The police arrived while she was outside and suddenly the bungalow was full of tramping feet.

'Ambulance?' one constable asked of Anne.

'If you mean do I want one the answer's probably no. But you'll need one for him,' Anne said, gesturing towards the body.

'Bit late for that poor bugger,' someone muttered, going back outside to use his radio.

I was praying that Patrick would wake up soon for the appallingly selfish reason that I didn't want to be around when the body was shifted. I had a feeling that it would fall apart and I would be sick again. Nausea was hovering even now at the back of my throat.

Dutchy was sitting up, head in hands, when Patrick's eyes fluttered open.

'Deep breaths,' Anne ordered briskly. 'On your feet in ten, out of the house in twenty.'

He was on his feet in twelve whereupon Anne took away the face mask and transferred it to Dutchy.

'Go on,' she said. 'Out. Go and sit in my car. Ingrid, you go with him.'

I took his hand when we were sitting in the back of the car and neither of us spoke.

'If they'd been armed with guns, we'd probably be dead now,' Patrick said, uttering what had so far remained unsaid.

'Just as well they didn't find yours,' Terry observed mildly but nevertheless getting across the message that he was unimpressed.

The gun harness had been beneath Patrick's sweater, worn next to his skin. The man who had questioned him and had pushed up the sweater in order to burn him a few times with his cigarette in order to make him talk, had not discovered it. I still could not believe that there had been time for this and could only reason that I had passed out for a few minutes when I was hiding in the airing cupboard.

'How incredible is village life,' said Anne, whose thoughts must have been similar to my own. 'One moment athlete's foot and old men with waterworks problems, the next terrorists and torture. You four are part of a team. I thought you might be. Special operations and all that.'

'Be our Somerset medic,' Patrick said with feeling. 'Oh God, why is the room still going round backwards?'

'What did you tell them?' Terry enquired with clinical interest.

Patrick commenced to whine in a weird Welsh monotone. 'It's just the rector's son I swear I am. I'm in the army and they sometimes let me drive a tank. No, honest to God, it wasn't me who took a shot at you the other day. That was the gamekeeper because he thought you were the poachers he missed the week before. He only shoots at people when he's drunk. We were all drunk because of the party. Mr Prescott was taken away to a psychiatric hospital. Why not? Half the village knows he's off his head. Please don't burn me anymore — I'm telling you the truth, aren't I?'

He stopped speaking to take a mouthful of tea from the mug he was cradling in both hands. 'Talk, they tell you during training.Talk about anything and everything. Act like ordinary panic-stricken Joe Bloke. Only I couldn't really let go on the hysterics because they already knew I was Major, army for the bloody use of. Then there was a sort of coldness on my face and that's the last thing I remember.'

Some sixth sense made me know what Terry was going to ask next.

'So how did they overpower you in the first place?'

'Two men and a girl,' Patrick said. 'One of the blokes was

61

big and strong. He literally strangled me to the floor. What else do you want to know?'

'How d'you reckon they knew your profession?' Anne said into the silence.

'Justin's christening was in the local paper,' Patrick replied. 'With a photo of the proud parents.'

I was still analysing the stab of alarm I had experienced upon hearing him talk of 'letting go with hysterics'. There could be no mistake in this, he had not said 'played up the hysterics'. So I gazed at him searchingly and recollected that the condition known as combat stress had, so far, not affected him.

'Is that a bruise or biro on your hand?' Dutchy said to Patrick apologetically. He still seemed to be blaming himself for what had happened.

Patrick set down his mug. 'It's ink,' he concluded, 'but I can't focus the eyes to read what it says.' He held out the hand for me to see.

'Words!' exclaimed Anne.

Even smudged, the neat writing was still clear enough to read.

'It says, "Alyssa Goldberg",' I said. 'The girl! It must be. She pretended she hadn't seen me in the bathroom.'

'Did she by Jove!' Patrick said.

'Are you people going to bed tonight?' said John, putting his head round the door. 'The police are coming back in the morning to ask more questions.'

'It's the padre himself,' chortled Patrick. 'Father, would you happen to have a drop of whisky in your pyjamas pocket? No?'

'No,' said John.

'It *is* the morning,' I said to myself.

It *was* the morning and my head hardly seemed to have touched the pillow before Justin started to make hungry noises. I slid out of bed, changed him and then took him back with me, propping myself up in bed and falling asleep again despite the fact that he was hungrily latched on to me. Then I became aware of Elspeth looking round the door.

'Sorry,' she whispered. 'I was going to give Justin a bottle if you hadn't heard him. I'll get you some tea.'

I offered Justin the other source of nourishment as he didn't

62

seem to be getting much milk where he was and then glanced down at Patrick who was still soundly asleep. He seemed peaceful enough.

When I woke up there was a cooling cup of tea on the bedside table and Justin was asleep at an angle of forty-five degrees, head downwards, in my lap. I put him back in his cot, went back to bed, drank the tea and slept until noon.

'It was almost certainly planned to finish Prescott right off,' Patrick was saying not too far away. 'I blame myself entirely that we didn't apprehend them. If I'd thought that they were in the house, waiting for him. . . .'

He was sitting on the bed, dressed, reporting to Daws over the phone. After a few more minutes of mostly listening he asked the Colonel to mention the name Alyssa Goldberg to David Prescott, and rang off.

'My name is mud,' he said.

'It wasn't your fault.'

'I've just had another roasting from the local police for not telling them what we were doing.'

'Since when did D12 tell the police what they were up to?' I snapped.

Justin was awake and working up to making more hungry noises.

'The milk's drying up,' I said. 'I'll take him down and give him some cereal.'

'Dawn's mother rang.'

Something in his manner caused me to go cold all over. 'Oh God,' I whispered. 'She's killed herself on those damn mountains.'

'Not as bad as that. She's broken her leg.'

But I simply couldn't conjure up any reaction to the news, not after what had happened the night before.

Patrick said, 'From our point of view it's just as bad.'

But I wasn't really listening to him. 'The body had no left arm,' I said.

'They're sending away for the one found at Brighton so a comparison can be made.'

'At your suggestion?'

'On Brinkley's advice. I phoned him late last night. Doesn't it worry you that Dawn's not coming?'

63

'Not right now. That girl – Alyssa – do you think she's some poor little rich girl who has run away from home and got in with the wrong company?'

'What on earth makes you say that?'

'The perfume she was wearing. It was very expensive. It was as though she was so sickened by the smell of the body that she'd poured the entire bottle over herself to counteract it.'

'Any idea what it was?'

'No. But it might be worth while walking around Harrods' perfumery department.'

'Then we will. Tomorrow. Just in case it's so expensive only half a dozen women in the country buy it. Justin can stay with Mother.'

'No,' I said. 'Justin comes with us. He's really no problem if I use disposable nappies all the time. If things get really difficult I'll take him to Sally.' Sally is my sister who no sooner sees a child off to nursery school when she comes over broody all over again. She and her husband, Derek, had been unable to attend Justin's christening and she was longing to see him.

A smile twitched the corners of Patrick's mouth. 'Successful writer can't face life without Oink, eh?'

I put both arms round his neck and pulled him down so I could kiss him.

'Still feel like death?'

'Warmed up a little,' he answered, kissing me back.

We didn't speak again for quite a while, seeking the solace and renewal of spirits that each knew the other could provide.

Chapter Eight

I suppose it was purely our defence mechanisms in the face of horror and tragedy that caused us to be taken with irrepressible giggles in Harrods the next day, regrettable behaviour – as the Scots put it – outwith our control. But I had already learned to my cost that trained beauticians, models and all such limp and over-groomed members of the female race, will reduce my partner to ill-advised smirks. Don't ask me why – he is not a misogynist. Come to think of it, I can recall an occasion when I mistakenly took him to a West End hair salon thinking that it was about time he started to have his hair cut properly. He had taken one look at the young male operatives within – satin shirts slashed to the waist, gold medallions, earrings glittering – and had bolted. At the time I had assumed this to be antipathy. Not so perhaps. There might have been the overwhelming urge to pee all over it like a rutting stag, yell 'Bullshit!' a few times, and depart howling with laughter.

'But you *do* know how to behave really,' I said as we trailed from one counter to another. 'You're involved with the most complicated forms of protocol when you're protecting the PM.' By now my nose was stunned into a state of complete non co-operation by the many perfumes I had offered to it.

Patrick pounced on yet another tester bottle. 'Would madam like to try Venom by Schlizt? Just the thing for Monday morning arse-hole. Only five hundred quid the half ounce bottle. Guaranteed tom-cat free and with no artificial additives.'

'Patrick!' I hissed when several heads turned. Ex-choirboys always have the most carrying voices.

'Or there's something bolder. Puke from the House of Von Pumpernickel. The promise that every man in the room will be like a dog with two —'

'Patrick!'

'Tails,' he concluded, all innocence, dabbing some on Justin's cheek, his son asleep in the sling around his neck. The delicate looking fingers replaced the tester in the rack but he wasn't watching what he was doing. 'Perhaps I shouldn't have done that,' he mused, gaze on Justin. 'He might turn into a toad at midnight.'

I walked off, pretending he wasn't with me. But this was difficult because lone men don't usually wear babies.

'You're not amused, Ingrid,' said he, peering through some silk scarves at me, whereupon I shrieked with laughter.

'This is hopeless,' Patrick said when we had both run down like clock springs. 'Let's find some coffee.'

We were near the exit to the department when he gripped my arm so hard I squeaked in protest. Then I saw what he was looking at. In large gold letters a foot high, glistening under the spotlights and surrounded by gold artificial bay trees in pots, was the word 'Goldberg'.

I didn't have to sample the latest perfume from this cosmetic company, the beauty consultants were misting it into the air. They too were dressed in gold; uniform, shoes and lurex tights. Their hair had sprayed on golden highlights, their faces were dusted with sparkling gold, as were nails, eyes, everything. And the perfume they were so generously wasting on us was called 'Alyssa'.

All I could think of were corpses.

We went back to Patrick's tiny flat just off Gower Street.

'There is absolutely nothing to connect Alex Haywood with this body,' said Colonel Richard Daws two days later. He was specifically addressing me. 'I appreciate that the fact that the arm was washed up not far from where he staged his fake suicide makes one look for a link. The police in Bude interviewed him again and showed him the wedding ring that was removed from it. He said he had never seen it before and the officer conducting the enquiry was inclined to believe him as he was wearing what seemed quite an old one which looked too tight to be removed.'

'But if the arm came from the same body that was used to frighten Prescott, what was it doing on Brighton Beach if the rest of it was in Somerset?' I protested.

'The entire corpse might have been in the sea at one time,' Daws said. 'The forensic people haven't sent in their report yet. Who knows? The arm could easily have been severed by the propellor of a boat while the body was in the water.'

'So don't we believe Prescott at all?' I asked, looking from Daws to Patrick.

Patrick took a deep breath and let it go gustily. 'But what has the guy actually *said?* Right, he mentioned that the man who owned the bike had been killed in order to obtain possession of it, and that he was shot. He began to go to pieces when I asked him if he was present when the killing took place. I know I then said that I thought he might have been forced to commit the murder but it was only a guess. Do we know whether the body had bullet holes in it, by the way?'

'Not yet,' Daws replied. 'But I've an uncomfortable feeling that even if we find out who this man was and everything about him, it won't lead us to the people who killed him. I'm much more interested in the girl − ' he slid his reading glasses on to his nose and consulted a piece of paper − 'Alyssa Goldberg. She's the eldest daughter of Eugene and Henrietta Goldberg. Together with a partner, they own Goldberg Enterprises.'

'Have you a picture of her?' I asked impatiently.

Saying nothing, Daws gave me a photograph.

'That's her,' I told him.

'Are you sure?'

I covered up all of her face but for the eyes with my fingers. 'Positive.'

'Her parents insist that she's on holiday, touring Europe.'

Again I looked at the picture. Alyssa Goldberg was a very beautiful young woman. Her shoulder-length hair was red-gold and styled for the photograph in masses of tiny curls. Her complexion was flawless, the bone structure of her face fine, the blue eyes enormous. They were the same eyes that had stared at me in boundless terror.

'I'm positive,' I said again. 'Her eyelashes are red-gold too and she had vestiges of eye makeup that had been applied just like this. Was this picture part of the advertising campaign for the perfume?'

Daws nodded.

Patrick said, 'You mentioned that she's the eldest daughter, sir. What other children are there?'

'Only another daughter.' Daws held out a second photograph to me. This one was a family snapshot of a girl playing with a puppy.

'Is this a recent picture?' I asked.

'I've no idea,' Daws replied. 'Her name's Raphaella.'

'And where can this young lady be found?'

'At a boarding school in Sussex. I checked. She *is* there and the woman I spoke to was adamant that none of the girls ever went AWOL.'

I didn't dare ask him what methods he used to elicit this kind of information from exclusive schools for girls.

'Prescott showed no reaction to either name,' Daws continued. 'Major, I'd like you to talk to him again. I'm not too worried about his state of health.'

'Now?' Patrick enquired.

'The car's waiting outside.'

When we were in the car and weaving through the traffic in the direction of Bushey Park, I said, 'I forgot to ask the Colonel about the hatemail that Haywood was supposed to be receiving.'

'You might just be mixing up your plot for *Echoes of Murder* with real life.'

This was uttered so coldly that I looked at him in shocked surprise. But Patrick wasn't giving me any of his attention, he was staring fixedly, seeing nothing, out of the window.

'What's the matter?'

'You were there. You heard him. He's not worried about Prescott's state of health. In his language that is an order to me to find out everything that Prescott knows without caring a damn what coming clean will do to him.'

During the meeting with Daws I had left Justin with his secretary but felt I could hardly expect the driver of our car to play with him while we spoke to David Prescott so I took him with us.

When we were halfway up the wide stairs to the first floor of

Rawlston House, Patrick said, 'I think we're going to have to contemplate using one of those nanny agencies. Dawn's mother recommended the one her daughter usually works from, and let's face it – if we hadn't heard about Dawn through a friend of a friend we would have had to have done that in the first place.'

'I'll look into it,' I promised, cuddling Justin tighter.

Prescott was already in the interview room and when we entered rose to his feet. He looked thinner than when I had last seen him but seemed composed.

'No, do sit, David,' Patrick hastened to say. 'You've met Ingrid. The small one is Justin.'

An inner door closed soundlessly.

'Not here to make me feel guilty about involving you all, I hope,' Prescott said.

'Justin's nanny broke her leg,' I said before Patrick could reply. 'And I'm enjoying a day in town. Patrick said he didn't think you'd mind if I sat in while you talked.'

'No, no, of course not,' he said and looked almost happy for a moment. It was then I realized that he was still under sedation.

'D'you know a girl called Alyssa Goldberg?' Patrick asked, making himself comfortable.

'The Colonel's already asked me that. No.' Prescott had answered the question quite cheerfully and I got the impression that he was glad to talk to someone. It was understandable for although he was not kept under conditions that could be described as solitary confinement, the people looking after him were forbidden to engage with him in meaningful conversation. This of course was official policy.

'What *was* the girl's name then?'

'They didn't call her anything. Just "Hey, you." One of them only referred to her as. . . .' And here Prescott said to me, 'Forgive me. He just called her "stupid bitch".'

Patrick's eyes closed momentarily in relief at the unforeseen readiness to talk but Prescott probably assumed him to be thinking deeply. 'Was she pretty?'

'I only ever saw her masked, but I think she had red hair. I felt sorry for her.'

'Why?'

'She was frightened of them. I think the man who was killed was a friend of hers.'

'So they forced her to stay with them.'

'They seemed to have some kind of hold over her.'

'D'you think it was drugs?'

Prescott thought about it for a moment or two. 'No, I should say it was fear of violence. The tall one used to hit her.'

'Did he have very dark brown eyes and big hairy hands?'

When Prescott's own hands clenched in his lap, I thought for an instant that Patrick had gone too quickly. But Prescott pulled himself together and said, 'Why — have you seen him?'

'In your bungalow. The three of them were waiting for you to return.'

'I was there too,' I said, trying to strengthen the fragile common bond. 'We know the kind of thing you went through now.'

'But what were you doing in my house?' he asked like a perplexed child.

'We went to make sure that it was safely locked up,' I told him.

'It wasn't,' Patrick added.

'What did they say to you?'

'Not a lot,' Patrick said abruptly.

'Major, you're keeping something from me.'

'They tortured him,' I said, taking the cue. 'He doesn't like talking about it really. Show him,' I instructed Patrick.

With a play of reluctance Patrick undid his shirt, thus revealing the burns across his stomach.

'The unspeakable. . . .' Prescott started to say, and then glanced at me, shaking his head. 'Why in God's name — ?'

'They wanted to know what we were doing there,' Patrick interrupted. 'And where you were and why you hadn't come back. I think I managed to convince them, but. . . .' He broke off and conveyed in quite the most heart-rending fashion that he could speak about it no more.

'My dear fellow. . .' David Prescott murmured, and then also became lost for words.

'But they weren't after money,' Patrick said, sighing. 'Otherwise they would have taken your quite superb collection of model steam engines and sold them.'

70

'They didn't want anything from me,' said Prescott after a long silence. 'Only to torment me to death.'

'Why didn't you say so before?' Patrick asked gently.

'Because of my memories.'

'Did they torture you too?'

'Not like that.'

There was another long silence during which the only sound was rain pattering on the window. Justin, thankfully, was asleep.

'Shall I carry on guessing?' Patrick said softly at last. 'I'll get there in the end. I've a really diabolical imagination.'

'What d'you mean?' Prescott asked, alarmed.

Patrick leaned forward, gazing intently at the other. 'The big man — that was a good word for him — diabolical. He offered to do some really fancy things to me if I didn't talk. Things that I wouldn't normally mention in front of Ingrid.'

Ingrid feigned boredom, stifling a yawn and examining her nails.

Prescott was nodding slowly.

'He's capable of anything,' Patrick said in a hoarse whisper. 'Drink, drugs, murder, filthy sexual practices. I can imagine him finding pleasure in setting up all kinds of revolting — ' He stopped talking for Prescott was shuddering perceptibly.

'Speak the unspeakable,' I said quietly. 'For Alyssa's sake. She's not a criminal but a lovely young girl taken from her family.' I took the picture of her from my bag and held it out for Prescott to see. 'Whatever it was, whether they made you commit murder or forced you into filthy acts, her fate depends on your telling us all you know so these people can be caught.'

'Her fate,' Prescott repeated very slowly.

'Yours is not in jeopardy,' I told him, words seeming to tumble from my lips. 'It never has been. All Christians know that.'

Prescott's forehead creased into a deep frown. 'Ultimate fate, you mean. Yes, of course, you're quite right. I — I hadn't thought of it like that before. If I can live with myself. . . .' His voice slurred slightly and trailed away, and with a slight shock I perceived the strength of the medication that he was under.

And then, haltingly, he told us. When it was nearly over Patrick pressed the hidden button on his chair that ensured the arrival of a steward with tea. Prescott talked on, at peace now that he could unburden himself of his nightmare memories. By the time he had finished and silence settled over the room it was nearly dark outside.

I rose to close the curtains, surprised to find myself utterly exhausted.

'Do you think your father would come to see me?' Prescott asked.

'Sure he would,' Patrick replied. 'I'll ask him if you like.'

'I'll sell the house. I couldn't go back there.'

'The village would be very sad to see you go if you moved away entirely,' I told him.

Patrick stood up and stretched. 'You don't happen to know any of these poor devils who killed themselves lately, do you?'

'*That's* what I was going to mention to you,' Prescott recalled. 'I was most distressed when I read that Colin Jones was dead. He and I were at university together. I was a very old student, you understand. He was brilliant — quite brilliant.'

'What about Peterson?' said Patrick, sitting down again.

'Gordon Peterson? No, come to think of it his name was Peters. Has someone else died with that name?'

'No, it was George Peterson. Kevin Cook was the other one.'

'I've never heard of that one,' Prescott muttered. 'Good gracious, I see what you mean. I hadn't realized that there might be a connection. One thinks of things like pressure of work and so forth. Now, wait a minute. . . . There was another name. I've been so distraught lately I haven't been able to concentrate on reading the papers but I was sure there was another name that rang a bell.'

'Haywood?' Patrick suggested lightly. 'Alex Haywood?'

'That was the name! Yes, Haywood. Now, Haywood was the kind of man who never looked as though he had a brain. But he was clever all right. I worked for him for a while when I first went to Bath.'

Chapter Nine

'My daughter is on holiday abroad — probably arriving in Switzerland some time today,' said Henrietta Goldberg.

I could imagine her answering the phone in a discreetly sumptuous drawing room, she herself groomed immaculately and sipping from a hand cut crystal glass her pre-luncheon aperitif. It was that kind of voice.

'Which paper did you say you worked for?' she enquired smoothly.

'I didn't,' I replied equally smoothly. 'I'm a freelance writer and I've been asked to create pen portraits of several young women who are regarded as having influenced fashion.'

'You're not *the* Ingrid Langley?'

I breathed a silent sigh of relief. At least now she wouldn't put the phone down. Affecting what I hoped sounded like the correct degree of modesty, I told her that I was.

'This is a great shame,' she continued. 'I'm sure that Alyssa would have been quite captivated by the prospect of a famous novelist writing an article about her. But she won't be home for several weeks as she's staying with friends in several countries.'

'It's not necessary for me to speak with her personally,' I said. 'I'm sure that as her mother you can give me all the relevant information. Anyway, the underlying gist of these articles is how families help and groom their offspring for the successes ahead.' I have discovered since working with Patrick that I am a regrettably glib liar.

'I'm not too sure that — '

'I'm afraid I can't offer you a fee,' I interposed. 'But the resulting publicity should more than. ...' I left the rest hanging in the air and made the resolve that I would write something that would be published even if I had to bribe the editor of a magazine to achieve it.

'Are you in London?'

'Just for a few days,' I told her, hoping that she couldn't hear Justin grizzling in the bedroom. The city air did not appear to be suiting him at all.

'Do you know Fitzmaurice Square, Chelsea? You must do, it's where they were going to demolish a derelict Regency terrace to build a block of flats. There was an *awful* lot about it in the papers.'

But not in the *Western Morning News*. 'The taxi driver will know where it is,' I assured her.

We arranged that I would call at ten-thirty the following morning.

'Clothes,' I said pensively to Patrick when he returned from yet another briefing with Daws, Justin still with the miseries.

'What about them?' he enquired, heading for his son.

'Patrick, if you pick him up every time he cries, I'll never be able to do a thing with him!' I complained, running in his wake.

Too late. Justin was up and goggling damply, like a myopic frog, at the paterfamilias. Seconds later he had brought up a good proportion of his feed. The perfect father had, of course, draped a towel over his shoulder first.

'There you are you see,' said Patrick triumphantly. 'Indigestion.'

It was a waste of time explaining that babies gulp air when they cry and being lifted quickly into an upright position can cause this to be expelled violently from the stomach, together with anything else that happens to be there at the time.

'What about clothes?'

I told him about the appointment.

'You're a genius.'

No, I did not smirk. 'I didn't bring the right sort of attire to project myself as a successful novelist,' I told him.

'So? What's the problem? You go and buy some.'

'You'll have to babysit. I simply haven't the time to buy clothes, feed and change him and get to Chelsea before ten-thirty.'

'But I'm going to work. I simply have to make enquiries about Jones and Peterson.'

'Take him with you.'

'Ingrid . . .' he began heavily.

'There's a phone here,' I reminded him. 'Isn't this flat mostly on expenses anyway?' I smiled sweetly. He hadn't known that I was aware of this fact, and always used the excuse of the cost of the upkeep of his London base when I suggested things like having the Devon cottage re-thatched.

'Okay,' he groaned. 'What's for dinner?'

I finished mopping our child, wondering if I would arrive at the Goldbergs' no doubt gold plated apartment delicately exuding the smell of sicked-up milk.

'Ten out of ten for noticing Prescott's model steam engine collection,' I said. 'I'm afraid I looked no further than the body in that room.'

'No dinner?' he said in a small voice, eyeing me curiously.

'I fell asleep this afternoon,' I admitted. This was an understatement. I had sat down for a few minutes to try to rid myself of a bad headache and had slumbered with a thoroughness that suggested exhaustion.

'It's not too late,' Patrick said. 'Hundreds of little shops stay open in the evening. I'll go out and buy some cheese and wine.'

'Can't we go out to eat?' I pleaded. 'We can take Justin with us.'

'That means I'll have to have a shower and shave first. Woman, I'm bloody starving!'

There was a short silence.

'I always fancy you when you're angry with me,' I said. 'You kind of fizz all over − like bare wires in the rain.'

One black eyebrow rose a fraction. 'I thought you only became randy when you were writing the naughty bits in your stories.'

'That,' I said, 'is a downright unmitigated fib. What if I were to tell you that when I awoke from my snooze I had a bath, put on this rather thin for the time of year caftan dress and omitted to wear anything beneath it because I planned to give you a small snack and then seduce you before we went out?'

Suddenly I had all his attention. 'Show me,' he drawled.

I put Justin down in his pram. Then I showed him.

The manner in which I did this, slowly and sensuously, the attitude of my body a blatant invitation, was a ploy I had not used since the very early days of our marriage. I had abandoned it after a short while because frankly it had proved too heady for a young man to handle, and the bride had finished up by being loved with a forcefulness and alacrity not very far removed from rape.

My motives were unclear, I didn't even consider them at the time. It was probably something to do with giving birth to Justin and the fact that after months of doubt we were a fecund pair. Motives were unimportant, of course, for the real reason was nothing more than body chemistry. Thus it was Nature that ensured Nature was ministered to, and I discovered that nothing had really changed over the years. Thus the woman no longer a bride clung and moaned and protested a little in the arms of the man bringing it about, and was finally driven to utter a great shout of pleasure that seemed to go on and on.

Trying on dresses the following morning, I gazed in the mirror. A dark-haired rather serious person stared back. No trace of a resounding bedding. Perhaps at my age it was illogical to expect to look different. I could recollect scrutinising myself in exactly the same fashion after Patrick had first made love to me when we were teenagers. He had been eighteen, I fifteen, and under a summer sky on Dartmoor we had both lost our virginity together. I had been convinced that everyone would know, almost as if the words PATRICK HAD ME were engraved across my forehead.

No one had known, not even when we had subsequently set off for picnics during that long hot summer. Looking back on those days it is easy to see why our friendship was assumed to be innocent for the extent of the vicar's son's interests were well known to be singing in the choir and going fishing in the Tamar with a boy called George. The rest of the time he studied.

First of all we had made love; increasingly expertly, and cajoling every last scrap of pleasure from our young bodies. Then we had eaten, sometimes buying a bottle of wine — and why should the man in the village store query the sale to a member of such a respected family? – and leaving it in a stream to cool.

After a short while, suffering a bout of conscience, Patrick had proposed marriage. I had shocked him momentarily speechless with the admission that I was under age. Then he had repeated the offer, come hell, high water, horse-whips or jail, and I had accepted.

We had married when we were both in our early twenties and Patrick well established in the Army. But a union that had depended almost entirely on sexual attraction was doomed, and after ten increasingly troubled years we split up. Ironically, one of the points of disunity was that Patrick wanted children and I didn't. Dreadful miserable years followed the divorce and in an attempt to find happiness I married Patrick's best friend, Peter.

Then Peter was killed just before our first anniversary.

Accepting Patrick back into my life had meant that I had had to face my own shortcomings and also him, maimed in body and a little in mind after an accident with a grenade during the Falklands War. He had been ordered to find a working partner as he had been recruited as a member of a new department being set up within MI5 to counter foreign interference with the running of that security service. It was to be called D12. The partner had to be a woman because the job would entail a lot of socializing. And the only woman whom Patrick could countenance being in close proximity with at that time was me.

Helping him regain fitness, and, yes, the self-confidence necessary to give a woman and himself pleasure in bed was the catalyst that had made me fall in love with him again – I had soon realized that he had loved me all along. We had remarried, older, and as far as I was concerned, much wiser.

In the end I eschewed dresses and chose instead a suit; fine red wool, a mid-calf length skirt and long blazer style jacket. New shoes, plain black leather, and a matching bag were essential. I had a white silk blouse at the flat that I could wear with it.

'Fed, winded, changed, topped, tailed and wide awake,' reported Patrick when I returned to the micro-flat. 'Look, I must dash.'

77

'Has Daws said anything about us interviewing Haywood?'
I called just as he was going.

'Not to be touched even with barge poles ten miles long,' he answered, and then had gone without further explanation. The front door banged.

I glanced at my ebullient infant and suddenly felt very tired. I could envisage my life in twelve or so years' time. Another male would be reverberating around the house, this one leaving a trail of unspeakably dirty rugby strip and deluged bathrooms, the entire demesne shuddering to the rock music of the hour and slammed doors.

'So what is the connection between Haywood and Prescott?' I muttered to myself, getting ready to go out. '*Is* there a link with the others — Jones and Peterson?' Patrick didn't seem to have had time to get on with his telephoning while I was out; he always draws dragons on the phone pad when he's talking and it was as virginal as before I left.

I decided that I couldn't face taking the pram and put Justin into the sling. But then I hesitated. It was better to be lumbered with the pram than for him to act as a bullet proof vest for his mother. I laid him down in it whereupon he bellowed his displeasure.

Together with a few other items, my gun and shoulder harness were in the small wall safe behind the print depicting the Charge of the Light Brigade. I returned the webbing and straps to the hiding place and put the Smith and Wesson in my new bag. All my bags smell of gun oil.

There are still parts of fashionable London that exude the same kind of stifling gentility as they did in the days of Disraeli. Fitzmaurice Square appeared to be in this category and, cruising around in the taxi, the driver searching for number 8, I wondered what the fate of a householder would be who had the temerity to paint his front door bright yellow instead of the regulation black.

The taxi driver unfolded the carriage part of the pram for me when I had made it clear that he would only be paid when I had both hands free.

'What's wrong with the 'erbert?' he asked, accepting a tip without thanks and having to raise his voice over Justin's, whose complaints were resonating off the surrounding stone buildings with interesting effects.

'Spoilt by Father,' I snapped.

I left the pram on the pavement outside number 8. There was not so much as a child's bike marring the perfection of the square. It was the kind of place that if one walked around it in an anti-clockwise direction, whistling and carrying a bag of flour on one's head, at least three ancient bye-laws would be flouted.

I climbed the steps, pressed the bell of Flat 2 and announced my identity over the intercom. Justin needless to say, had switched off hysterics as neatly as turning off a tap as soon as I had picked him up. The door clicked open.

Flat 2 was on the first floor. I mounted the stairs slowly, totally occupied with the matter of the small person in my arms. He never seemed to cry when Patrick was around and this was not just because Patrick sometimes lifted him when he did. But for me he was either asleep, actually being attended to or yelling blue murder.

A Brown Burmese cat sauntered down the stairs to greet us, and, on the wide landing above, a blue member of the same breed stretched luxuriously and tried to pat the pompoms on Justin's woolly hat through the banisters.

'Look,' I said. 'A cat — a great big pussy cat.'

He turned his head, saw it, and then beamed gummily at me — a complete fluke but it made me feel all soppy and maternal.

'Ye gods, that's what it is,' I said out loud. 'Patrick talks to you — all the time.'

The perfume called Alyssa met me at the top of the stairs and for a moment I was quite unable to continue. I stood on the landing, hugging Justin and trying to banish the mental images of a bloated corpse. I suppose I only paused for a matter of seconds but it seemed like hours. In the end both child and animals exorcised my ghastly memories, Justin crowing at the Burmese who were both rubbing round my legs, throbbing a welcome.

One of the two pale green doors opened, the one nearest to me, and Henrietta Goldberg came out. So did her husband. A sickening wave of the perfume engulfed me and I almost retched. But I swallowed hard and smiled at them, the thought uppermost in my mind that here were not nice people, they were the sort from which a young daughter would want to run forever.

Chapter Ten

Whether to impress me or not, a couple of my novels had been placed in a prominent position on a coffee table, *One for Sorrow* and *Two for Joy*. But I only noticed them vaguely as I crossed the room to where Eugene Goldberg invited me to sit, I was too involved with attempts to quell the memories that the gusts of the perfume were resurrecting. Outwardly, I suppose, it was a normal-looking Ingrid Langley who propped her baby in cushions in one corner of a vast, squashy bright pink sofa but in reality the lady wanted to throw up.

'Damn cats,' Henrietta Goldberg said, after the introductions. 'Always trying to sneak in and strop their claws on the furniture. I've mentioned it to my neighbour several times but she couldn't care less.'

A reflection on the creatures' excellent taste, I couldn't help but think. 'Sorry about having to bring Justin,' I said, my own cat's whiskers, as my father used to call a certain sensitivity to vibes, convincing me that an apology was in order. 'He's long overdue for a nap so if we just ignore him he'll go to sleep.' I looked sternly at my son as I said this and he gazed back at me in a fashion I had observed in his father, with the innocence possessed by a newborn boa-constrictor. Perhaps, on the other hand, I was overwrought and imagining things.

Ignoring him with ease Henrietta Goldberg said, 'Coffee, Miss Langley, or are you one of those who prefer something stronger at this time of day?'

I am not easily brow-beaten and right then could have put a small measure of whisky to good use. But I smiled and told her meekly that coffee would be lovely, thank you.

80

This was all ready, it seemed, and while she organised crockery and percolator I had a chance to study them both. Without question she dominated. Is it possible for a woman to be a time capsule? From the top of her back-combed peroxided beehive hairstyle to the tips of her peep-toed high-heeled shoes, she was the fifties personified. Writing down the words 'her tightly corseted figure' takes me back to my childhood and misty recollections of the fashion of those days. And Henrietta Goldberg was a hard woman, the thinly compressed carmine lips and bright blue eyeliner both emphasising not feminising or softening the spitefulness of her face.

Her husband was not the archetypal hen-pecked spouse by any means. In a muted way he echoed her disenchantment with life: a sour twist to the mouth, a way of closing his eyes for a few moments with an air of finality when presented with an object or subject less than agreeable to him. Justin had been thus erased from his view of the world, as if by doing so the child could be eradicated. I found it chilling.

This aside, Eugene Goldberg was a shrewd-looking man and I could imagine his retaining sufficient mastery of his own life to exclude Henrietta from his business dealings. But at home, and in everyday matters, he deferred. He did so now concerning the choice of a small table to be placed near me upon which I could place my coffee cup. But why wasn't a business tycoon in his office? Was he at home in order to help his wife answer tricky questions?

I busied myself finding my writing pad and pen in my bag. It had taken only one quick glance around the room to discover that there were no framed photographs of either Alyssa or her sister. There was not what I call a homely clutter at all: a few artificial plants − very expensive silk ones; a few tropical shells with pieces of bright green dried fern sticking out of them, and one of those glass lighthouses that you fill with different coloured sand from the Isle of Wight. The focal point of the room − and it was so ghastly I could hardly tear my gaze from it − was a veneer and plastic fireplace surrounding a gas fire, the edifice crowned with a false chimney-breast in gleaming dimpled copper sheeting that went right up to the ceiling. The ornaments enshrined on the tacky little shelves of this looked as if they might have been won at a fairground during Goldberg youth.

81

'Oh, sorry!' I hastily closed my bag and took the cup of coffee from Henrietta Goldberg, hoping that she hadn't noticed the Smith and Wesson residing darkly at the bottom of it.

'Sugar?'

'No thanks,' I replied. 'What charming china. Did Alyssa give it to you?' It was Coalport, pure white and delicate, with leaf patterns on it.

'That was a good guess,' said Eugene Goldberg with an attempt at joviality.

I could hardly say that it wasn't vulgar so they couldn't have chosen it. 'I can imagine this appealing strongly to a young girl,' I said. 'Would it be possible for me to see her room before I go so I can form an idea of her character?'

There was an awkward silence before her mother said, 'We took the opportunity of her being abroad to have it decorated. The furniture's all in store.'

'You know what these girls are, Miss Langley,' said Eugene. 'All the walls covered in posters of pop stars and the floor knee deep in clothes. It hasn't had a real turn-out for years.' His pale blue eyes snapped closed on me.

Totally unbidden, a picture came into my mind of a completely bare room, the walls white-tiled like a mortuary, no curtains at the windows, and the sun pouring like a searchlight on to the naked dead body of a girl on the floor. She was arranged very tidily, hands by her sides, her hair combed, toes pointed. No, I am not psychic, this was just my writer's imagination running in over-drive.

'You don't look like a perfume tycoon,' I said to Eugene with my very best smile. 'I always imagine such men to be dapper Italians dripping with their own products and gold ingots on chains.'

He laughed humourlessly. 'I'm no such thing really. Goldberg Enterprises is a food park.'

'I'm not with you,' I confessed.

'A food park. You know – cold stores, processing plants, factories. All on one site. We supply high street stores and the hotel industry.'

'I didn't know there were such things,' I said, genuinely interested.

82

'Mine's one of the first in GB. We're opening another in France in three months' time with a third planned for Germany next year.'

'So the perfume business. . . ?' I prompted.

'Just a small experiment.'

'Inspired by having two lovely daughters?'

He glanced at his wife. 'Not really.'

I made a joke of it. 'So it wasn't a question of Dad being nagged into something more interesting.'

'They have no opinion on their father's private business interests,' said Henrietta.

'Really?' I asked, utilising one of Patrick's expressions, that of polite disbelief.

'They're not here — so they can't offer opinions can they?' she said, slightly desperately.

I thought back to the telephone conversation I had had with her and wondered whether she was regretting gushing that Alyssa would be captivated by my writing an article about her. For the next few minutes I asked routine questions — her childhood, schooling, hobbies and so forth — taking all the information down in shorthand.

'Have you a photo I can use?' I finally enquired, and there was another heavy silence.

'There's a couple in the advertising folder,' Eugene said nervously to his wife.

When this was produced, Henrietta flipping through it, irritated, and the pictures given to me, I saw that they were the same as the one Colonel Daws had acquired.

'Lovely,' I commented brightly. 'Just the thing. Now — just one or two more questions and I think I'll have a fairly good idea of Alyssa. You say she did well at school. Was there a chance of her going to university?'

'It was arranged,' said the girl's father after another of the silences that I was beginning to dread. 'She was going to read law — here in London. But she suddenly decided she didn't want to do that after all and announced that she was going abroad for a holiday.'

'Just like that?'

'She was very difficult,' said Henrietta, her voice sounding a little cracked. 'You will appreciate that it was quite out of the question that she should live in at the university. I mean, a girl whose face is on every advertising hoarding and in every magazine can't just walk about as if she were anyone. We arranged that she should live at home and travel to her lectures every day by car but she would have none of it.'

I wrote down 'insufferable bitch' in shorthand and said, 'I'll just say that she won a place but hasn't yet taken it. It doesn't matter, though. People love to read about young people being rebellious, especially when they're both clever and attractive. Tell me — does Alyssa have her own set when she's at home?'

'Set?' said Henrietta Goldberg blankly.

'Friends. A young group.'

'No.' Her tone made it sound as though I'd suggested that the girl had VD.

'Does she have no friends?' I asked, careful that my manner did not reflect my feelings.

'One or two,' said Eugene hesitantly.

'We have to be so careful,' Henrietta told me smoothly. 'With all the money that will be hers one day. . . . '

'Ah, right,' I mused. 'I see what you mean. I can imagine plenty of young men queueing at your front door.'

'No boyfriends,' snapped Henrietta.

I decided there was no point in pursuing this line of questioning and said, 'So I take it that she has an allowance until she's twenty-one? That's in a few months' time, isn't it?'

'I don't think that has anything to do with anyone, Miss Langley.' This was from Eugene.

'Unless I mention it there are some people with the kind of mind that will wonder if she's paying her way around the Common Market countries by working in clubs and bars,' I said, allowing a little of my anger to surface. 'You don't want people to think that, do you?' I was almost convinced now that the girl had indeed run away from them and had nothing to live on. Worse, Alyssa *was* the girl I had seen in David Prescott's home, and worse still, her parents knew she was in trouble and were doing nothing about it.

But I didn't possess Patrick's courage to bring out the truth.

When no information appeared to be forthcoming concerning money, I said, 'I get the impression she had boyfriends of whom you didn't approve.'

84

'Whatever makes you think that?' Henrietta asked.

'Most girls do, don't they?' I replied blandly. 'I know I did. I went round with a crowd of bikers. My mother threatened to throw me out.'

The air left the woman's lungs with a whistling sound and when she opened her mouth to speak no sound came out.

'There were one or two we didn't see eye to eye on,' Eugene said, filling in quickly. 'But our daughter's more mature now.' He brightened visibly as an idea occurred to him. 'That's why we allowed her to go abroad.'

I wrote busily, abandoning all ideas of writing an article. If my worst fears were confirmed, the newspapers would do it for me and until that happened there was nothing to write that wouldn't result in my being sued for libel.

I gave them a vacuous television presenter's smile. 'It's not as exciting as I would have liked but I'll make something of it. May I use your phone?'

Henrietta Goldberg looked at Justin as though he might be sick on her pink leather if not closely supervised. I deliberately followed her gaze to where he lay. He had slithered down in the cushions and was in the process of trying to pull off his bootees, an expression of ferocious concentration on his face.

'Yes, of course. . . it's in the hall.'

I drained my coffee cup and went out. The phone was one of those onyx and brass creations and was housed on a table so low that I had to stand with my knees bent to dial Patrick's work number.

'Garstang Autobits,' said that well remembered voice, obviously bored.

'It's me,' I said. 'If you're not busy, could you pick me up from here in a taxi?'

'Problems?' he asked.

'Come right now,' I told him. 'I've plenty of material but I'm short on brainpower. I didn't get much sleep last night after Justin woke us.'

Justin had been an angel and I was merely using our ploy of telling obvious lies in order to warn. Patrick's favourite is, 'Agatha rang. No, not your mother. . . Agatha Hendricks.' My mother's name is Marion.

'Roger and out,' he said.

I returned to the Goldbergs' sitting room feeling not at all guilty at having unleashed upon them one of the British Government's hardline inquisitors.

'Will you be mentioning the perfume in your article?' Eugene enquired when I had told them that my husband would be picking me up shortly. 'There must be quite a few people who haven't heard of it. And we're bringing out a range of toiletries soon with the same name.'

'Will Alyssa be promoting it personally?' I countered.

'We don't know yet,' he said with a sickly smile. 'If she's not . . . available then her sister Raphaella could do it. Here, I'll show you.' He rose and fumbled through the contents of a nearby drawer. 'There she is,' he went on, handing me a photograph. 'Henrietta and I both think that she's going to be even prettier than Alyssa when she's older.'

I stared at the picture. It had been taken at a wedding, Raphaella a bridesmaid in pale green taffeta. She had the same colouring as her sister, her hair gleaming like newly minted copper coins and swept up and gathered into a head-dress of silk leaves, white roses and pearl droplets. Yes, one day she would be far more beautiful than Alyssa. Perhaps this was one of the reasons why Alyssa seemed to have been written off.

I asked them about their younger daughter and they became much more interested, animated even. Henrietta was telling me how well she was doing at her boarding school when the front door bell rang.

'It'll be Patrick,' I said. 'Shall I go?' I got up first anyway and went into the hall to let him in.

He had changed into uniform, and if there hadn't been a Burmese cat on each shoulder would have looked quite formidable.

'They don't live here,' I hissed.

'Haven't I seen you before?' said Eugene after I had introduced Patrick.

Patrick sat down, hoisted Justin on to his lap and smiled at the speaker. No, I didn't imagine this, it was one of his stock in trade smiles, like a shark, showing all his teeth, his eyes like living, mad, polished pebbles. Heaven only knows why he's in the Army and not on the stage.

'My brother was carrying the banner in a teacher's demo the

86

other day. You probably saw him on TV.' He spoke very quietly with just a hint of a lisp, the effect, even with the baby in his lap playing with his fingers, unbelievably sinister.

I showed Patrick the pictures of the two girls and he held them at arms' length, one in each hand, studying them, eyes slitted. Then, in an uncanny moment of what could only be described as telepathy, I saw Alyssa as he had observed her on that night in Prescott's bungalow. Not just terrified as when I had seen her but in the state of trauma of someone being forced to witness torture.

'The big man struck her,' murmured Patrick. 'She tried to make him desist and he punched her to the ground. I'm afraid the entire episode was a lot more nasty than I've so far. . . .' He stopped speaking and I realized with a shock that he wasn't acting now. 'This girl,' he said sharply to the Goldbergs. 'The eldest . . . Alyssa. Is she about five feet eight inches tall, slim, left-handed, and wears a gold signet ring on the little finger of her right hand?'

'Who are you?' Henrietta demanded.

Patrick showed her his ID card. It doesn't, of course, state that he works for MI5 but there's a photo and a very official-looking gold crown stamp with his name, rank and the information that he's a member of the Security Services.

'You're not the police,' she snapped. 'I don't have to talk to you.'

'I'm worse than the police,' she was informed. 'Answer the question.'

'Let me see that,' said Eugene.

It was given to him.

'The description could fit any number of girls,' the man said, handing it back. 'As we've already said – '

'She wrote her name on my hand,' Patrick interrupted. 'To put the thing in context she was with two men who were burning me with a cigarette at the time, and had been instrumental in nearly driving a government scientist out of his mind by making him shoot a man and then cut his left arm off before he was quite dead.'

Henrietta Goldberg uttered a loud shriek, startling Justin.

'Really!' shouted Eugene. 'This is – '

'Masked.' Patrick's voice cut through the other's effortlessly.

'But with that hair showing, those eyes. It was her all right. Why didn't you go to the police when she left?'

'Oh God!' wailed Henrietta.

Eugene Goldberg shakily lit a cigarette, and from the look his wife gave him I reasoned that this wasn't usually permitted in the flat. 'She's twenty,' he said. 'You don't call the police when your daughter leaves home.'

I said, 'Not when her face is on every advertising hoarding and in every magazine and with all that money to come to her when she's twenty-one?'

'Money?' asked Patrick.

'There isn't any,' I said disgustedly. 'That was the excuse they gave me for never letting her have any freedom. They don't care a damn about her. She's only a body who promotes chemicals in a bottle.'

We sat out the predictable storm of protests and then Patrick said, 'What was the name of the man whom she left with?'

'There was no man!' shouted Eugene, dropping the cigarette and having to snatch it from the carpet.

'He's dead,' Patrick added. 'Had an almost brand new Kawasaki motor bike. He was the one who was murdered.'

'Oh God,' said Henrietta again.

'It'll all come out in the end,' Patrick told them. 'And I'll make damn sure the papers print precisely why you haven't gone to the police — because she defied your orders as to how she should conduct her life, and now she's gone you're choosing to forget that she ever lived. I wouldn't mind betting that she's rung once or twice, begging for help, and you've told her to go to hell.'

'Oh, no,' said Eugene. 'No. I'd never do that.'

But Patrick was looking at the girl's mother.

'Henny, she hasn't tried to get in touch with you, has she?' blurted her husband.

The woman didn't have to say a word, the answer was right there on her face.

'Alyssa phoned you?' Eugene said. 'She phoned and you. . . .'

'Shut up!' his wife yelled. 'She's stupid and a trollop! She's been a trollop ever since she was old enough to be one.

88

Boyfriends at fifteen. Parties when we weren't at home. Wine bottles under her bed. Good riddance to her! I hope she gets what all trollops deserve.'

'What was the name of the man she left with?' Patrick asked again. Something in his tone made me glance at him quickly and I saw that his eyes were glittering with tears of anger.

'She — she knew a boy called Len,' Eugene said, and it seemed as if he was mentally already packing his bags.

'Len who?'

'I've no idea.'

'Come on! You can do better than that.'

'I'm sorry — I don't know his surname.'

'Friends then. Someone we can ask. For pity's sake, think!'

'Deidre Crocker,' said Henrietta with huge distaste. 'She was the one who organized all the parties. She's one of those Sloane people. Really fancies herself as a lady. Her number might be in the notebook under the phone.'

Patrick shut the door after him and was gone quite a long time. No one spoke while he was out of the room and I was wondering whether I dare turn a chair away from view and endeavour to feed Justin, who was by now burrowing into me in an unmistakable manner, when Patrick put his head round the door and asked to borrow my notepad and pen.

I gave it to him, taking Justin in my arms and then, following a signal from him, went out into the hall, closing the door.

'She *is* a lady,' Patrick said quietly, hand over the mouthpiece. 'Her brother's the Honourable Leonard Crocker and she's worried frantic because he hasn't returned from holiday. She said Alyssa might have been with him but apparently they weren't that close. She's gone to find the details of his bike.'

'You haven't told her?' I said, appalled.

'No, of course not. We can't even be sure it is him until the dental records are examined. I just said that a stolen bike had been found with her phone number in one of the panniers. I'll get on to Brinkley in a minute.'

I went out on to the landing, sat on the top stair, undid my jacket and blouse and gave Justin, a hair's breadth from unhappiness with tiredness and hunger, something to think about. The Burmese appeared silently from nowhere and

89

rubbed themselves against me purring throatily, the Blue then sitting down and regarding Justin with the utmost fascination.

I didn't want to go back into the Goldbergs' flat. Within it was a woman who had borne two children, at least one of whom she hated because the girl wanted parties, friends, and a little light relief from stultifying company.

'Brinkley's going to put out a description of her,' said Patrick when he eventually joined me. 'He's getting in touch with the Avon police to try to establish if this guy Crocker was the murdered man.' He sat down on the stair alongside me. 'It shouldn't be *that* difficult to find Alyssa.'

How wrong he was.

Chapter Eleven

I think I'm fairly safe in saying that at this point Patrick became obsessed with finding Alyssa. He had had no success with tracing the families of either Colin Jones or George Peterson; the former had been unmarried and the uncle with whom he had been staying when he had shot himself was abroad. Peterson's wife had moved away, leaving the house in the hands of an estate agent.

It seemed logical to me to visit the places where the two men had lived and try to find more information. At the back of my mind was the worry that someone else might be on this deadly list and by the time a connection was found between all the victims it would be too late to save another life. I pressed both Daws and Patrick about the necessity to question Alex Haywood but was ordered to contain my impatience. Haywood *was* being watched, Daws stressed. The threatening letters — for this was what they were, not just hatemail as the policeman, Forbes, had told me in Bude — were a good excuse to do so, and the letters did seem to be genuine.

'Haywood's a very eminent man,' Patrick said during one of these discussions. 'And the world these people move in is very small. It's almost inconceivable that Prescott wouldn't have heard of or worked with some of the men who have died.'

The discussions became arguments and, when I perceived what he proposed to do next, outright rows. I should have been warned, of course, when he had obtained permission to borrow the Kawasaki. But nevertheless it was an enormous shock when, with Terry's active help, Patrick set out to turn himself into a Hell's Angel.

Never, ever, has he done things by halves. Over a period of days – and I'm prepared to swear that as these days went by he was praying that the police would be unable to find the girl – he had his ears pierced, rings and studs in each, and got himself tattooed. I wept, noisily and at length, when I beheld the latter ghastly, grisly disfigurements on his arms and hands. Those lovely expressive pianist's hands! Alarmed by my reaction and still bloody from their application, he promised to have them erased when they were no longer needed.

I was so horrified at the lengths to which he was prepared to go that I distanced myself from both him and Terry. Thus I was not there when he rode away on the bike, which had been disguised by subtle respraying and given false number plates. I didn't ask how the latter had been achieved, I went home. Terry rang me to say that Patrick had left but I could hardly bring myself to speak to him I was so angry. The police were there to find missing persons, I managed to get across, and then slammed the phone down and cried.

A week later, when I was still in a mood of furious despair, Terry rang again.

'Has the Major contacted you?' he asked guardedly.

Sarcastically, I said, 'You mean Alpha One hasn't reported in?'

'No. We arranged that he would contact me every four days or so.'

'Not Daws? I thought you were supposed to be on sick leave.'

There was a very long silence on the other end of the line and I interpreted the reason for it correctly.

'The Colonel isn't in on this,' Terry said at last.

'But I take it that he is now and you've had a hell of a carpeting?'

'That's about it,' he acknowledged.

'Terry, I could wring your neck!' I exploded, my feelings getting the better of me.

'Daws already has,' he said. 'This is a ghost grovelling for mercy.'

But I couldn't simply feel sorry for him and laugh it off. 'You don't really know what you've done,' I told him. 'This isn't just a matter of dressing up your boss like a dog's dinner and the pair of you falling about with the giggles at what he looks like. If those people whom we ran into in Prescott's bungalow recognise him, he's a dead man. If you had only stopped to think you could have talked him out of it – even gone yourself, you're young and fit, not a man of forty who was blown up in the Falklands.' I was crying as I spoke these last few words though I hadn't intended to get really carried away.

'Oh God,' Terry whispered hoarsely, and before I could say anything the line went dead.

'Oh God,' I echoed, resting my head on the wall. My mind was a dull blank as I tapped out his number. It rang for a long time. At last he anwered, his voice thick.

I said, 'Would you come down and look after Justin for a few days while I go to Wales?'

He didn't hesitate. 'Of course. Tomorrow?'

'Tonight if you can make it. I'll meet you at Plymouth.'

He sniffed and then, surprisingly, chuckled. 'Okay.'

We rang off after arranging what time train he should catch.

'Good,' I said to my reflection in the mirror, not worrying that he had guessed I knew he would otherwise have gone out and drunk himself blind that night. Right then it didn't seem to matter that he was aware I had a soft spot for him.

'You're lucky to find me here,' said Idris Jones, looking at me over the tops of his reading glasses. He took them off and handed me back my D12 ID card. 'Isn't it about time you people let Colin rest?'

'No one has interviewed you from my department,' I said. 'My husband tried to contact you but your housekeeper said you were in the States.'

'Department?' he growled. 'They're all the same to me...police, MoD investigators, Special Branch and now you, Mrs Hoity-toity, and your departments.'

When bullied by burly Welsh farmers, look fragile.

'You'd better come in for a minute,' he said, shaking his stick at a bunch of collies who were endeavouring to round me up, grinning, tongues lolling. They bounced away and commenced to play tig with each other in the immaculate yard.

Caerfyllin Farm was only just in Wales and was situated a

few miles east of Mold, some ten miles west of Chester. I had taken the train the morning after Terry had arrived, changed at Crewe and hired a car in Chester. It was still only early afternoon, the Clwydian mountains indistinct in the blue misty distance.

Colin Jones' uncle was probably in his early sixties but as with many people who spend a lot of their life outdoors did not look it. I guessed that he had been educated over the border for his Welsh accent was barely discernible. Entering the house confirmed another guess, that he did not have to rely on his hill farm for a living. The rooms gleamed with cherished antique furniture and old silver. Paintings with their own small brass lights hung on the walls, and also on the walls in the alcoves of the living room were several very fine oriental rugs. A well-stocked drinks trolley stood in one corner.

'Sit down,' he ordered, moving a pile of *Country Life* magazines from a wing chair for me. He did not want me there but he was a gentleman.

'I only arrived home two days ago,' he said, seating himself. 'Still feel as though I'm on the damn plane. Would you like some tea?'

'That would be lovely,' I told him, making myself comfortable.

'You don't look like a department woman,' he said when he returned after requesting tea from his housekeeper, Mrs Parry. I knew her name because I had heard him shouting for her.

'What *do* I look like?' I enquired.

'Intense,' he replied. 'Too quiet and introspective to be a civil servant. You listen a lot and say little. Let others do all the talking and trip over their own stupid tongues.'

'It wasn't a phoney card I gave you,' I said, having to smile.

'That's as may be,' he retorted. 'But it doesn't mean that I have to talk about poor Colin.'

'It might help save the lives of others if you do, Mr Jones.'

He hunted around and found his pipe, filled and lit it and then gazed at me impassively through a haze of smoke. 'Department people aren't usually given to making dramatic statements either.'

'Having someone shoot themselves on your property *is* dramatic,' I countered.

He stabbed the air in my direction with the stem of the pipe. '*With* my property, Mrs Department. Let every fact be absolutely correct.'

'Your shotgun. Yes, I know.'

'But at Caerwys Reservoir – not on the farm.'

'Is that far from here?'

'About two and a half miles.'

'And is it near your boundary?'

'The lower pasture fence borders the road that leads to the lake.'

'Then surely you're splitting hairs.'

'No. There's a subtlety that also defeated all the other department folk. Colin hated the reservoir – he could remember what the valley looked like before it was drowned so that you damned English can have two baths a day.'

'So you don't think he went there *because* he loathed the place, because the site was somehow fitting for what he intended to do?'

'That too is subtle. . . but no.'

Somewhere outside a cow was bellowing mournfully.

Idris Jones said, 'It was like this, you see. Colin once said to me, "Uncle, if I could choose where I must die, it would be in the ring of pines." Here, come to the window and I'll show you.'

I went and he pointed out a copse of trees on a hill overlooking the farm.

'So he *was* contemplating suicide,' I said.

'He said that when he was twelve years old.'

I sat down again, thinking.

'It was still his favourite place, even when he grew up,'

'So why did he go to the reservoir?'

'Why, indeed,' said the farmer sadly.

'You've already made up your mind,' I persevered. 'Tell me.'

He shook his head slowly. 'Perhaps I'm a stupid old man.'

'Why did he kill himself? There must have been a reason.'

'There was a reason. . . but I never got to hear of it.'

I tried another angle. 'Were you his only relative?'

'I suppose you can say that. His sister can hardly be described as living.'

I waited, knowing that he had more to say.

'Colin's parents were both killed in a car accident when he was five. The little sister, Glenys, was found in the wreckage with head injuries. She's had to be in a special hospital ever since.'

'And Colin?' I prompted.

'He was thrown clear . . . just a few cuts and bruises. I think he's always blamed himself.'

'But why?'

'He seemed to remember being naughty and difficult and his father turned round to scold him. Then the car crashed.'

'And he never married?'

'No. But it was early days for him really . . . he was only twenty-nine.'

'Did he ever mention a man called Alex Haywood?'

The tea arrived while he pondered. Not just a silver pot, hot water jug, sugar bowl, creamer and bone china cups and saucers but home made scones, butter, strawberry jam and another plate loaded with chocolate biscuits. Mrs Parry was one of those spare — almost pared to the bone — Welsh housewives, her grey hair skewered mercilessly into a bun but she gave me a thin smile that for her was probably one of profuse welcome.

'Haywood, you said?' Idris Jones asked when I had poured the tea.

'He might have worked with him,' I said.

'I've heard of the name, but not from Colin. In the papers, was he?'

I hoped that my disappointment didn't show. 'He pretended to commit suicide because he wanted to start life afresh with a woman in Bude.'

Jones snorted contemptuously. 'Yes, *that* Haywood. Not the sort that many would be friendly with, I've no doubt.'

'So Colin never mentioned the newspaper story?'

'I hadn't seen him for five months before the weekend he died. He phoned me every week or so but I can't remember him talking about it.'

'Mr Jones, have you *any* idea why he came to see you and then killed himself?'

'Come down to the reservoir before you go,' he replied.

No, Caerwys was not a happy place. The flooding of the valley had not yet been healed by time even though it had happened ten years previously. It seemed as if Nature was still outraged by the deed and was refusing to cover the raw scars on the hillside where the road had been blasted through. A small group of trees were dying slowly where the natural drainage had been destroyed and they now stood with their roots in the bed of a stream. On this sunny day the water of the lake was a sullen, dead blue. In the rain it must look like the last place on Earth.

'He was found on the road across the dam,' said Idris Jones, pointing through the windscreen of the Land Rover.

'Who found him?' I asked.

'Some men on motorbikes.'

My expression must have given me away for he stopped the vehicle abruptly.

'Is that it, Mrs Department? Men on motorbikes?'

'Was there a girl with them?'

'Always questions and no answers,' he growled. 'Is it the Russians getting rid of our scientists . . . the brightest brains in the land? Is there some filthy plot amongst the Left to do away with all those with a good head on their shoulders?'

'What makes you say that?' I almost shouted at him.

'I'll tell you why,' he said, yanking on the handbrake. 'Yesterday I had a visit from another of your damned department people. This man was riding a motorbike and when I first saw him I was of a mind to get my shotgun and send him on his way. Then, nice as pie, he wished me good day and started to ask questions. He seemed to know quite a bit about Colin and what had happened to him.'

'What did he look like?'

'What do any of them look like with those helmets on? Tall, I suppose. I noticed that his hands were tattooed when he took his gloves off.'

'Did he show you a card like mine?'

'No. But then again I didn't ask for it. I didn't ask his name either.'

'What made you think he was from officialdom?'

'By his manner. Well-spoken. Not a ruffian despite what he looked like.'

I never carry a a photograph of Patrick with me. That really would be asking for trouble if it fell into the wrong hands. 'Did he have grey eyes?'

'I can't remember,' said Jones placidly, seeming to relish my confusion.

'You didn't happen to notice if he had a slight limp?'

'He might have done . . . he was a bit stiff from riding the bike.'

'D'you mind telling me what you said to him?'

He hesitated. Then he said, 'Not much. I didn't trust him. It's the only reason I let you in . . . because I liked the look of you.' He got out of the cab and stumped off down the road in the direction of the dam.

I stepped out into a cool breeze and followed him. Above my head a skylark soared, its throbbing song answered by another on the far side of the lake. The breeze ruffed the smooth, dead surface of the water and whispered, raspingly through the twigs of the trees that were struggling to survive.

The visitor had not been Patrick. I was quite sure of this now. For one thing Patrick would have introduced himself, using either his own name or a false one. Also, with people like Idris Jones he never resorts to cunning or what he calls weasel smiles but is himself. Thus those being questioned are hardly aware of it and confide in him. Idris Jones hadn't trusted him so it couldn't have been Patrick and that was that.

I shivered.

There were still dark stains on the dam wall where Colin Jones' brains had been blown out. His uncle gestured towards them helplessly and then walked away for a short distance, hands rammed into the pockets of his jacket.

'You think they killed him, don't you?' I said, my voice taken by the breeze to where he stood.

'Yes,' he said without turning round.

'Did you say as much to the police?'

'They would not be interested in the ravings of an old fool.'

'So what would Colin have been doing down here with the gun if he hated the place?'

'I have no idea. I lost several nights' sleep thinking about it.'

I gazed up to the hills and saw the young man's favourite

view point was just visible from where I was standing. What if he had seen someone on the dam when he was up there, someone he loathed and feared, and had brought the shotgun with him to try to drive him away?

Chapter Twelve

Two months later Patrick still hadn't returned. During this time he contacted me three times, one phone call and two letters. The message was virtually the same in all; he was quite safe, had not yet located Alyssa, said that he loved me and hoped Justin was behaving himself. On the occasion when he rang I had the opportunity to pass on Colonel Daws' message to him, to report immediately in person. Patrick ignored the request.

The content of Daws' calls to me were becoming stronger by the day until at last he threatened to fire Patrick.

'I'm sorry but I can't communicate with him,' I said.

'Really?'

'Really,' I told him angrily. 'Surely we're not getting to the stage where you're doubting my word? It isn't a lot of use your shouting at me every few days like this. Can't you imagine how worried I am?'

'It's reached the stage where he's disobeying orders,' Daws retorted, no less coldly. 'He's doing a police job now — not working for me.'

'Then stop his pay,' I said desperately. 'I'd rather pay you back everything he's earned these past few weeks than have to tell him he's fired.'

'Oh, I'll tell him,' the Colonel said sinisterly. 'When he finally makes contact.'

When he rang off, having said that he'd give Patrick one more week, I had a really good howl. When he had ridden off on the bike it had been spring. Now it was early summer and a nanny whom I had employed to replace Dawn was so unsuitable I felt that I was going out of my mind.

This young woman had arrived from an impeccable agency. I say young but in fact she was only a few years younger than me, in her early thirties. Justin was teething, sobbing to himself half the night with a chunk of chewed sheet for company. Whatever I did – teething jelly, rusks – he spent nearly all his sleeping time fretful and crying.

When Annette had arrived I had moved out to the barn flat for there wasn't room for me indoors now unless I slept on the sofa downstairs. In my room in the barn I could still hear him crying, hour after hour. He would drop off to sleep for half an hour or so perhaps and then I would start awake at his tiny thin scream of pain and it would begin all over again.

Annette did nothing. She argued, correctly I suppose, that continually lifting him would not achieve very much. She herself seemed to sleep like a log – that's if her fresh appearance was anything to go by – while Justin became hollow-eyed and pallid.

Somehow I got through each day, running to the phone every time it rang in case it was Patrick, shopping in the village and writing not one single word. The first of these calls was from Terry, reporting for work after his period of sick leave, to tell me that the body in David Prescott's house had been positively identified as Leonard Crocker. He had been killed by several bullets in the chest.

In desperation I started work on re-writing the film script for *A Man Called Céleste*. This was a fairly mechanical procedure requiring no creative skills, the words were already in the mouths of the characters in the rough draft of the novel. I had already sent off the first few scenes with a covering letter to the agency dealing with it and had received their go ahead to re-write the rest.

On Annette's days off I brought Justin over to the barn with me and he spent the night in his pram next to my bed. Even after five weeks the problem had not abated and now he had nappy rash too, his bottom aflame. Bathing him one day towards the end of May, I was shocked to see that he was losing weight.

On the Friday of that week I had to go into Plymouth to buy paper and typewriter ribbons. It was a beautiful day, the

101

Sound glittering in the bright sunshine, Plymouth Hoe ablaze with flowers, and I lingered, treating myself to a cream tea in a seafront café. When I arrived home Justin was in the garden in his pram, screaming, stinking, the pram covers clotted with stale vomit, his face crawling with flies. When I discovered his nanny reading on her bed, the radio going full blast, I think I went slightly crazy.

I turned the radio off and fired her, using words known occasionally to have escaped Patrick's lips when he is driven too far. My diatribe finished, she looked at me in disdain and loftily informed me that the countryside was enough to make anyone bored with their job. She packed and left but I wasn't there to see her go. I had paid her wages and informed her that she could take a taxi or walk to the station, I wouldn't be giving her a lift.

For a week I worked on Justin and after that he began to get better. The nappy rash soon abated when he was changed regularly and often, and the cream I had given Annette actually applied. A bottle of painkilling syrup looked as though he had been given three doses out of it and I blamed myself for this for I had assumed upon noticing how full it was on a previous occasion that she had asked at the doctor's in Tavistock for a repeat prescription.

His appetite was next to non-existent in the hot weather, all he wanted was cuddles and milk. Feeding him myself was out of the question now as not only did I not have any milk but he had three tiny front teeth, two at the top, one at the bottom. So I cuddled him closely when I gave him his bottle until the day came when he nearly bit the rubber teat in half, retched, and then roared his frustration.

'To hell with you, Richard Daws,' I sobbed, suddenly remembering that his deadline had come and gone. I got on the phone to Elspeth, knowing that she was due home after a three week holiday touring Scotland. When I had finished giving her the news there was an appalled silence on the other end of the line.

'Poor little mite!' said Elspeth when she could speak for indignation. 'Oh, *do* bring him here. No one in this house is disturbed by babies. And I've a friend who brews up all sorts of old country remedies − all made of herbs and natural things.

I'm sure she'll have something for teething.' She chattered away comfortably and I was so drained of energy that I agreed to visit them even though I had a deadline of my own on the film-script.

Just before I left, Elspeth phoned me back.

'Patrick rang,' she said. 'He hadn't any more change and asked me to tell you that he's found the girl and is bringing her here as the Bath police will want to interview her. I couldn't very well say no but I've a feeling things might be a little difficult.'

'Did he say when they would be arriving?' I asked.

'No.'

It was a huge relief to know that he was safe. But my own vague misgivings refused to be dispelled.

I commenced the journey at a little before nine that night, aware that Justin would sleep well in the soothing motion of the car. I was half expecting when I drew up at the Rectory that I would see the Kawasaki propped up by the back door, but unless Patrick had put it back in the old stable he and Alyssa had not yet arrived.

'Ingrid, I wish I'd known,' said Elspeth, speaking in an undertone to avoid waking Justin after giving me an appraising look.

'You were on holiday,' I said. 'There's no way I would have said anything.'

'This is Patrick's fault,' said she, tight-lipped.

'No,' I protested. 'It's not. It's my fault. I was blinded by the woman's qualifications. It's horrible when you're feeling your way all the time and don't know if you're doing the right thing.'

Patrick did not come back the next day, nor the next. Summer had definitely arrived and for hours Justin lay under a big sunshade on the lawn, not even wearing a nappy, ate his first real grown-up food, carefully puréed, and slept peacefully at last, his inflamed gums rubbed with a weird unguent tasting and smelling mostly of garlic.

'If he can't have Mum he doesn't want bottles,' Elspeth pronounced, and went out to buy him a plastic beaker, one of those with a lid and shaped mouthpiece. I expected battle royal but he was soon trying to hold it himself by both handles and also attempting to knock it on to the floor when it was empty.

'It is time,' said his grandmother thoughtfully, observing this, 'for him to learn what no means. Never be frightened of saying no.'

On the Sunday, worry was gnawing at me like rats on a bone. Thankfully, John and Elspeth had ceased to say, 'Perhaps he'll come today,' every morning and in my preoccupation with imagining the worst I think I forgot that they too must be frantic with worry. Terry had arrived on the Saturday for the weekend and it was only on the following morning that I thought to ask him why.

'The rector rang me,' Terry replied. 'He doesn't like the idea of that girl coming here and no one to fend off anyone who might be following her.'

'It's the village carnival on Thursday,' I said. 'I wonder if Patrick'll wait until then?'

'Any particular reason?'

'It's an after dark affair,' I explained. 'Fireworks and illuminated floats. If he wants to come back with a girl on the pillion and not attract attention to himself, that would be the night to choose.' I looked sharply at Terry. 'What did his father mean. . .no one to fend off any followers? Patrick will be here, won't he?'

'Just playing safe, I suppose. And we must face the fact that the Major might not be in very good shape.'

'John's a realist,' I murmured. 'Yes, I've no doubt Patrick will be very tired.'

I attended the morning service, harrowing myself with the thought that the last time I had done so Patrick had been by my side, overwhelmed by the occasion and thinking that one day, possibly, he would be standing where his father was now, up by the altar, taking the service. Now for all I knew he was a rotting corpse in a ditch; lost to me, the world and his Maker.

I waited for John afterwards. It seemed offhand not to do so as Elspeth had been to the eight o'clock service. While I waited I wandered around the church, reading the inscriptions on the old brasses and those on ancient stone tablets set in the flagged floor, the words almost worn away be the passage of countless feet over the years.

John, half out of his robes, put his head around the vestry door. 'Have you ever thought about Confirmation, Ingrid? I'd be delighted to instruct you.'

I'm afraid that I ignored the question and shouted my worst fears down the short passageway.

'Round the other way,' he corrected gently.

'All right,' I said, still shouting and making the discovery that tears were coursing down my cheeks. 'His Maker, the world and me. That's probably the order Patrick would put us in.'

He shook himself free of the clinging material and started to fold it up. 'Patrick will never be dead to his Maker. Right now he's not lost to anyone. If he was, I think...somehow...I'd know.'

But my mind would not produce arguments and I accompanied him back to the house without further comment. The endless day wore on, the sun a glare in a copper-coloured sky, and older village folk shook their heads and warned of thunder. By tea-time there was hardly a breath of moving air, all the windows of the Rectory flung open to catch the slightest breeze. Every now and then a sudden wind came and went, causing the beech trees around the garden to sigh, their branches moving up and down so that they looked as though they were lifting and lowering long skirts.

At just after seven the storm broke, surprising us all with its abruptness and ferocity. Elspeth and I ran from room to room, slamming windows, unable to hear each other speak for the thunder. We stood by the French windows of the sitting room, watching the rain sluicing down the glass.

'Like in the films,' Elspeth said under her breath during a lull. 'when something really ghastly is about to happen.'

'Only writers are allowed to have that kind of lurid imagination,' I said, trying to joke her out of the mood of foreboding.

At nine the storm had not abated and we had had to roll back the carpet in the hall and lay old towels on the floor to mop up rain driven beneath the front door. Coming down the stairs from checking that the same wasn't happening at the bedroom windows, the light out but my progress illuminated by almost incessant lightning, I paused to look out of the small window on a half landing.

105

Just coming to a standstill in the driveway at the side of the house was a motorbike.

'Someone put the yard light on!' I shouted down the stairs. 'They're here!'

I stayed where I was for a moment, long enough to see the pillion passenger dismount, walk round to the front of the bike to steady it while her companion stiffly climbed off. She pushed the machine towards the back door but not before being taken lightly by the shoulders and given a tender and lingering kiss.

Chapter Thirteen

I didn't run to the kitchen. For one thing my legs had suddenly become weak and it was vital to have a little time in order to be composed when I arrived. He had kissed her. It was a kiss that had spoken of gratitude, affection, homage even.

This shock was driven out of existence when I beheld Patrick sitting at the kitchen table. He was huddled up, leaning on his arms in an attitude of utter exhaustion. As I stared it seemed that in fact I might be imagining things and that here was a Patrick who would look like this one day when he was old and dying. His face was grey, dark lines beneath eyes that had once lit expressive features and were now sunken and dulled. The matted beard made him look like a stranger.

Then, I noticed Alyssa. She was not the girl in the glamorous advertising agency photograph but a bone thin child, the wonderful hair as dirty and tangled as that of her rescuer, the visible areas of skin grimed and bruised. Yes, bruised, I saw with horror as Elspeth gently helped her remove her soaked outer garments.

'The doctor for that one,' Patrick said, his voice hoarse as though he had been shouting.

'And for him!' Alyssa said shrilly. And then her face contorted and she rushed over to Patrick, almost knocking him off his chair with the force with which she flung her arms around his neck. Then she cried, terrible racking sobs.

By the time I had found Terry in the Ring O' Bells − the inn next door to the church − John had come in from visiting a parishioner suddenly bereaved and, not at all sure what to do, was surveying the scene in the kitchen. Even Elspeth seemed at a loss so I went into the hall and phoned Anne.

'It's one of those emergencies we appear to keep on having,' I explained.

'Is the girl's condition serious enough for her to require hospitalization?' Anne enquired after I had elaborated a little.

'I think she's been knocked about...possibly raped,' I told her.

'I'll decide when I see her,' she said briskly and rang off.

Alyssa was still crying, her head on Patrick's shoulder, his on hers. When Anne arrived, almost immediately, she and I set about prising the two apart, talking to her soothingly all the while. She released him eventually, and when he sprawled quite unconscious on the table it became apparent that she had been crying not for herself but for him.

'A bath,' Anne snapped at Elspeth, leading Alyssa to her. 'I'll give you a sedative for her in a minute.'

'They beat him,' Alyssa wailed. 'They tied him up to a gate and beat him half to death.'

Patrick regained consciousness when we started to undress him. This was unfortunate for he had no reserves left to tolerate it. Now there was no patience, self-control or his normal iron will. Just trying to remove his leather jacket caused him to whimper and swear, attempting weakly to strike away our helping hands.

'I can't stand this,' Terry blurted out. 'Can't you give him something?' he shouted accusingly to Anne.

'Not until I find a vein under all this lot,' she replied coldly. 'If you can't stomach it, clear out.'

'Patrick!' I said, holding his face on either side. 'For pity's sake co-operate or we can't help you.'

But he was beyond my reach, half fainting, sobbing with pain every time we moved his arms. Somehow he found the strength to fight us off.

'This is hopeless,' Anne muttered finally. 'I'll get an ambulance.'

She met Elspeth in the doorway who said, 'Alyssa's a lot calmer now. She's soaking in a bubble bath.'

The very last person I wanted to see Patrick like this was his mother.

'Problems?' she asked, standing on tip-toe to see over Anne's head.

'He's in a lot of pain,' I said lamely.

Sometimes even a wife can be an intruder in her husband's relationships with his family. The measures that Elspeth now took, quickly, deftly and without fuss, were almost certainly the same that he himself would have carried out in the circumstances. Reading the situation at a glance she took a bottle of smelling salts from a cupboard, gathered him up from the table where he had slumped and held the bottle to his nose. Patrick gasped, choked, and his eyes opened.

'You once stitched up a very nasty cut on my hand,' she said in conversational fashion. And then to Anne, 'He's very good at stitches, you know.'

'That's more than I am,' Anne commented dryly.

'Morphine in the backside or bite a bullet was the anaesthetic on offer, if I recall correctly,' Elspeth continued. 'I declined both with gratitude. Ingrid, please do as you did then and make some tea. I think we could all do with a cup. John, be your usual practical self and bless the patient with a short prayer to give him fortitude. Terry, you can help me remove this dreadful leather so Anne can treat the injuries that lie beneath.'

I am sure that I was observing this amazing piece of organisation round-eyed but I did as I was told. Patrick, surrounded both spiritually and physically, found fortitude and submitted to the ministrations. But he gazed warily in the direction of the bottle of smelling salts that Elspeth had left encouragingly on the table before him. Later I discovered why. They were another concoction of the lady with rural remedies and one tentative sniff nearly lifted the top of my head off.

Looking back, I'm not sure how he had tolerated wearing the jacket at all. When it was unzipped a smell of stale warm meat filled the room. Removing Patrick's arms from the sleeves was achieved quickly for he passed out again momentarily as soon as Terry began to pull the jacket from his shoulders. No one resorted to using the smelling salts. I held his head until Anne told me to allow him to fall forward across the table.

'Bloody hell,' Terry breathed.

109

'Hospital,' Anne decided taking one look at the blood soaked tee-shirt.

'No...please,' I said. 'I'll look after him. He's spent too much of his life in hospital since the Falklands War.'

'He'll need a general anaesthetic,' Anne told me impatiently. 'The cloth is well and truly stuck to his back.'

'Then let me soak it off with warm water,' I pleaded. 'Please. Give him a mild pain killer and let's get a cup of tea laced with whisky inside him. He's only fainting like this because he probably hasn't had a hot meal in weeks. Please, I know more about him than you do...he's never had a spare ounce of fat on his body to live on.'

She wrinkled her nose doubtfully. Just then Patrick's right hand travelled spider-wise across the table and grasped one of mine that was resting on it.

'Please,' I said. 'If I'm wrong, I'll phone for the ambulance.'

'We'll try it,' Anne said. 'But bear in mind that you might be causing him a lot more pain this way.'

Terry caught my eye with a look that echoed my own thoughts, that Patrick's stamina was not so good as it used to be. But that, I reasoned, still meant that he had more resilience than average, the main reason for this his ability to take nourishment in situations when most people would be incapacitated by nausea and shock.

Therefore I was the only one not surprised when, with a lot of assistance, he drank a large mug of sweet tea spiked with his favourite tipple, watched calmly as Anne gave him an injection and then pillowed his head on his arms as we got to work on his back.

It took half an hour to cut and unstick the cotton fabric from the mangled flesh beneath during which time I heard him catch his breath twice. As the last corner of the tee-shirt was eased away and we saw the full extent of the beating he had received, Elspeth started to cry quietly.

'Belts,' Anne reported in her laconic fashion. 'The buckle ends of metal-studded belts. There...look, you can see where the sharp edges have cut into him.'

And the dents still oozing blood where small studs had smashed into skin and muscle. He would be scarred for life.

'Is Alyssa all right?' Patrick asked faintly.

'Oh heavens!' cried Elspeth. 'I'd forgotten all about the poor child.' And scrubbing at her eyes with the hem of her apron, she fled upstairs.

For three days Patrick lived on the settee in the living room, lying on his front, carefully dosed by Anne so that occasionally he slept lightly but did not exist in a drugged daze. When necessary Terry assisted him to the toilet, a protracted process even though there was a small cloakroom downstairs next to John's study.

His back was left uncovered to speed the healing process and only smoothed lightly with an ointment that lubricated the lacerated flesh so that he could move. By the second day the bruising started to appear and soon he was a terrible sight, black and blue even on his chest.

I reported all this to Daws and Daws remained silent.

When I took Patrick in his breakfast on the fourth morning – for true to my predictions he was eating everything we gave him – I found him perched delicately on the edge of one of the armchairs, a good fifteen feet from the settee.

'Thank you for keeping me out of the blood wagon,' he said.

I carefully set down the tray and tried without success to swallow the lump in my throat. This was the first spontaneous remark he had made since starting his recovery. During the previous three days one of us had been with him constantly, even during the night, but other than responding to queries about his needs he had said nothing.

And of his state of mind I was very uncertain.

'How's Alyssa?' he asked.

'Quiet well, considering,' I told him. 'Anne's been with her a lot...and your mother, of course...just talking. Elspeth's going to take her into Bath today and buy her some clothes.'

'She was gang raped while they beat me,' he muttered.

'Who rescued you?' I said, attempting to draw him away from the worst memories until he was stronger.

'No one. She managed to get free and ran off and they scrambled to get away, thinking she'd gone for the police. Alyssa came back after they left and released me.'

111

'Eat your breakfast,' I urged. 'Cold bacon and eggs is downright nasty.'

I didn't help him as he levered himself to his feet and travelled the short distance to my side, just held my breath.

'Why is Terry still here?'

'He's on leave,' I replied. The real story, that Daws had ordered Terry back to London and Terry had demanded leave, could be conveyed to Patrick later. One mutiny was quite enough to worry about at the moment.

'Make sure Terry goes with Elspeth and Alyssa. Tell him to wear his gun.'

But he was hardly concentrating on what he was saying, just gazing at me as if torn by some ghastly dilemma.

'Please eat,' I said.

'Ingrid . . .'

Oh God, what was he going to say? That he'd fallen in love with Alyssa?

He tried again. 'What would you say if . . . ?'

'Can't it wait?' I enquired gently when the words died in his throat for the second time.

He shook his head.

But whatever it was had to wait for just then Alyssa came into the room. The change from when I had last seen her — for all my time had been taken up with looking after Justin, sitting with Patrick and doing most of the shopping — was incredible. Here was a top-to-toe groomed Alyssa, her beautiful hair gleaming and squeaky clean, wearing my new green silk dressing gown and carrying Justin. I have written about jealousy and at this moment it coursed through me in its purest, most unfettered form.

'He was crying,' she said, turning to close the door. 'Sorry about borrowing the lovely robe . . . I only had a towel round me at the time.' She took one of Justin's hands. 'Look, there's Daddy.'

I held out both arms for Justin when his face began to screw up as he caught sight of Patrick but the girl kept hold of him.

'It's the beard,' I said. 'He's going through a phase of crying at men he doesn't know.' I was furious. To avoid what I had foreseen as almost a certainty — Justin apparently rejecting Patrick — I had planned either to allow the meeting to be

112

accomplished in stages or to suggest that Patrick shave off his beard first. Normally, of course, it wouldn't have mattered but with Patrick obviously going through some kind of private hell, adding to it, even in small ways, was crazy.

Now though, not all all sure of anything, I could only sit there feeling angry and watch while Alyssa placed herself on Patrick's other side, our son on her knee. Ever since entering the room she had gazed at Patrick adoringly.

Justin grizzled, throwing himself away from Patrick so that his head banged into Alyssa's chest. He needed changing and was hungry. Patrick ignored him and started to eat his breakfast. Seeing this, the total disinterest, my heart sank.

'Perhaps you'd better have him,' Alyssa said to me. 'You won't want the wet nappy coming through on to your robe.'

No, quite. I relieved her of the squirming child and reseated myself. Nothing was going to make me leave them together in the room, not even Justin's empty stomach. I knew I was behaving stupidly but couldn't stop myself.

Even closer now to the object of his fear Justin shrank back towards me, his fretting noises threatening to become real crying. Then, quite suddenly, he stopped. On the plate nearby a knife had probed into an egg yolk and a morsel of bread and butter been dipped therein. It was held out to him, golden and succulent but with not a trace of solicitude, his name not cooed enticingly. When he didn't immediately open his mouth, Patrick ate it himself.

'That's cruel!' I burst out. 'He's too young to understand.'

Patrick said, 'Survival. If Alyssa hadn't fed me Mars Bars on the way home, I'd have died a thousand deaths. Only a few more miles, she kept on saying, only a few more miles.' Another piece of bread and butter was dipped into the egg and proffered and this time it found a ready and waiting participant.

'He's only just started having eggs,' I said when most of the egg yolk had been eaten by Justin. 'But please don't give him the white of a fried one.'

'I'm not stupid,' Patrick said mildly, cutting up a slice of bread and honey into squares.

I simply didn't know what to make of this. A few minutes previously he had been in a desperate mood; now he was happily engaged in giving Justin his breakfast.

113

'Is this your house?' Alyssa asked.

'It's the home of my parents,' Patrick said.

'Are you really in the Army? I thought you might be a policeman.'

'Yes – but I work for MI5 now.'

'So my parents didn't report me as missing.' Clearly, she was still too shocked to take in properly what he had said.

Silence.

'To me they did,' Patrick eventually said.

'I bet you had to twist their arms,' she burst out.

There was another silence and then Patrick said, 'You'd better get dressed. My mother's going to take you out and buy you some clothes. Ingrid will give you the money – a stipend doesn't run to that kind of thing.'

Alyssa looked at me fearfully, as if I might refuse. She was raped, I reminded myself savagely. Her boyfriend was brutally murdered before her eyes and her parents were utterly beastly to her. Yes, of course I'd buy her some clothes.

'You ought to phone home,' Patrick said, when Alyssa's hand was on the door knob.

'They don't care a bloody damn,' she said. Her eyes filled with tears.

'Your father does.'

'Good old Dad,' she commented sarcastically and went out, banging the door.

'She's still pretty shaken up,' he said, but more to himself than to me.

Before I could comment Elspeth came in. 'Patrick, it's the Colonel. He's insisting on seeing you.'

He was and his good manners seemed to have deserted him for he was right behind Elspeth. Terry, who presumably had seen his car arrive, was only seconds in his wake and stationed himself protectively by Patrick.

'I won't detain you,' said Daws. He opened his briefcase and extracted two envelopes, one for Patrick, one for Terry. 'Your resignations from D12. All you have to do is sign.'

'All I have to do is sign,' Patrick echoed to himself. 'All I need then is a pen.'

Daws gave him one and watched while Patrick wrote.

'Just like that?' asked Terry angrily. 'No arguments, no fight?'

114

Gazing at him, Patrick shook his head. A strange mood seemed to have come over him since Alyssa's exit. 'No,' he said. 'Not from me. What you do is your affair.'

But Terry signed and threw both letter and pen on to a low table.

Daws, obviously, had not expected this. He sat down rather heavily in an easy chair and surveyed us all. Elspeth remained where she was in the doorway, torn between curiosity and the awareness that what she was witnessing was not really any of her business.

The Colonel's eyes raked Patrick, his manner making it quite clear that he had become inured to all sights of injured personnel whilst serving in Malaya and Northern Ireland.

'In the words of the prophet,' said Patrick calmly, 'I have hit the wall. I'm counting. With a bit of luck I'll get to fifty before I start screaming but can make no promises. Please leave unless you wish to be presented with such a distressing spectacle. Sir,' he added on an afterthought.

Daws sat tight. 'Has the girl been to the police?'

'Not yet. But they're informed and I understand will come to her.'

'Please go, sir,' Terry said to Daws.

'Major . . .' Daws began.

'They beat me,' said Patrick in a whisper, keeping himself under a restraint terrible to see. 'They beat me until I nearly shit myself. I've been done over before but never to the extent that I thought I was going to die. I never want to clap eyes on any of them again.'

'Please go!' Terry said again.

'Very well.' Daws got to his feet.

I said, 'Are we just going to leave it like this? Before we even listen to what Alyssa has to say? What on earth's the point in demanding resignations at this time?'

Coldly courteous, Daws said to me, 'Whether everyone likes it or not, D12 has a military structure in so far as those in command give orders and those beneath them obey. This is not the first time this group has refused to obey orders, and not the first time, Meadows, that you have asked for leave in order to support the Major in following his own devices.'

115

'I haven't resigned,' I heard myself say into the ensuing silence.

'No,' Daws agreed. 'You have twenty-four hours to find someone to look after your child and report to me in London.'

Chapter Fourteen

Daws let himself out, Elspeth was too stunned to move.

'Magic,' I said to the room at large, finding that I was very angry indeed. 'Suddenly all my team mates are going down like nine-pins and all because of a little dolly bird who flew away from home.'

Patrick had had his head in his hands and now looked up at me with a mixture of hurt and what I can only describe as numbed shock.

'Are you still counting?' I said to him. 'Lost for words?' I snapped when he didn't reply.

'Ingrid...' Elspeth said, but I was coming right up to the boil.

'What has it achieved?' I asked. 'Does she know the names of any of the men who abducted her? And just as a matter of interest, who was it who gave you permission to use the bike?'

'Brinkley,' Terry mumbled.

'Better and better,' I said. 'Daws' brand new idea of a liaison officer within the Yard. A good idea too when you think about it but I'm sure he's not there to lend pieces of evidence to D12 operatives who fancy a ride round the countryside. What number are you up to now?' I shouted at Patrick. 'I'm not surprised Daws left. God above, he must have had plenty of shell-shocked soldiers weeping on his shoulder in his time. He was just sick with embarrassment that someone he'd regarded as grown-up had gone and got himself beaten up doing a knight errant act in deepest England.'

'That's most unfair!' Terry protested.

'It's the truth!' I said, still shouting. 'And Patrick knows it's the truth. Every time they hit him, he knew how stupid he'd been.'

Patrick jerked himself to his feet and went to the window on the far side of the room. Supporting his weight with his arms on the window ledge he stood there, and one didn't have to be very clever to realized that he was fighting back tears.

'You haven't hit the wall,' I said to his back. 'I thought for a while that you might have done when the grenade exploded and tore you apart. If you had stayed the sort of person you were before it happened, you probably would have. But you didn't.'

He slowly turned round. 'What do you mean?'

'The reasons I divorced you,' I went on, 'were that you were an all-too-perfect, scathing snob, very fond of your own voice. Hard as nails, always ready to show you were better than the next man. Every little hitch in life was like water off a duck's back. A man of action. . . . Writing books was what weak, soft people did for a living.'

His eyes were just like holes in his head as he stared at me.

'But then it all changed,' I continued. 'In one split second you were reduced to a bloody torn wreck and became human...someone who suddenly began to think of other people's feelings. Do you remember when you came to see me just after Peter was killed to ask if I wanted to work for D12, and you fainted at my feet because you'd only just come out of hospital after treatment?'

Dumbly, he nodded.

'You were so grateful when I gave you a cup of tea and let you lie on the sofa. What was it . . . about four years after we'd been divorced?' I felt a tear trickle down my cheek. 'Right then...just for a moment...I think I would have died for you.'

I brushed away the wetness on my face. 'So now you're soft and cry a little when things go wrong. Sometimes you do things on a whim and usually it all comes out right in the end. This time it hasn't because you let yourself be blinded by a girl's big blue eyes and pretty hair. If it had been Terry, you would have said "Serve him damn well right." It served *you* damn well right!'

I knew I was really going to cry at this point so I walked out of the room.

Tears brimmed and overflowed when I was in the hall and I made for the front door to escape into the garden. But I stopped for on the hall table were the two envelopes. I picked them up and took them outside with me, hugging them to me with Justin.

'Poor little baby,' I sobbed into his silky black hair. 'You're all wet and still hungry and munching your fingers because your gums hurt.'

I sat on the rustic seat by the arch that led to the vegetable garden. Would Patrick ever forgive me for saying those things in front of Terry and Elspeth? It seemed to me, miserably reviewing what I had said, that I had merely been unleashing my resentment at his looking for Alyssa and had sounded no more than a jealous shrew. The tears rolled down my cheeks. There was nothing worse than kicking a man when he was down.

Daws had given us another chance.

I opened the envelope with Patrick's name on it and scanned the letter it contained. Daws had been scrupulously fair in his composition. The reason for the resignation was that Patrick no longer felt he ought to take such personal risks now he had a family. He had also decided that his duties with the Downing Street security team and working as my agent merited more of his attention than he was able to give at present.

All very correct. But had Daws really intended him to sign it? And had the Colonel paused to give thought to a question that others might ask — what was to happen to the distaff side of the partnership?

Then I noticed the signature at the bottom.

'Oh my Godfathers!' I exclaimed aloud.

I tore back indoors and burst into the living room. All was as before except that Elspeth was sitting in the chair vacated by Daws.

'Ingrid, you mustn't run with him,' she said crossly. 'Here, give him to me and I'll do something with his nappy.'

Regrettably I dumped Justin in her arms without further ado, with eyes for no one but Patrick. 'I was beastly to you too,' I gabbled. 'During our first marriage, I mean. I smashed your guitar, didn't I? And I've never replaced it. Come to that, I was beastly to you just now...Patrick, why in Heaven's name did you sign the letter "Alex Haywood"?'

119

Patrick lowered himself gingerly so that he could sit on the window ledge. Then he said, 'I had no hunches – no ideas at all really. I still thought you were confusing real life with Langley fiction. But Haywood's the leader of the gang – the two who had Alyssa are his henchmen. He's grown a beard but I'm sure it's him.'

I gave him back the letter. 'Please tear it up. Daws left them in the hall.'

'I don't think I'm strong enough,' he said under his breath, and I remembered what he had said about not wanting to face the gang again.

'Let's get this in perspective,' Terry said. 'You went in there on your own and got a hell of a pasting. Next time you'll have your own henchmen – me, and a few strong blokes who owe me a favour.'

'And if I order *you* to go in alone?' Patrick asked.

'If you say so,' Terry replied stolidly.

'What if I tell you to destroy your own letter and go back to London cap in hand, with Ingrid but without me making any promises concerning my own decision?'

'I'd give it thought,' Terry answered after hesitating.

'Then think. Now. I trained you but that doesn't mean your career hangs on mine. Majors are supposed to be able to raise a few strong blokes of their own too.'

Terry snatched his letter from me, ripped it to shreds, threw the pieces up in the air and stalked from the room. He nearly knocked Anne over in the doorway.

Shakily, Patrick said, 'This is getting to be like one of those very bad plays that people act in village halls to an audience of three. Doctor, take my paw and put me down for today I am a very old dog.'

'I don't know how you got over there,' Anne scolded. 'Men are all the same – putting a brave face on things when it's a serious injury and making a fuss when they have a cold.'

Concluding dully that the only one who had been presented with a brave face was Alyssa, I said, 'What am I offered for Justin then? He's very young at the moment but in about twenty years' time he'll be able to dig the garden and mow the lawn. If he's anything like his father there'll be quite a good brain too and you may depend he'll be a real whizz at – ' But it

120

wasn't funny and the rest of what I had been about to say remained unsaid when I saw the way Patrick was watching Anne prepare an injection.

I went away again.

Richard Daws smoothed out the top sheet of Patrick's ten-page report and read the first few paragraphs again. Then he shook his head slightly and closed his eyes for a moment. 'You wrote this?'

'Patrick dictated it to me,' I told him.

He smiled equally slightly. 'No, I wasn't accusing you of making it up. It flows, that's all. A pleasure to read if the contents weren't so appalling.' He flicked the paper with his fingers. 'I can't find it in me to continue to remonstrate with him after reading this.'

I said, 'He still won't even tell me what he's going to do.'

'And it's such a waste.' Restlessly Daws rose and began to pace up and down. 'What on earth was the man thinking of? I'm aware, in retrospect, that I regarded finding the girl as of paramount importance and I said as much in his hearing. But to take it upon himself to. ...' He broke off and shrugged helplessly. 'I was warned, though. Before he came to me I was made aware that. ... But what the hell's the use of going through that now?'

The Colonel sat down again. 'I've seen it all before. Men who were prisoners of the Japs. Bomb disposal people who suddenly couldn't be in the same room as a clock. All at once the brain says "never again".'

'He is nevertheless quite sure it was Alex Haywood.'

'Who has been at home all this time in Bude.'

'The police are still watching him?' I gasped.

'Yes.'

'Then why did you leave the letters of resignation behind?'

'Because I'd no idea when I entered the house that the Major was so badly hurt nor Meadows so fiercely loyal to him. People shouldn't be expected to sign things under those circumstances.'

I picked up the report I had carefully typed, and scanned through it, suddenly drained of energy. For the first couple of weeks Patrick had toured likely haunts of people who might know of Alyssa's whereabouts; camp sites used by those who drifted from one pop concert to another in the summer, peddling drugs and stealing whatever they could find. He had asked tinkers, fairground staff and groups of bikers. He had soon discovered that those calling themselves Hell's Angels often had jobs for most of the time or were registered unemployed; they couldn't afford to run their bikes otherwise.

He had visited the Salisbury Plain area which he knew pretty well from early days in the Army. Then he travelled the old drove roads of Wessex — wide paths across the hills over which cattle used to be driven to market. Here he encountered real gypsies with horse drawn caravans who would have nothing to do with strangers and set their dogs on him.

After drawing a blank there Patrick had journeyed to Savernake Forest in Wiltshire, another favourite stopping place for travellers. In a lay-by he had come across a convoy of caravans and had stopped to ask questions. Just then the police had raided it, searching for drugs. The army officer had stuck to his disguise and had found himself in a police van. Wishing to search him for forbidden substances they had taken no chances and made sure he was on the floor, horizontal, with the application of boots and fists. Finding nothing of interest — as for obvious reasons Patrick had been carrying neither identification nor a lot of money — the good upholders of the law had kicked their find out on to the road.

That hadn't been the worst day. It hadn't taken him very long afterwards to find real bikers as he had been given the names of various cafés in seaside resorts. But the ones he had come across wouldn't have anything to do with him. They refused to answer his questions even when he said that he was looking for his girlfriend whom someone had stolen. He wasn't one of their group and that was the end of it, they hadn't wanted to know.

Patrick hadn't gone into details about living rough and long wet nights followed by longer wet days. Nor about being taken ill, probably the effect of drinking polluted water. For a week he had lived in a small copse, racked by diarrhoea and vomiting for the first couple of days and for the rest of the time too weak to ride the bike. The disguise again was to blame for the weakness as a couple of village shops had refused to serve him and he had run out of food, having not taken much with him. Very bad planning, he had agreed ruefully.

Then he had had a real piece of luck. A postman whom he had asked — and he asked everyone who would speak to him — remembered a girl with long red hair. Finding Alyssa after that had been a long, long slog. Then one day, probably the Monday of the previous week — Patrick wasn't sure because his watch had stopped — he had come upon the gang resting at the side of the road.

No one recognised him, not even Alyssa. He had requested permission to go along with them for a few days, and when his assurance that he had been kicked out of the SAS had been satisfactorily proved by his fighting and beating the men who called him a liar, he had been more or less accepted. Patrick insisted in the report that this group were not real Hell's Angels. They were a collection of criminals of one sort or another, mostly of the violent kind. One of them was almost certainly a murderer on the run, another an escaped convicted IRA man.

The rest of the account glossed over the end of the affair. From what Patrick had told me — sometimes haltingly — and using my own intuition, it seemed that he had deliberately set out to get to know Alyssa, openly flirting with her. This had been difficult as the group travelled great distances every day — sometimes hundreds of miles — on what he could only describe as vague errands. But one thing he was certain of, it involved organized crime, possibly the delivery of stolen money or drugs.

And the finale. A botched escape with Alyssa, the arrival of the leader of the gang whom Patrick was still insisting was Alex Haywood, and ghastly retribution. A six-bar gate had been lifted off and leaned against the wall of a barn, hinges end down. Patrick had been stripped to the waist and tied, spreadeagled, to it. Haywood and his two henchmen had then beaten him with their belts while the rest of the gang had taken it in turns to rape Alyssa.

Her ordeal might have been worse, Patrick had finished by saying, but I hadn't noted it down. Most of the men were so drunk that at a guess only one or two had succeeded in penetrating her. He himself hadn't been so fortunate, those beating him were stone cold sober.

123

'I still don't understand why you didn't call the police,' I had said.

'I didn't want to bust Haywood right there and then,' Patrick had replied. 'There must be others. It's a bigger set-up than just a few thugs on bikes.'

'Are you sure they didn't recognize you?'

'Positive. They'd have killed me slowly and thoroughly if they had. I didn't even tell Alyssa until we were nearly home.'

'But you must have still had those cigarette burns on your stomach.'

'I made sure I rubbed some mud over them.'

I came out of my reverie to see that Daws had reseated himself and was surveying me closely. 'Patrick hasn't hit the wall,' I said.

'Do you know what PTSD is?'

'Post-traumatic stress disorder,' I said. 'They called it shell shock in the First World War and battle stress in the Second. I've been thinking of very little else for the best part of a week.'

'Recklessness and seeking out danger is one of the symptoms,' Daws mused.

'I think I'm ahead of you,' I observed apologetically. 'The Gillards' GP put me in touch with a psychologist who is making a study of PTSD for the Ministry of Defence. He was all ready to drop everything and come over to see Patrick but I managed to get him to talk first. He asked me if Patrick suffered from sleep disturbance, exaggerated startle response, or feelings of guilt. I said no three times. Then he went on to talk about heavy drinking, broken relationships, becoming reclusive and getting into brawls. That wasn't really our man either. He then asked when Patrick had last seen active service and I said the Falklands where he'd lost part of his right leg. I had to say that he now worked for the Security Service and had seemed to go to pieces after being badly beaten up by thugs. At which point the psychologist asked me how old he was.'

'What has age to do with it?' Daws interrupted.

'He seemed to think it important. We got rather deeply into middle age restlessness and subconscious longings for change and excitement after that, and when I could get a word in edgeways I thanked him very much and said I'd be in touch.'

'Poppycock,' Daws huffed.

124

'But he hasn't got PTSD,' I declared. 'All I can suggest is that if you want him to go then say so and he will.'

'I'm not sure that I was asking for your advice,' he said, but quite kindly and with another tiny smile.

'Blame my sympathetic nature,' I retorted. 'I always try and help when folk look perplexed.'

Daws removed his glasses and polished them furiously on his handkerchief. 'All the information about this bike gang. . . I take it that Brinkley's been made a party to it?'

'Yes. There are several very good descriptions of men almost certainly wanted for serious crimes. From that point of view the search was a success.'

Sarcastically, Daws said, 'Perhaps I ought to suggest that D12 be made a small investigatory unit for the Metropolitan Police.' He gestured towards the report before him. 'What did the girl have to say? There's no mention of any information she gave.'

This quite innocent question found a target right at the heart of my misery. 'Her story's coming out in dribs and drabs,' I told him. 'Anne Walker, the GP, is insisting that she is only to talk about what happened to her when she wants to and that she's not to be bombarded with questions. And she's acting for the local police surgeon at the moment as he's ill so no one can argue with her.'

'It doesn't sound as though you approve,' Daws suggested.

I gave him what must have been a sickly smile. 'She and Patrick have been sitting down together and Patrick's been making a note of the gist of what she says. It isn't really a lot of use because the men all had nicknames – Loopy, Dirty Joe and so forth. Nothing to identify them. To be honest I think they doped her. She's very hazy about everything – even the murder of her boyfriend.'

'Does she remember David Prescott?'

'She said a man whom she hadn't met before killed Leonard Crocker, but that's all. There's none of the awful horror of what Prescott says he was made to do. If the killers have access to drugs – and they *do* seem to, Patrick and Tom Holland were made to inhale something in Prescott's home – I'm wondering if Prescott was doped too and suffered hallucinations.'

125

I thought back to the evening before and how Patrick and Alyssa had sat together while she talked in a low monotone, he occasionally prompting her gently. The only time either of them came alive, it seemed, was when they were in one another's company. Seeing their two heads closely together, in exactly the same fashion as when she had embraced him in the kitchen. . . .

'Ingrid,' Colonel Daws said, breaking into my thoughts.

'I'm sorry,' I said. 'Did you say something?'

'You think he's attracted to her, don't you?'

'I'm not sure,' I said, after deciding not to lie.

'People who have suffered together *do* share a bond,' he pointed out. 'I know you think I'm an old fuddy-duddy but I've been in the army long enough to have seen it all. You can throw all sorts of folk together and they'll possibly stay in small groups of those with something in common. But once they've shared an experience – fought a battle, been under the same artillery bombardment, suffered as prisoners of war – then the whole lot have a close bond. And they *have* to talk it out. That's what all these reunions are about, really. People are still talking about the First World War – never mind the Second or the battles for the Falklands.'

'Patrick's never talked about – '

'No,' Daws interrupted. 'I was thinking about the girl. At a guess he's concerned for her mental state if she keeps it to herself. I should imagine he'd worry about that rather than the possibility of ruffling your feathers.'

I looked at him speechlessly and saw the accusation in his pale blue eyes. And then I recollected how Patrick *had* started to tell me about what they had gone through and I had stopped him, thinking it ought to wait until he was stronger.

'Where are you going?' the Colonel asked when I got to my feet.

'To jump in the Thames,' I said.

Chapter Fifteen

After a long meandering walk I *did* end up on the Embankment. Exactly where I had wandered is still a mystery to me but I don't try very hard to remember, one doesn't want to bring back moments of real misery.

'All that patronizing crap,' I said out loud, and a woman nearby gave me a sideways look and walked a little faster.

'Pure bloody jealousy,' I went on. 'Seen from close-up that poor kid is just skin and bone. It was me who was blinded by her hair and big blue eyes. Patrick hadn't even noticed. He was only thinking of her in the hands of those bastards.' Ready tears blotted out a dull, humid afternoon.

But not for long. A piercing whistle – one of those with which the less timid summon taxis – shocked me into turning round, fumbling for a tissue. It was Terry, already ensconced in one, the door thrown open, beckoning to me frantically.

'What's wrong?' I asked when we were speeding in the direction of the East End.

'Just getting you away from the river,' he replied evenly. He eyed my abortive rummaging in my bag for tissues and produced his handkerchief, a square of perfectly ironed pale blue lawn.

'This is too good to blow on,' I said.

'Just blow, there's a good girl.'

I blew. 'Did Daws order you to follow me?'

'Yes.'

'Terry, I wasn't really going to – '

'I know that,' he interrupted in rather a bored tone. 'But Daws was scared silly.'

Feeling rather small, I concentrated on removing the signs of my moment of weakness. But why had he been waving at me so urgently, I wondered, if he knew I wasn't really going to throw myself in?

I glanced at him surreptitiously. Terry is regarded as an eventual highflyer within D12; the fact that he has been chosen one day to replace Patrick is an indication of this. But to both of us — Patrick and me — and except when not engaged in openly fooling about, he had always remained slightly distant. To me especially he was scrupulously polite. I had often wondered what he was really like, how he behaved with close friends. Now, it seemed, I might be about to find out. He had never spoken to me like this before.

'Where are we going?'

'I'm taking you home.'

Neither of us spoke again until the taxi reached its destination. I stayed dumb. Always having assumed that Terry inhabited a garret bed-sitter in a less than fashionable area, it was with a slight shock that I entered a warehouse conversion on Canary Wharf. He had, I now noticed, an armful of shopping, a French loaf sticking out of the top of his brown paper supermarket bag.

'Did Daws give you hell?' I asked when we were on our way up in a lift.

'No.'

'Didn't he say anything?'

'He didn't say a word. Never even mentioned his visit to Hinton Littlemoor or why he'd gone.'

'Didn't he even ask you if you'd made up your mind to stay on?'

'Nope.'

Still in a daze I was ushered into the flat. It was on the top floor with stupendous views across the river. It occurred to me, standing with what I hoped was an intelligent expression on my face, gazing out of the window, that I had never bothered to ask Terry where he lived or, come to that, anything about his domestic arrangements. Perhaps I had distanced myself from him, instead of the other way round.

'Drink?' Terry spoke to me from the far end of the living room, at least thirty feet as the crow flew from where I stood.

'D'you just have orange juice?'

'With ice?'

'Please.'

He went into the kitchen, giving me the opportunity to examine my surroundings. The room was decorated in different shades of cream; plain walls emulsioned directly over the brick, a plain ivory carpet, a pale honey-coloured leather three-piece suite. The curtains were boldly patterned in black and scarlet. But it was the pictures that held my gaze. No, not pictures, icons.

'Like them?' he said, returning with the ice and I'll swear a mischievous twinkle in his eyes.

'Beautiful,' I murmured, really lost for original comment. 'Quite lovely.'

'My sister chose them,' he said, giving me my drink. 'She sort of dabbles in antiques. Please sit down.'

Ye gods, he was enjoying this! I thought. My bewildered gaze drifted over small works of art on the shelves, mostly antiquities. Priceless.

'D'you live here alone?' I asked, gathering my scattered wits with an effort, adding. 'Not prying, just interested.'

'At the moment.'

There was an awkward pause.

'There's a woman who comes in to clean but she doesn't have a lot to do really as I tend to clear up after myself. I can't stand living in a pigsty.' He was drinking white wine, the glass not from Woolworths either.

Another silence.

'What are you going to do?' Terry said.

'Do?' I responded unhelpfully.

'Are you going to stick with D12?'

'I don't know.'

He carried on being extremely patient with me. 'Until the Major makes up his mind. . . .' He shrugged, his expression unreadable. 'There *is* work to be done.'

I said, 'I think I managed to persuade Daws that Patrick hasn't flipped.'

'That's a mite cruel if he has.'

This really took my breath away for a moment. 'Surely you don't think that?'

129

He ignored the remark. 'No, but then again you might not have torn into him like that if you thought he was telling Daws the truth.'

'Terry –'

'But why should he lie?' Terry continued as though I hadn't started to speak.

'He wasn't lying in the sense that he was deliberately deceiving Daws,' I replied heatedly. 'It was just a temporary loss of nerve because he felt so rotten.'

'You simply can't face the thought that he's gone chicken. Fine, I realize that you went for a walk by the river because you felt a right heel for what you said to him. I can understand a woman getting fighting mad with a man whom she thinks has ruined his career, rescuing a silly little dolly bird from God knows what, but. . . .'

'But what?'

'He has nothing to be ashamed of. Even if he has to see a shrink before he finds the courage to go through his own front door into the street.'

'I made enquiries about combat stress,' I said after a brief silence. When I looked up – for frankly I had been unable to meet his gaze – I saw that he was smiling at me in a fashion I could only describe as faintly mocking.

'There you are, you see. If you can call it combat stress you can sleep at night. It's the thought that he's scared shitless of a bunch of hoodlums who beat the living daylights out of him that you can't live with. How do you imagine he's facing himself?'

'OK,' I said. 'I'm wrong, wrong, wrong! I was jealous, scared because I thought he might have turned into a coward, and I simply don't deserve to have such a wonderful man in my life.' I jumped up from my seat and went to look out of the window, seeing nothing.

'Daws has promoted me,' Terry said. 'Just while the Major decides what to do.'

I was ice calm now. 'You mean we're to work together? Just the two of us?'

'If you want to.'

'And if I don't?'

'I'll answer that when it happens.'

130

I needed time to work out what I was going to do. I sat down again and said, 'D'you think he's right about it being Haywood in charge of that gang?'

'You tell me,' Terry replied dryly. 'You're the expert on PJG.'

'I've never known him make a mistake with names and faces.'

'Then who are the fuzz watching in Bude?'

'It's not that difficult to disguise a man to make him look like someone else. Especially if Patrick *is* right and Haywood's grown a beard.'

'That probably means that the hatemail and threats story is all lies.'

'Right,' I agreed. 'To make it appear that he's on the line. In the same way as his fake suicide, he's drawing attention to himself ... first as a rather weak character and now as a victim.'

'It's a pretty fragile theory.'

'The whole thing's a mess from our point of view. I'm not even sure how Patrick managed to botch getting Alyssa away at the first attempt.'

'The bike wouldn't start. The carb flooded. Then of course everyone woke up and they were caught.'

'Wasn't he armed?'

'Not with a gun. Just a flick knife. Reading between the lines, I get the impression that he hadn't really recovered from being ill and having to fight his way in. You were right in what you said on the phone. I should have gone. It simply wasn't the sort of job where he could use his real talents. More my kind of thing, where a bit more brawn and less brain would have succeeded. And on top of that he got the thrashing and that really knocked him for six. I blame myself. Youth really does tell when it's a question of taking punishment.'

'So what do we do?'

'That's a very leading question.'

'Didn't Daws give you any orders?'

'No. There's not a lot on at the moment. He did mutter something about a job that involves checking on the extramural activities of a certain MP, but there's no real need for us to do it.'

'The police can check up on Haywood's . . . there's no need for us to do that either.'

'I'm not so sure about that. As soon as a police car hoves over his horizon he'll split up the gang and they'll never be caught. Anyway, that's what Brinkley said to the Major when he gave him the descriptions. The police'll have to send in undercover people as well if they want to pick them up.'

'I think I'd rather climb Everest without oxygen than look for that lot,' I said. 'Anyway it's out of the question for me. Can you imagine me, at my age, as a biker's doxy?'

Terry surveyed me critically. 'You'd get away with it. With a bit more make-up and spiked-up hair, you'd look in your twenties. No problem. But we needn't play it like that. You could be just some woman I'd picked up on the road.'

'Are you serious?' I shrieked.

'Why not?'

'Terry, I didn't join D12 to do that kind of thing!'

'Nor did I. It isn't really our brief. But I'd like to get into that gang and see what goes on.'

To succeed where Patrick had failed, I thought. But it was only natural that he should feel like that. It was also quite natural for me to want to keep right away from the idea. The thought appalled me. But, deep down, I felt compelled to go. After the unforgivable things I had said to Patrick, I owed it to him.

'We could do it,' Terry said, setting down his glass and joining me on the settee. 'But it would mean that as far as they were concerned you'd be my woman. We might have to play on it a little.'

'Not if I was just someone you'd given a lift to,' I pointed out.

'Lifts are paid for in their way of life.'

'You seem to know an awful lot about it.'

'You hear things in pubs, don't you?' he replied with a smile.

I was about to say that I didn't in the kind of pubs I frequented when he took me in his arms and kissed me. I should have felt ashamed not pushing him away but didn't, just relaxed and, to be honest, enjoyed what was on offer. If I was to change my mind and take to the road with him. . . .

'I've always wanted to do that,' he said, drawing away.

'You're a very attractive woman. I've never been surprised at the Major going back to you after you were divorced. Frankly, Mrs G, you're sexy.'

'Rubbish,' I said weakly.

'I've caught you eyeing me up a couple of times. When you thought I wasn't looking.'

This was absolutely true and I know I blushed.

'Neither of us is promiscuous,' he went on, 'but a man can become curious about a woman if he doesn't have a harem at home.'

He broke off and kissed me again, satisfying a little curiosity of my own. And again I allowed him to linger, realizing with a shock that I wanted him to. There would not even be a conscious decision. I would merely permit him to continue. His kisses would become more fervent and soon he would be fondling my breasts and removing my clothing. In as little as five minutes or even less we would be making love right where we were on the settee. And I had seen enough of Terry's body to know that the experience would be very, very satisfying.

'I mustn't do this,' I said, pushing him away. He immediately desisted.

'Stay to dinner?'

'No. Thank you. Please call a taxi and I'll go to the flat. I've stayed too long already.'

'I'm quite a good cook,' he said, disappearing into the kitchen, I thought to use the phone. But when I went to the door of the kitchen a few moments later he was chopping mushrooms.

'I'm going after Haywood,' he said. 'If it is him. If it isn't nothing will have been lost.'

'Can you borrow a bike?' I asked, endeavouring to take my mind off his broad shoulders. 'That Kawasaki's had too much of an airing already.'

'I've a friend called Dave who *might* lend me his BMW.'

I fetched the glasses we had used and placed them on the draining board. In my mind's eye we were still on the settee. He was sliding off my black lacy panties and. . . .

'What about leathers?' I snapped.

'Dave's about my size, Terry murmured, pausing in his chopping. 'Pass me that opened bottle, will you? I enjoy a drop of wine when I'm cooking.'

I should have dumped the bottle down in front of him and left.

But I didn't, I stayed.

We both drank white wine while I watched him cook. He cut pork fillet into medallions, beat them flat with a rolling pin and then marinated them in oil, lemon juice and garlic. Finely chopped onions and mushrooms were then sautéd in butter until transparent and transferred to a dish in the oven to keep warm. A pan of rice boiling gently on the back of the cooker, Terry then cooked the pieces of pork until they were lightly golden on each side. These too were put in the oven to keep hot and the vegetables put back into the pan together with a couple of tablespoons of sherry. When it was bubbling he stirred in a swirl of thick cream, poured it over the meat and it was ready.

'Still going home?' he teased.

We ate in the kitchen where there was a most unusual black lacquered table and four chairs. I thought when I first seated myself that the top was glass, such was the high polish. All through the meal, which we finished with baby French melons, I felt mentally breathless at the sheer style of Terry's living arrangements. And afterwards, when he had refused to let me clear away because there was a dishwasher, I went to look for the bathroom, turned the wrong way and found myself in his bedroom.

If there had been a suspicion lurking at the back of my mind that I was the victim of a leg pull and this was in fact his sister's flat it was now dispelled. I knew enough about Terry to be convinced that this was his room. There were framed enlargements of photographs of Norway that I knew he had taken. His camera tripod stood in one corner together with a handcarved Welsh shepherd's crook Patrick had bought him as a joke, only to discover when he fell upon it with cries of admiration that woodwork was one of his interests.

How he loved black with vibrant colours. The carpet was black and the bed covers striped in purple, scarlet and black. Hidden spot lamps beamed on to a couple of strange 'sculptures' made out of pieces of scrap metal. These too were finished in matt black.

I went over to the window where the lights of London blazed before a seemingly limitless horizon. My writer's imagination

134

would not let me enjoy the scene before me. Terry and I were lying on the bed and we were naked. I opened my body to him and he slowly and tantalizingly. ...

I banged the palms of my hands on the window and turned to run from the room.

'What's up?' Terry asked, coming quickly.

You are, I thought. Magnificently. Oh God.

'Ingrid. ...'

'Please don't touch me,' I said.

But he came over to stand close by me.

'A cold shower should do the trick,' I told him. 'Preferably fully dressed.'

He put his hands lightly on both my shoulders. 'We can't work together with this bloody stupid on-going situation. For as long as I can remember, ever since the team was formed, I've drawn back from you for fear of sparking something off. There was a time when I guarded you for five weeks without a break and I thought I'd crack up if we so much as accidentally rubbed shoulders.'

'It was nearly seven weeks.'

'It felt like seven years! And now it's getting dangerous. How the hell can we work together if we can't relax in one another's company? One of us is going to end up making a fatal mistake because we're concentrating on keeping at a polite distance.'

A pulse beat at the side of his throat. But it was steady, he was neither angry nor really agitated. Nor, come to that, sexually aroused. Not yet.

His hands slid round the back of my neck and he pulled me towards him. Then, when our lips had sundered, he turned me round to face a long mirror. Standing behind me he unbuttoned my dress and slid it slowly off, his fingers straying inside the lace of my bra and then following the fabric down to my waist and hips.

I stayed.

Chapter Sixteen

Terry's friend Dave lived in Richmond, and judging by the contents of his double garage couldn't make up his mind about hobbies. To reach the motor bike entombed within he and Terry fought their way past a sailing dingy, water skis, a set of golf clubs, fishing rods, a rowing machine, two racing bikes and what looked like the remains of a badly dented hang glider.

Contrary to my expectations, when Dave wheeled the machine out, to a chorus of muted crashes as the other contents of the garage settled into the space it had vacated, it was apparent that it had been carefully mothballed. Both men set about stripping off the plastic wrapping and when the bike was revealed I saw something with which I was familiar.

'An R80,' I said.

Dave gazed at me with more interest than he had displayed when we were first introduced. 'You know about bikes?'

'Only this one,' I admitted. 'My husband had one a couple of years ago.'

Dave gave Terry an old-fashioned look.

'Ingrid is just a friend,' Terry said heavily. 'She writes books. I promised to take her for a ride on a bike. You know . . . material.'

'I believe you, old son,' Dave told him. 'Thousands wouldn't.'

Oil was checked and a restored Humber Sceptre plundered of petrol. When the bike failed to start Dave burrowed again in the garage and emerged with a tool box and spare set of plugs. When these had been fitted it still refused to burst into life so Terry was dispatched to buy a new battery. Three-quarters of an hour later it fired at the first attempt.

'Holy cow,' said Dave morosely. 'Just listen to that bucket of scrap.'

It sounded all right to me but he fiddled and tuned for another half an hour. Then he handed me a helmet.

'I'm not dressed for biking,' I protested, mindful of new white cord trousers and red sweat shirt.

'It's dry. You won't get dirty. Besides, you're not going on it with *him*,' he jabbed a grubby thumb in Terry's direction, 'until I'm sure you can stay on it with me, and he can stay on the road with the pair of you.'

I wasn't convinced that I would be able to stay aboard with anyone but quelled rising panic and mounted the pillion seat. Certain home truths concerning riding as a passenger came back to me when Dave climbed aboard. One was the close proximity with which my thighs were tucked in behind his. It was a great relief not to feel the slightest bit curious about *him*, proof possibly that spending the night at Terry's flat had cured all curiosity. With a bit of luck I'd never look at another man again.

When one has learned to ride a pedal cycle and a horse the necessary balance technique required for more exacting two-wheeled transport comes as second nature. And a motor bike does not shy at plastic bags in hedges. Speed is the thing, however, speed.

I had expected a short spin down the road and back but we hit the A3 and headed in the direction of Chobham. I was beginning to think that Dave was experiencing some curiosity about me, and a motel was the next stop, when he slowed and turned off down a country lane. A little later we drew up at a pub.

'Terry will wonder where we are,' I said, removing the helmet to make myself heard.

'He won't fret for an hour or so,' said Dave imperturbably. 'He knows I sometimes call in here for a quick half at lunchtime. It's an interesting old pub ... I never have to have my arm twisted to come here.'

I could see why Dave liked the place. The entire premises were festooned, within and without, with what looked like every item of impedimenta required for all the country pursuits known to the population of the British Isles. There was heavy horse harness with all the brasses, instruments for cutting peat, ploughs, guns, threshing flails, hunting horns, ram castrators, cow bells, man traps, gin traps, mole traps and pony traps on the lawns outside. There were framed advertisments extolling the virtues of stallions long dead, picture postcards of the district depicting children playing with hoops and spinning tops in a peaceful dusty street, stuffed pike, foxes' brushes, carved decoy ducks, and, over the public bar, a hand-blown yard of ale.

I ducked under a row of Navy rum measures, almost dislodged a copper warming pan from its hook on the wall, and sat down. Probably the most important part of the collection of artifacts as far as the customers were concerned were Real Ale Society awards singing the praises of Old Peculiar, Owd Roger, Pedigree, Old Timer, and other quaint-sounding thirst quenchers.

And sitting in one corner of this cathedral to the glory of beer, with what looked like a gin and tonic on the table in front of him, was Daws.

'It's rather complicated,' said Dave quietly when he saw where I was looking. 'Suffice to say that I work for Special Branch.'

I had no choice but to go to the table where Daws was sitting and take a chair next to him.

'There's nothing sinister or complicated in this,' Daws murmured when Dave had departed to the bar.

'You've had me followed,' I said accusingly.

'No. I said there was nothing sinister. I had a hunch that Meadows might get the idea to carry on where the Major left off. I also know that David Greenaway has been a close friend of his for many years, and possesses a motor bike. I contacted him. It was as simple as that.'

'So you intend to put a stop to it.'

'Not at all. The experience will do Meadows good. Mainly because I don't think he realizes what he's let himself in for.'

'There's a but in there somewhere,' I said.

'If it's going to be done, it must be done properly.'

'I'm going as well.' I had only made up my mind at that moment.

'It will be very hazardous for a woman.'

'Terry will be with me.'

Daws frowned. 'From what I understand, this gang shares its women.'

'From whom do you understand that?'

'From the Major.'

'He didn't say anything about that to me,' I declared.

'Surely he would be unlikely to worry you with distasteful facts like that.'

Well, no I thought, usually Patrick would tell me. He believes in giving me all the facts connected with our work. Perhaps for the sake of his cover he had been forced to roll in the hay with some girl and this was what he had been about to tell me when Alyssa entered the room. I would worry about it another time.

I said, 'You seem to have changed your mind about D12's involvement with this investigation.' I knew I was on thin ice by saying this; Daws doesn't admit to changing his mind even when it is blatantly obvious.

'It will be good training,' he replied, evading the question as I had expected. 'But I insist that you wait a couple of weeks . . . ten days at the least. Inspector Brinkley's in touch with Special Branch who are about to mount a surveillance on these people, and he's also suggesting that they infiltrate one of *their* members into the gang. They must be given a chance to do this without interference. Of course the police are far more interested in this than I am but if the Major's right and it *is* Haywood. . . .' He smiled, a faraway look in his eyes.

'Terry ought to have a refresher course in bike riding,' I said. 'It's years since he had one and he said that was only a small machine.' Self-preservation dies hard. Terry had told me some time previously that he had been involved in a bad accident with a bike when he was in his teens.

'Oh, he will,' Daws replied, still uncharacteristically dreamy. 'Our usual arrangements for training with the army can't be used this time. Apparently their facilities, for some reason I couldn't fathom, are stretched to the limits. You're both going to the Police College at Hendon for a week.'

'Both!' I exclaimed, the protest rather spoilt when the word actually emerged as a faint squeak. Dave, approaching with a tray, grinned as he heard me.

139

'For your own safety it's vital that you brush up on a few things.' Daws finished his drink. 'I suggest that this weekend you stay with your in-laws near Bath. I've a little job for you in Bristol for a few days before you go to Hendon. If you call in at my office tomorrow morning, I'll brief you.'

Over and out, I thought. He had guessed that I would want to go with Terry.

'Oh, and I nearly forgot. The Major rang and asked me to tell you if I saw you that the nanny – the young woman who broke her leg – has been in contact with him and intimated that she could cope with the baby if she had a little help. The plaster's off and she's walking with a stick. He suggested that she go to stay with his parents to see how she got on. I believe she's due to arrive next Wednesday. That's tied in rather neatly, hasn't it?'

Elspeth, of course, was aware that I helped Patrick in his work. We had only ever told his parents that I went with him on assignments where socializing was required and John was unimaginative enough to accept this.

'I don't like the idea of you working on your own,' Elspeth said when I mentioned the reason for my quick return from London as I entered the Rectory.

'It's only to keep an eye on someone,' I said. I put down my case and took Justin from her. He immediately seized one of my dangly earrings and yanked hard. During the ensuing hubbub John came out of his study to see what was wrong.

'Really, I can't hold a Church Council meeting with all this noise going on,' he complained.

Elspeth and I scuttled into the kitchen, Justin still with an awesome hold on the silver filigree threaded through my ear. He was finally bribed with a chocolate button to let go.

'Why aren't they in the vestry?' I said in a stage whisper, looking in a mirror to see if my ear lobe was bleeding.

'It's being decorated,' replied Elspeth, no louder. 'Heavens, why on earth are we whispering like this? They can't possibly hear us with the door closed. Now, you mustn't worry about Justin. Dawn and I can manage perfectly. I'm quite looking forward to meeting her . . . she sounded most pleasant over the phone.'

'We're lumbering you with yet more visitors.'

'Company,' Elspeth corrected with a smile. 'It really is a bit quiet for me with just John and me.'

'Isn't Patrick here then?'

Elspeth hesitated fractionally before answering. 'He escorted Alyssa to London to where she's to stay with a friend. Deidre Crocker, I think he said the name was. The police are going to keep a round the clock watch on her until this awful business is over.'

'Was he well enough?' I said, utterly amazed.

'No. By no means. But there was another reason for his going to town. Anne had booked him into one of those clinics for injured sportsmen. She says it will cost a small fortune but as far as getting someone fit again, the place is unrivalled.'

The cost didn't bother me at all for I was fairly sure D12 would pay. Even if Daws did demur we weren't exactly broke. But why hadn't Patrick rung me at the London flat to tell me what he intended to do? Except for the one night I had spent at Terry's, I had been there every evening.

'Which day did they travel up?' I enquired, trying to sound off-hand.

'It was all rather sudden,' Elspeth said, frowning as she tried to remember. 'Yes, I know. It was the same day you had to report to the Colonel. Last Friday. John drove them to the station for the four thirty-five.'

Which meant that Patrick had been in town the same night I had stayed with Terry. Ye gods. But I could recollect no sign of his having slept at the flat when I returned there. Normally he would have left a note. So had he gone straight to the clinic or been parked across the river opposite Terry's flat with powerful binoculars trained on that young man's bedroom window? We hadn't closed the curtains.

'Is something wrong, Ingrid?'

I decided to give the other fear an airing. 'D'you think he's in love with her?'

Elspeth's frown became a trifle deeper. 'If you'd asked me if she's in love with him, then I'd have to answer yes. But it's only natural when he rescued her. But as to the other. . . . You never know with Patrick. Even I don't sometimes.'

*   *   *

141

The next morning I hired a car and drove to Bristol. I had been given the job of helping to keep surveillance on the MP. This entailed staying at the same hotel as him for a couple of days, watching his movements and gaining entry to his room to place a small listening device therein. All conversations within the room would then be relayed to a van parked in the street near-by, the markings of which would suggest that it was there in connection with the repair of telephones. In fact it was one of D12's undercover units.

On the surface this assignment hadn't sounded as though it ought to have been dumped on our doorstep, and to be honest before I had been to see Daws I hadn't been interested. I am sometimes given a small job during a lull in a much more important one. But when he had begun to explain, I had become more and more intrigued. For the man was a friend of his, one of the few who had championed the original setting up of the department. There were whispers, from a source that Daws hadn't mentioned, that moves were being made to dis-credit this ardent supporter of the smaller, less publicised security groups.

Everything went exactly to plan. The Honourable Member arrived by taxi from the station about an hour after me and went straight to his room. I shared the lift with him to the third floor but kept my nose firmly in the crossword of a newspaper I was carrying. When he reached his room, number 142, I strolled past and then went down the stairs to my own on the floor below.

Part of my brief was to eat in the hotel restaurant for it was known that our man usually did so when away from home. I was to observe him accordingly and note if he received visitors. During the afternoon he went out and others took over with the surveillance so I spent rather a boring afternoon in the hotel as it was raining heavily.

At six thirty-five I observed him return, still alone. He went to his room, I guessed to change for dinner, so I did likewise, but waiting this time until he was out of sight. At a little after seven fifteen the phone rang twice. I didn't answer it. It was my signal that he had gone to the restaurant.

A minute or so later I was inside his room. I had not had to resort to illegal methods to open the door, a key had been

142

pushed beneath my own door while I was changing. I didn't put the light on in case there were cameras.

Astoundingly, I found one. But not for this Peeping Tom the cunning lens hidden in a locked drawer with a hole where the handle had been removed or looking down through a light fitting in the ceiling. No, by the beam of my tiny flashlight I found it tucked behind the pelmet over the window, a tiny hole having been bored through it for the lens. It seemed to be wired up so that it only functioned when the lights in the room were switched on.

Still standing rather precariously on a chair I took the camera down, shook out the spool of film it contained and dropped it in my bag. The camera I consigned to a water grave in the toilet cistern. This was joined by a bug I found in the phone when I went to insert my own and another that had been fitted behind the ventilation grille in the bathroom. By this time I was feeling a little breathless. MI6, KGB, CIA or who?

I was just leaving the bathroom when I heard a key being inserted in the lock of the outside door. My insides performed a ghastly loop the loop.

But it wasn't the rightful occupier of the room for whoever it was didn't put the light on either. Through a chink in the bathroom door I watched, holding my breath, as a shadowy figure went over the window. Checking on the camera? Had removing it and my own movements around the room been picked up by the other devices? If the snoopers were in a room close by it would explain their quick arrival.

He had left the outside door ajar.

I bolted.

Number Two was in the corridor keeping watch. I didn't take any chances. He folded in half quite gracefully when my knee met his stomach and it was the work of a moment to shove him backwards into the room and pull the door shut.

By the time I reached the restaurant the Honourable Member had company. A lady, and I use the term without hesitation. Not his wife, however, whom I knew to be firmly at home in Harrow with her wobbly false teeth and baggy cardigans. No, this young woman was almost certainly his secretary, wearing a black wig to cover her own blonde hair. Oh dear.

I decided to risk phoning Daws from a call box.

'Who are they?' Daws grated when I had reported that someone had beaten us to it.

'No idea,' I confessed. 'I think you ought to get your chum out of here.'

'So do I. I'll ring him at the hotel. I'd like you to leave as well. But stay right where you are until someone comes to escort you to your room. The safe word will be "cuckoo".'

After I had explained exactly where I was, he rang off. A couple of minutes later a man in blue overalls approached the phone box. He pulled the door open.

'I thought I heard a cuckoo just now,' he said, without looking too embarrassed.

'Up in Room 142?' I countered and he grimaced. 'You're Steve, aren't you? I've seen you running with Terry in the park at lunchtime.'

He grinned an affirmative. 'Would you know these guys again?'

'I'd know the one who was standing outside the room. He was about four feet six inches tall ... all right, five feet, and had stringy grey hair.'

Steve borrowed the phone box to remove his overalls. Beneath them he wore a well-cut grey suit, white shirt and red tie. Together we went back into the hotel where the usual air of affluent calm seemed undisturbed. Then I saw the man I had been ordered to watch talking on a phone at the reception desk.

Steve and I nudged each other simultaneously.

'Snap,' I said.

We turned aside to go to the lifts, and out of the corner of my eye I saw the phone call concluded and the MP hurry back through the door that led to the restaurant.

'Do we apprehend those men if we see them still hanging around?' I asked.

' "Pulverize" was the word the Colonel used,' Steve answered shortly.

'But they might be MI6 or Special Branch!'

'He doesn't particularly care who's *side* they're on. He just won't truck with anyone treading on his oppos' toes.'

Any dread on my part that I was about to witness the pulverizing — in friendly fashion, of course — of other upholders of law and order soon faded. The two were either stupid, inept or both, and were still in Room 142, apparently trying to dry out the camera. And when one shouted a warning to the other it wasn't in English.

Finally Steve alerted the hotel security staff who called the police. When he showed them his identity card the two intruders were removed, horizontal, and no questions were asked concerning their poor state of health.

'One thing . . . ' Steve said quietly to me as we were leaving.

I couldn't help but smile at the way he was carefully blowing on his knuckles.

'Yes?'

'Forgetting for a moment that you work with two other members of this organization, one of whom is your husband. . . . '

'Go on,' I prompted when he stopped talking.

'I never gossip, but where someone's safety is concerned I do tend to pass on what I hear. The grapevine has it that when young Terry returned from Somerset he was saying to Daws that it was about time he took over from Gillard. According to him, and in the most respectful way, the Major failed because he's over the hill. So Daws has given him his head and from what I hear it's to teach him a lesson. Don't go with him, Ingrid. For God's sake, don't go with him!'

Chapter Seventeen

The Bristol affair having come to rather an abrupt end, I decided to use the time left to me to do a little private investigation on another matter. The following day I drove down to Blandford Forum in Dorset.

I am reasonably familiar with the old town's narrow streets because when we were first married Patrick had been stationed at Warminster. *En route* to Poole and Bournemouth for shopping trips one had to drive through Blandford. The Maltravers Arms Hotel on the southern side of the town was a favourite place to stop for coffee and on this particular morning I found myself pulling into the willow-lined drive for reasons of pure nostalgia.

It all seemed exactly as I remembered; grandfather clocks, faded carved coats of arms on the staircase, the suit of armour that Patrick had once given a raffish salute, the Victorian conservatory where one was served with morning coffee or afternoon tea.

There was the same scent of crushed geranium leaves and jasmine and of hot floor tiles dampened by a recent spraying. I sat where I could see the garden through a thick tracery of vine leaves; the same smooth lawns, a tiny sunken garden with a fountain and, on the far side, a magnificent *Wellingtonia,* a Giant Redwood, at least fifty feet high.

I gave my order and watched a cat climb the *Wellingtonia.* But I was thinking of the Haywood case. In order to justify accompanying Terry, I had to have a good reason, some further link between the scientist and the gang of bikers than my own husband's punch drunk identification. I was sufficiently hard-headed not to rush off with him on a mad-cap whim. Terry, after all, could look after himself, and by tagging along I was only presenting him with further problems. I had to have *evidence.*

But what exactly was Daws up to?

This question kept coming to the forefront of my thinking. Again I pushed it to one side. There was no doubt that the Colonel would want to clip Terry's wings if he thought him becoming uppish. But I must not let this cloud my judgement; Daws wouldn't deliberately put his life at risk.

In truth, I was scared. But I had made myself come to Blandford to try to find George Peterson's widow as a last effort to get at the truth. If I failed to locate her, or if she didn't have anything interesting to say, then I would be able to look Terry in the eye and tell him that I thought there was no point in my going with him. I knew already, of course, that he wouldn't be able to fathom this weird female logic.

Another factor was that I felt totally lost without Patrick's guidance. He had phoned Elspeth to tell her that he was responding well to the treatment and was spending most of the time eating and sleeping. Just what a mother would most like to hear, I though wryly. He hadn't mentioned me or asked her to give me a message. But I couldn't stop thinking about him.

The cat had attained the first branch of the tree and was lying full-length, tail swishing, as it watched sparrows who were chirping a monotonous warning. Observing it and its barely suppressed desire to rend the birds feather from feather, I thought of Patrick again. Had he seen Terry and me together?

I forced myself to concentrate on the job I had reluctantly set out to do. Ten minutes spent with the records computer in the D12 office had been fairly fruitful. It had given me the Petersons' address in Blandford and also the name of the estate agent who was handling the sale of the house. The property had been sold to a couple by the name of Lawson but only subject to contract, the deal hadn't actually gone through. According to the computer the Lawsons were quite beyond reproach so at least there seemed to be no question of Amanda Peterson having been forced out of her home by anyone connected with her husband's death. But I wanted to make quite sure that she wasn't being made to hand over any money from the sale.

I had bought a street map and experienced no difficulty in finding the house in Maple Drive. It was a conventional semi-detached property, well looked after and with a neat front garden. I found it difficult to believe that the man who had pruned the pink and cream Peace roses and mowed the lawn was now dead. But perhaps Amanda was the gardener.

There were no curtains at the windows but a car was parked in the drive to the garage. As I unlatched the front gate I saw movement within one of the downstairs rooms.

'Mrs Peterson?' The question was merely politeness on my part for most certainly it was Amanda Peterson who answered the door.

'Yes.' Weariness and being widowed hadn't spoilt a fine English complexion and cornflower blue eyes.

I produced my identity card and saw her frown slightly.

'Really, this is too much! I spoke to someone from the security service yesterday.'

'Did whoever it was show you a card like this?'

She gazed at me penetratingly for a moment. 'I seem to remember it being exactly the same. How is it that you're not aware of his visit?

'Small cogs in a big machine,' I said humbly, wondering if it had been Daws. 'I'm sorry to have troubled you.' I turned to leave, ashamed at my relief.

'No, don't go. I didn't mean to be rude. It's just that I can't get on with packing.'

'There's no point in my asking questions if someone's asked them already.'

'Oh, bother questions. Come in and have a cup of coffee – I'm dying for some.'

Realizing that she needed female company, I went in.

'You'll have to put your jacket on the banisters, I'm afraid. Jeremy asked if he could have the old coat rack.'

'Your son?'

'Yes. We've – or rather, I've – only the one now. He's at university doing Engineering. In a way I'm glad he's not at home and has plenty to keep him busy.' She gave a slightly forced laugh as she went into the kitchen to put on the kettle.

148

'You love your children, but teenage boys either seem to be eating you out of house and home or sprawled in front of the television. Do sit down. You might have to move a few things, though.'

I wouldn't normally have asked her about that telltale word 'now'.

'Elizabeth died from a brain tumour four years ago,' Amanda said, unconsciously perhaps cradling the kettle in her arms. 'She would have been twelve in another week's time.' She then apologised for having consigned the best bone china cups to a tea chest.

After insisting that I help while she made the coffee, I went into the living room and filled two more tea chests with books, packing cushions wrapped in polythene on the top. I had started on a third with a table lamp, more cushions and ornaments rolled up in tissue paper when Amanda came in carrying two mugs.

'I can see you're a woman after my own heart,' she said, clearing the settee of folded curtains so we could sit down. 'Methodical. It's because I'm making lists and labelling everything that the job's taking so long.'

'Are you moving far?' I asked.

'Back where I came from. Suffolk.'

'Is that far enough?'

She gave me another of her straight looks. 'That's a slightly sinister question.'

'It was meant to be.'

With a nervous little shrug, she said, 'I understand I'm to be given police protection for a while. Until this business is over.' She gazed about for something upon which to place her spoon. 'George was the most unflappable man who ever lived. "Never lose your cool," he always used to say. I know it sounds pathetic but I'm trying to live like that at the moment.'

'Of course it isn't pathetic,' I told her, remembering how I had drawn on the memory of Peter's sang-froid after he had been gunned down by terrorists in Plymouth. Then I added, 'That doesn't sound like a man who would take his own life.'

'Oh no. George didn't kill himself. He was murdered.'

The completely calm way she made this pronouncement enabled me to see precisely the kind of man he had been and how his strength was living on in his courageous pretty wife.

'There was no evidence, of course,' Amanda continued. 'Just a car with a piece of hose connected to the exhaust pipe and put through one of the windows. But for such a normally happy man to end up like that was obscene. And he thought people who killed themselves were cowards. Not from the point of view of jumping off the bridge or under the train but afterwards. Think of the poor devils who have to pick up the pieces, was his attitude.'

'But there are no pieces when you die from carbon monoxide poisoning,' I pointed out gently. 'Nothing nasty.'

'Having to identify your dead husband is nasty,' she said simply. 'He wouldn't have done that to me.'

I tried to recollect how I had first reacted when I heard that Peter had been killed. Disbelief, mainly, utter disbelief.

Amanda said, 'When someone you don't know personally is called George you always imagine them to be a pipe-smoking, cuddly old duffer with not much of a sense of humour. George wasn't like that. He was an untidy whirlwind of a man who bubbled over all the time with ideas and laughter. Sometimes he was quite exhausting to be with. He almost fizzed with nervous energy and could never remember where he'd put anything. It took me ages to get the place straight after he'd . . . gone. And then I hated it, as though I'd finally removed all traces of his ever having lived here. I think that was when I really cried.'

'Was it possible that someone was putting some kind of intolerable pressure on him?'

'I'd have known about it if they were. George couldn't keep anything concerning his feelings to himself. He was too much of an extrovert.'

'So this came right out of the blue? He was murdered and it was made to look like suicide?'

'I suppose so. But why on earth should someone want to kill him?'

'I was hoping you could give me some clues about that.'

She shrugged wordlessly.

'The police must be suspicious of the circumstances surrounding his death or they wouldn't be giving you protection.'

'An Inspector from the local police said something about the deaths of other scientists, and that there might be a link. It seems to me that it's one of those things that's blown up out of all proportion by the press.'

'D'you know if your husband had met any of the others who died?'

'No idea. I don't care really. It's awful when people try to lump the man you loved together with strangers. I don't even know who they were — I stopped reading the papers afterwards because every time I did his name was there.'

George had been only the second to die, I suddenly remembered. 'It *is* important,' I said.

'For whom? More strangers? I know it's appallingly selfish but now that my life's ruined I can't worry about the world at large.'

'How about Jeremy?'

'Jeremy has nothing to do with this,' she said, beginning to show signs of losing her composure.

'Nor did a girl called Alyssa Goldberg,' I murmured. 'Until the gang responsible for terrorizing David Prescott wanted her boyfriend's motor bike. He was murdered and the girl ended up being forced to join them.'

'Did you say David Prescott?'

'Yes.'

'Doctor David Prescott who works in Bath?'

I told her it was.

'What on earth's been happening to him? I don't remember hearing anything about that.'

'You stopped reading the papers,' I reminded her, perhaps unkindly. 'No, I don't suppose anything got into the media. They didn't quite succeed in driving him out of his mind. D'you know him personally?'

'We met at a computer software presentation in London. It was some years ago now.'

'And you were accompanying George.'

'Oh no. I work for the MoD too. Senior to George really but he didn't hold it against me.' This final remark with a tiny, fond smile.

My pulse began to beat hollowly in my ears. 'Was Prescott's boss Alex Haywood there too?'

She grimaced. 'You could say that.'

151

'Amanda, for God's sake tell me what happened.'

She looked surprised by my fervour. 'Happened,' she echoed. 'Well, yes ... Haywood decided that he couldn't live without me. We'd been there a couple of days – it went on for four if I remember correctly – when George got an anonymous note to the effect that Haywood and I had slept together the first night. George had arrived on the second morning as he'd come straight from a meeting at Rolls-Royce at Derby. Haywood *had* propositioned me, as a matter of fact, and I told George about it. George wasn't stupid. He immediately buttonholed Haywood and accused *him* of sending the letter. Haywood used a lot of bad language but didn't deny it. Then David Prescott overheard him and told him to moderate his language. I got the impression he was religious and couldn't stand blasphemy. The row became even more public after that. It was awful.'

'Prescott said nothing about this. The only person he mentioned besides Haywood was Colin Jones who shot himself in Wales.'

There was no stopping Amanda now. 'We were a group! You know, you all sit at small tables for dinner and tend to make friends. Yes, Colin was there too. He and David had met at university. David was a very senior student. He'd left Ferranti to take another degree. I should imagine that David would be the sort of man who would want to forget an episode like that, especially as it became so unpleasant.'

'Was a man called Kevin Cook one of the group?'

'No. I can't remember anyone with that name.'

'Sorry to interrupt. Then what happened?'

'The letter was posted up in the lecture hall and printed underneath was: ALEX HAYWOOD WROTE THIS BECAUSE HE CAN'T KEEP HIS HANDS OFF OTHER MEN'S WIVES. It put him in a very bad light. It was surprising how many people knew him and how unpopular he was already.'

'Have you any idea who put it up? I take it George didn't.'

'No, but he gave it to the person who did – Colin. Yes, I heard about Colin's death. I wonder what made him do it.'

'Perhaps he didn't,' I observed. 'No more than George did. Amanda, do you know if this episode affected Haywood's career?'

'I've no idea. George and I never discussed it afterwards. Some things you can, can't you, and have a good laugh over? But not this, it was just plain nasty. But I should think it must have done. Bound to really. I mean, you sign the Official Secrets Act. They do keep tabs on you and the way you behave. Surely you're not thinking that Haywood. . . .'

'Is anyone threatening you?' I asked when her voice trailed away. 'Any letters, phone calls or demands for money?'

'No.' She replied unhesitatingly.

'What was the name of this man who came to see you yesterday?'

'I'm afraid you'll think me quite stupid. I've forgotten. I'm hopeless with names.'

'What did he look like?'

Amanda stared into space, eyes narrowed. 'Around forty, I should say. Quite tall. Dark. Well dressed. His eyes were blue, I *think*. I'm not quite sure because he was wearing gold-rimmed glasses with tinted lenses. He was very softly spoken. I thought afterwards that he might have been Irish.'

She was far more observant than Idris Jones had been. Amanda's visitor was probably the same man who had called on Colin Jones' uncle. He was one of those Patrick had de-scribed to the police, a face out of necessity imprinted into his own memory. O'Neill, the ex-IRA man.

'What did he ask you?'

'When I was leaving here. Where I was going.'

'Did you give him an address?'

'Two, actually. The friend with whom I'm staying here in Blandford. It's no good, I can't sleep in this house now. And that of the new house I've bought, near where my parents live in Stowmarket.'

So if she wasn't being threatened – and I was quite sure of this from her manner – then she too was going to be murdered.

'Would you describe your work as having a high security rating?'

'Oh rather ... I'm helping with design work on the next generation of submarines after Trident.'

'And how will you carry on if you're moving to Suffolk?'

'I'm being transferred to London. It means I'll just go home at the weekends.'

153

'Amanda, do you trust me?'

'Yes, of course. Why shouldn't I?'

She was far too trusting. 'Will you stay at my cottage in Devon until your house sale goes through?'

'But surely —'

'Please,' I interrupted. 'Go today. Now, if possible. No, even better, I'll take you myself. I could do with a few hours at home.'

'But it'll take me the rest of today to finish packing,' she protested.

We did it between us. It took two and three-quarter hours and every time I heard a motor bike I broke into a cold sweat.

Chapter Eighteen

I didn't recognize Terry when he arrived at Hendon after four days at the police unit at Barnes which provides motor cycle outriders for the Royal Family and visiting dignitaries. This was not because of anything that had happened to him there but as a result of an appointment at a London hospital on his way between the two establishments.

Someone whom I discovered much later to be an expert on disguises had secretly observed Terry at Barnes and had decided that even with his hair cropped really short he still looked too law-abiding. Therefore, at the hospital and under local anaesthetic, the crowns were removed from two of his front teeth, one at the top and one at the bottom but not opposite each other. These were a legacy from the bad accident he had had as a teenager when in possession of his first motor bike. Taking advantage of the anaesthetic, a three-inch cut had then been inflicted in his cheek and badly stitched so that it would heal with a scar. Terry isn't vain but was not at all happy with his reflection in the mirror afterwards. His only consolation was a written promise from Daws that medical restitution would be forthcoming when the case was concluded.

All this I found out later, of course, but when he first slouched in dressed in tattered black teeshirt, leather jacket and trousers, and adorned with chains and leather bracelets studded with spikes, I really thought that here was someone who had come to the wrong address. Then I recollected that everyone has to have a pass.

'Ingrid,' said the swimming instructor.

I looked down from where I was standing on the lowest of

the three diving boards and felt dizzy. Together with the probationers, I was now required to jump off it and into four metres of water.

I couldn't.

I can swim quite well and don't mind being under water. But the sensation of falling. . . .

'Who the hell are you?' demanded the instructor when he beheld the stranger.

'Meadows,' said Terry.

'You're MI5 too?' But clearly he didn't believe what was on his list.

Terry nodded slowly three times like something mechanical.

'What do you lot use for discipline to get people to do as they're told?'

'It's not like that,' Terry answered, ignoring the sarcasm. 'We each have our own fields of excellence and don't tend to stray outside them.'

'So when someone's drowning you consult your fields of excellence directory and get on the blower.'

There were a few titters.

'You misunderstand,' Terry said urbanely. 'And, anyway, I can't order Ingrid to do anything as strictly speaking she's my boss.'

The titters ceased abruptly.

'But in an emergency,' Terry continued, 'the ones with skill in a particular subject lead those without.'

And with that he took off his Doc Martins, raced up the ladder to the highest board and, leathers and all, dived in.

'What on earth happened to your face?' I enquired when he was bobbing a few feet below me in the water.

'Sadistic dentist,' he replied. 'Come on, arms out, stick your chest out and just step off. If you make it off the high one, I'll put my name down as a blood donor.'

'Did you — ?' I began.

'Yes, I still pass out when folk come at me with needles.'

I stepped off.

A few days later I had my own encounter with needles. As I had already pointed out to Terry, it is impossible to turn a thirty-six-year-old woman into a biker's doxy, no matter how well preserved she may be. So we were adopting his suggestion that I should be just a person to whom he was giving a lift. I was to be made into a drug addict, trying to kick the habit, hitching lifts to a rehabilitation centre in Exeter recommended by a friend. Therefore there had to be fair number of needle marks on my forearms and thighs. Almost painlessly these were applied by D12's own medical officer, an ex-army surgeon, when I went to him for a check-up.

'Thought about going on the pill for a few weeks?' he enquired, having pronounced me fit and well after a week of almost unrelenting circuit training and running round sports fields. 'There *is* a risk of − '

'Rape?' I interrupted, saying the difficult word for him. I had always felt that he was absolutely at home with anything encountered on the battlefield, from severed heads to trench foot, but when he had come across the department's first female operative his thin ginger moustache had been seen to twitch nervously. I could imagine him addressing a group of WRACS during the War. 'Not from one of our chaps of course, but. . . .'

'It's a bit late for that now,' I told him. 'We're starting out tomorrow and I'm sure you have to take them some time in advance.' The idea didn't appeal in the slightest. Previous experience with such things had resulted in my becoming an over-emotional disaster zone − probably, on reflection, one of the reasons Patrick and I had broken up the first time.

There remained little to do but wash my hair with cheap washing up liquid until it resembled an unravelled ball of wire wool, apply dark lines beneath my eyes with make-up, and attire myself in the old clothes I had brought from home. When kitted out in an ancient pair of jeans muddy from gardening, a baggy sweater, a pair of Patrick's socks and a headscarf, it was a real mess that gazed back at herself in the mirror.

Terry fell about laughing.

'You're still lisping through those gaps in your teeth,' I commented tartly.

Almost exactly forty-eight hours later, he said, 'Good of Brinkley to come and see us off.'

I glanced at him quickly but he wasn't being sarcastic, just miserable. The stitches had been removed from his cheek but it still hurt when he spoke or, for that matter, moved his face muscles at all. Terry has very mobile features.

'Yes,' I agreed. 'I enjoyed meeting him.'

Brinkley had briefed us, and listening to him I had been left in no doubt as to the danger of what we were endeavouring to do. One member of Special Branch had been order to infiltrate the gang, another to watch him and report back with the group's movements. Adam Wells, the first of these, had had a tough time. According to his colleague, whose life depended on remaining invisible, the gang had taken him and his bike apart to make sure that he was what he was pretending to be, a thug down on his luck looking for a job. The man watching with the aid of powerful binoculars and also infra-red nightsights, Philips, had reported tersely that Wells had been tied to a tree for two days and beaten. And there was no sign of the man Patrick was insisting was Haywood, nor his two minders.

'Be careful,' Brinkley had warned. 'Philips said he had a hunch there had been changes in the command structure so God above knows what's going on. He and Wells have no idea that you're about to arrive on the scene, though. It's too risky as we can't guarantee they could stay silent if their cover was blown.'

This last remark had had a dreadful effect on me for I was not sure if I could do the same for them if Terry and I were exposed and forced to talk.

I had already informed Inspector Brinkley of the whereabouts of Amanda Peterson. Contrary to what I had expected he had made no comment, merely thanking me and assuring me that she would be watched over.

'Philips is due to be relieved today,' Terry remarked. 'Poor bugger's probably desperate for a bath. I know I am and I've only been on the road for two days.'

It went without saying that we had Philips to thank for pinpointing the location of the gang. We would not have to search for them as Patrick had done, and if they were travelling in the same direction as they had been the day before they would find us.

'I'm scared, Terry.'

'They can't suspect us. They'll come upon *us,* remember?'

'What if they go right past?'

'They won't. According to Philips they stop all other roughneck bikers unless there's a whole lot of them, and relieve them of money and valuables. We've only got a little cash and my old camera which will look OK.'

'I know that,' I said peevishly. 'I was at the briefing as well.'

We had travelled from London to Southampton on the first day and from there, slowly, to Lyndhurst in the New Forest. If anyone questioned our slowness – and police in a patrol car already had – it was because we were having trouble with the bike. And now it was the excuse for us sitting soaking wet under a clump of trees on the Lyndhurst-Brockenhurst road, the sparking plugs on an oily rag at Terry's side as he crouched by the bike.

Waiting.

The rain had ceased and but for the swish of passing cars the only sound was that of water dripping from the leaf canopy above my head and pattering amongst last year's leaves on the forest floor. Some of the drops were going down my neck and some weren't and at that moment my thinking wasn't progressing much beyond this. Fear gnawed at my stomach.

'How has Philips been keeping track of Wells?' I asked.

'Wells has a homing device around his neck on a bit of string,' Terry replied. 'Make no mistake, out of the two Philips is the expert. He has a car for roadwork and there's a mountain bike for when they head off down farm tracks at night to sleep in barns. They seem to know every path and by-way in the south of England. But I don't think Philips is his real name. I also think they've borrowed him from the SAS.'

'So who's relieving him?'

'One of his chums. Who else?' He picked up one of the plugs and cleaned it on another rag. 'Why did you decide to come?'

'Because I said it was Haywood all along and I want to be in on the act when he's caught.'

'As a result of loyalty to the Major on your part, or fresh evidence?' Terry asked shrewdly.

'It goes back some years to when Haywood decided he wanted Amanda Peterson and certain people who are now dead – Jones, George Peterson – or scarred for the rest of their lives – David Prescott and Amanda herself – saw to it that he didn't have her and exposed him for what he was.'

Terry whistled softly. 'What did Daws say?'

'I didn't tell him.'

'Why ever not?'

'He would still have said there wasn't enough evidence, and he's right. There isn't. There must be more to it than just a grudge.'

Then, in the distance, we heard the roar of motor bikes.

'Coming from the Brockenhurst direction,' Terry muttered. 'They spent the night near Christchurch . . . it must be them.' He gazed at me calmly. 'Do I get to play this my own way? Will you follow my ideas as though I was the Major?'

'Daws promoted you for the duration of the job,' I reminded him. 'And strictly speaking I've never been your boss.'

They were almost upon us and Terry had to raise his voice over the noise. 'So what would he be doing now? Saying a little prayer?'

'More than likely,' I replied as the first of about twenty bikes went by. 'He's not a Catholic but I've often noticed him crossing himself before a hazardous undertaking.'

I was thinking that they hadn't seen us when one of the riders at the rear of the bunch peeled off and slowed. He stopped at the side of the road near where we were, switched off the ignition and looked at us. At least I assumed that was what he was doing, he was wearing an old-fashioned crash helmet and a pair of sunglasses with mirrored lenses so I couldn't see his eyes.

'Lost?' Terry growled, straightening from the bike.

By now others had turned back. Some rode around behind us and others approached from the front. We ended up by being completely surrounded, the noise and fumes overwhelming. Then one by one they switched off their engines.

'What are you doing here?' asked an individual with red hair, this being revealed when he removed his helmet to scratch his scalp.

'Fixing the soddin' bike,' Terry said. 'Is this your private road?'

'Just answer the questions, laddie,' whispered the one with sunglasses.

Just then I noticed that there were two women riding pillion and also a man. At the moment I looked at him he keeled over sideways and fell to the ground. His hands were tied together.

'Shit,' someone said from behind me.

'Chuck him in the stream,' ordered Sunglasses. He seemed to have some authority for two others dismounted, lifted their bikes on to the stands and yanked the man to his feet.

'Is he drunk?' I demanded to know. But I knew the answer already for his face was bruised, his lips split and bleeding. It was Adam Wells, the Special Branch man.

'Ever so drunk,' said one of those holding him up. They both released him and Wells sank to his knees. One man began to kick him to get him up again.

'Stow that!' shouted Sunglasses, betraying a naval background. He glanced along the road. 'What's wrong with the bike?' he asked Terry.

'Nothing now. It was mis-firing so I cleaned the plugs.'

'Too many strange faces with neat excuses around us lately,' chimed in another voice from behind me.

'That's why we're checking on people,' he was informed. 'Shut your trap.' Another quick look along the road in the direction from whence they had come. 'Where the hell's he got to?'

'Thought he had a faulty valve on one of the tyres,' Redhead disclosed. 'Whatever it is, we wait.'

'This is a public road,' I said to Sunglasses. 'Leave us alone.'

'Where are you going?' he said.

'Mind your own damn business.'

'She lives on any street corner,' piped up a voice, and there were roars of laughter.

Sunglasses got off his bike, came over and shook me. 'Answer or I'll break your boyfriend's neck.'

I could see two of me reflected in the lenses. I answered him. With language that actually made him take a step backwards.

'Exeter,' Terry said quickly, and with the manner of a man with his neck in mind. 'She's not my girl though. She was hiking and I gave her a lift.'

'For services rendered,' observed Redhead with a raucous laugh. 'Can't you just see it eh? She's old enough to be his Ma. Like screwing scrag end of mutton.'

161

I'm an excellent shot with stones at close quarters and scored a bullseye on his sweaty pink forehead before he could duck. There were howls of laughter while he tried to mop up the blood. When he could see, he headed for me purposefully.

Terry got to him first.

'No fighting,' said Sunglasses. 'D'you want half the county's police here?'

'I'm not fighting,' said Terry, and threw a punch that sent Redhead sprawling.

During the shouting that followed another bike drew up. It was a Kawasaki with transfers of twin-headed eagles on each side of the petrol tank. The rider dismounted and as he turned to remove his helmet and hang it on the handlebars I saw that there was another eagle outlined in brass studs on the back of his jacket. When he faced me my knees almost gave way.

Terry saw what was about to happen to him and waited, remarkably bravely, to be despatched to utter oblivion.

It was Patrick.

Chapter Nineteen

I'm not sure what prevented me from throwing myself at his feet crying that Terry and I hadn't slept together. For that was what the vicious jab to the side of Terry's jaw had been all about. In retrospect I would have been wasting my breath for just seeing us seemed to have unleashed a vast bottled-up resentment. Oddly, I too remained calm and then there was only a fleeting sensation of a paralysing grip on my neck. After this, nothing.

I was only unconscious for a couple of seconds but lay quite still. There was earth grittily in my mouth but I dared not spit it out. A tiny pebble, however, that was threatening to slide down my throat I lodged between my back teeth until the opportunity came to get rid of it. Infuriatingly, my mind always records this kind of minute detail in moments of stress when it could be far more usefully employed in working out strategy.

The shock of seeing Patrick was worse than his subsequent reaction. But he had used the absolute minumum force to render me senseless. I was quite sure of this because it had happened to me before during training. Forget what he had said or do something stupid while learning self-defence and that was what was handed out. There would be no bruises.

I didn't have long to get my breath back. Someone, probably the owner of those bloody wiry fingers, grabbed my ankles and towed me along the ground. We went downhill, along a path of sorts. The whole gang were with us by the sound of it, pushing their bikes. I didn't open my eyes. After encountering just a little mud and only one patch of nettles we stopped.

'This'll do,' said Patrick's voice. 'We'll make sure they're who they say they are, and then if the guy wants to come along with us that's fine. He looks as though he might have done this sort of thing before.'

'What about her?' A foot nudged me in the ribs. It was Redhead speaking.

There was a pause. 'I'll think about it. We'll get rid of her somehow.'

'The boss won't be happy if you rub her out and the police come looking for her.'

'Neither will he want her released to go bleating to them about her boyfriend.' Patrick retorted scathingly.

'She's just some hooker he picked up on the road.'

'Then no one'll miss her if I cut her throat.'

Another silence. Then Redhead said, 'I've knocked about rough but I'm damned if I've met the likes of you before. I can't say I've ever laid into a woman either.'

'Which is why you spend all your time trying to kick this lot into line instead of being given the interesting jobs. Go away and play with yourself while I ask young gap teeth a few questions.'

'Why did you come back?' The question was spat at Patrick.

Patrick bent down and began to go through my pockets. 'The Goldberg girl's parents gave me ten K to find her and I did. I made a hash of getting her away but survived to collect the money. I reasoned while your boss and his two paid thugs were giving me a hiding that a lot of money could be made on this side of the organisation too. What do you do now? A post office here and a security van there. Peanuts.'

'He won't like it.'

'He'll have to. His muscle-bound protectors were picked up by the police yesterday.'

'What?' Redhead hissed, also bending down so they were talking across me. 'That's impossible.'

'It happened,' Patrick said imperturbably, removing the cheap wristwatch I had bought specially. 'I gave their descriptions to the police, and where I'd last seen them, plus of course the numbers of their bikes and they got scooped up in no time.'

'You bastard!'

'A bastard with brains,' Patrick said through his teeth. 'And

164

you're clever enough to know that if you co-operate with me, the world's yours.'

'We could kill you.'

'No. You couldn't. And if you tried to get them to do it, they'd kill you instead. D'you know why? I'll tell you. It's because you're a lousy leader. Another reason is that men respect someone who goes back after what was handed out to me. Stir them up, Red, and I promise you that if they don't kill you, I will.'

Muttering, Red went away.

Under my breath I said, 'You must get that dreadfully corny patter from watching all those old gangster films.'

When there was no response to this I opened my eyes. Patrick was unzipping a top pocket of his jacket. He slipped the watch within and withdrew what turned out to be a photograph. He held it for me to see, hand and photo shaking slightly. I tore my gaze from it to observe that he was trembling slightly all over, like the vibration of a purring cat. No, he hadn't lied to Daws about not wanting to go back.

The photograph had been taken at extreme range and in very bad light so was dark and blurred. Because of this the two people depicted in it were unrecognizable. Just a vague outline of a man and a woman standing near a window, the man apparently slipping off the woman's dress and fondling her breasts as he did so.

'We didn't sleep together,' I said. No one was paying any attention to us, all busy involved some distance away with Terry being tied to a tree.

The picture went back into Patrick's pocket and still he didn't speak. He didn't trust himself to, I saw with mounting fear, over-stretched nerves and blind fury combining to get him to such a pitch that he could do anything.

'The phone rang,' I blurted out. 'Terry went to answer it but it was a wrong number.'

The mad gaze snapped away from Terry and on to me. 'I know. It was me. I asked to speak to Agatha Hendricks. I thought he might mention the name and then you'd know I wasn't far away.' He stood up.

'Don't throw this job away,' I begged.

'I'm not going to. I'm going to question that man over there.'

I struggled to my feet and waited until a bout of dizziness abated before I spoke. 'Patrick, if you hurt him out of spiteful revenge, I'll – '

'You'll what?' he interrupted.

'It was as much my fault as his,' I said in an anguished whisper.

With the flat of his hand he shoved me down again. Then he took a flick knife I had never seen before from his pocket and sprang the blade. Looking at me as he did so.

'When the phone rang I dashed into the shower,' I sobbed, aware that anyone overhearing would assume me forced to relate details of my sex life. 'I turned it on to cold and stood there under it in my pants and bra. When Terry came in I shouted things along the lines of how we'd been chosen for our integrity and we were rubbish if we couldn't resist going to bed with each other. Then we behaved like a couple of kids ... drank a lot more wine and Terry got in the shower too and we stood under the freezing cold spray and took everything off and touched each other all over to prove that we could without wanting to make love. By the time we'd finished fooling about we were both drunk and the bathroom was flooded and I'd never laughed so much in my life.'

From the glassy way he was looking at me, I wasn't sure that he'd even heard.

'That's the truth,' I said.

Patrick took a fresh grip on the knife and walked away. 'You shouldn't have come,' he said over his shoulder. 'And I can't think of any reason to keep you here.'

I could.

Terry was conscious and raised his head when he saw Patrick coming, this despite a little preliminary softening up by Red and a slovenly-looking man referred to as Loopy. Waving them to one side Patrick gripped the knife between his teeth in order to leave both hands free and administered two stunning slaps to Terry's face, whip-lashing his head from one side to the other. Then, stiffly, as if reluctant, he took himself off to lean against an oak several feet away.

'Speak, sonny,' he said.

Visibly, Terry fought down the nausea that the blows had induced.

166

'Unless you want the same again,' Patrick added.

Terry told his story. It was plausible and he looked the part. He would have been awarded, I found myself thinking, at least eight out of ten at one of D12's very exacting rôle-play sessions. He even remembered, eyeing the knife, to roughen the edges off his public school accent.

When he had finished, Patrick said, 'So if you're going round the country looking for work on building sites, you need money.'

'Who doesn't?' Terry replied sullenly.

'Where did you do time?'

'Parkhurst.'

Adam Wells started to shout from where he also had been tied to a tree. 'So he's in, is he? And yet I'm still under suspicion. Do I look like a bloody cop?'

'Does this man?' Patrick asked him.

'Let me loose and *I'll* ask him.'

Wells did blench slightly when Patrick approached with the knife, but to his relief was cut free.

'Why is he still under suspicion?' Patrick asked no one in particular. 'Ah, I remember now. Red told me. It's good for morale to have someone to beat up when you feel like it.' He gave Wells the knife. 'Go on, ask him. But be careful, it's very sharp.' This last remark was uttered in a mincing tone and a few of those watching tittered. But from nerves; this was not the kind of mindless violence to which they were accustomed.

'Give him hell,' Patrick urged. 'With those teeth he must be a Chief Commissioner at least.'

Wells saw that he was being mocked and returned the knife. He stayed free. No one moved to restrain him again.

'Is she your woman?' Patrick said suddenly to Terry, making him jump guiltily.

'No.'

'Never?'

'Never.'

The knife was held before Terry's eyes and then made an indescribably evil movement. Terry gasped as the blade then drew a thin red line across his throat.

'Never?' Patrick repeated.

'Never!' I yelled. 'Are you deaf or daft?' I ran over to them.

167

'This is all my fault. If he hadn't picked me up at Reading, he wouldn't have come this way.' There was loud laughter when I got down on my knees and grabbed Patrick round the shins. 'Don't hurt him anymore — he's only a youngster. I'll do anything if you'll leave him alone. Anything.'

'You'd need to be desperate,' Red commented, spitting on the ground near me.

Patrick chuckled. It was one of the most cold-blooded sounds I had ever heard. 'But not even hookers will give me what I want — not often, anyway.' He yanked me to my feet. 'D'you hear that?' he shouted in my face. 'Anything, you said. Whenever I say? As often as I want?'

I nodded, wondering desperately if we would have to do things in public that we didn't normally do in private. Kinky sex hadn't been quite what I'd had in mind. He'd been so busy acting he hadn't noticed precisely what he'd said. But perhaps he had, I reasoned in a quite unwarranted moment of mad levity, and this was easier than having to cut my throat.

It is not generally known that as well as thousands of acres of woodland, farms and picture postcard villages, the New Forest has large areas of bleak heathland that is as inhospitable as some of the wilder areas of Dartmoor. In a stony river gulley roughly at the centre of one of these, not far from the isolated railway station Beaulieu Road, the gang, The Hunters, as they called themselves, had set up temporary headquarters in a group of derelict farm buildings.

I gladly relinquished my hold around the waist of the man with whom I had been riding pillion. He stank. His greasy hair hung in lank strands beneath his helmet, so greasy in fact that it looked as though it had been smeared with lard. His name was Joe, I had been told, Dirty Joe, another of the men whom Alyssa had remembered.

Terry had ridden with Patrick, his hands tied together in front of Patrick to stop him falling off. I was unsure if he was really as dazed as he was pretending, especially when I noticed that it was the passenger who actually kicked down the stand of the bike and lifted the machine on to it.

Dirty Joe said, 'The women get food ready while the men drink. Get to it.'

A large brick barn was the only building with a roof in a reasonable state of repair. Holes in the original slates had been patched with sheets of corrugated iron, some of them tied to visible timbers with that universal standby of marginal farming, baling twine. Inside at one end the roof beams had been boarded over to provide storage space and this was partly filled with bales of hay and straw. At ground level pallets had been put on the beaten earth floor to provide a dry place to stack paper sacks of animal feeding stuffs. The two women were dragging some of these to one side.

'Want a hand?' I asked.

'Give the men this,' one of them puffed, hauling a cardboard box from a recess in the sacks. It contained partly full bottles of spirits and tins of beer. 'You'd better make sure Red has control of it.'

'He doesn't seem to be in charge anymore,' I pointed out innocently.

'But he's still in charge of me, and I don't want my block knocked off, thank you.'

'Then you take it,' I countered, achieving a frightened look in Patrick's direction. 'I haven't the slightest desire to offend the other one.'

She was a big brawny girl and stood up straight to stare at me, arms akimbo.

'No, you're right,' she acknowledged. 'I wouldn't swop places with you in the hay-loft tonight for all the money in the Bank of England.'

'What's his name?' I asked when she returned. The other woman had turned her back on me.

She began to pull aside more of the sacks. 'Well, he was Paddy when he first arrived. I told Red he was up to something but as usual was ignored.' She sniffed meaningfully. 'Then he took a fancy to Des's girl and tried to make off with her. They nearly killed him. I think he's come back to get even.'

There was more commonsense behind her dark brown eyes than in all the men put together, I decided. I gestured worldlessly in the direction of the other girl, still with her back to us.

'Her? Oh that's Paula. I'm Red's, you're Paddy's, she's everyone else's. Aren't you, Paula? You dozy trollop.'

169

Paula mouthed a few ugly remarks at us. She didn't seem very bright.

'Mind you,' my new friend went on as though Paula was deaf as well, 'if you're nice to Paddy, he doesn't look the sort to sell you like Joe did her. A fiver all round he got. Kept him in fags for weeks.'

I didn't actually pinch myself but couldn't believe what she was saying. Were we or were we not living in the twentieth century?

Paula found her tongue. 'You heard what the guy said: she's a junkie. He was taking her to one of those places where they sort them out. She's probably full of disease. Go on, sod off you. I don't want you near my food.'

'Where's the bloody nosh?' roared Red.

The provisions packed into black plastic bags and hidden in the recess proved to be of better quality and variety than I would have imagined. There was ham, boned chicken and sausages in tins, fruit pies, Swiss rolls and pounds and pounds of biscuits. One bag contained enough sweets to open a confectionery shop. Several of the men had emptied their panniers of the day's purchases of bread, milk, fresh fruit and butter.

'I've never shared needles,' I said, driven by both women's looks to act the part. 'And I've kicked it. I stopped because I'd run out of money. It was hell. All last week. ...' I stopped talking, ostensibly choking on emotion, and went to sit by myself near the door to get some fresh air.

'I could possibly be of service to you,' said Joe, leaning over a pile of fence posts to speak to me.

'How?' I asked sullenly, but knowing all too well what he meant.

'So you've no money,' he went on smoothly. 'But I'm sure we could come to a mutually satisfying arrangement.' He smirked, revealing the stumps of blackened teeth.

'The only satisfying arrangement I'd come to concerning you would be with an undertaker to burn your stinking carcase,' I yelled, for some reason enjoying myself immensely but at the same time hoping Patrick would quell any violent reaction on Joe's part.

'Go and shut her *up!*' Patrick shouted across to Terry.

170

'She needs drugs,' Joe said to him. 'Perhaps we could do business.'

'I'll let you know,' Patrick replied after a long pause.

Terry came over and sat down heavily. 'Shut up,' he said, leaning back and closing his eyes.

'Feel rough?'

'Not for the reason you're thinking. He's not strong enough yet to hit me hard.'

'What then?'

'We're to have nothing to eat or drink except water for two days. It's the rules for all new entrants. I don't think our Paddy would have gone along with it but Wells is all ready to kick up a fuss if we're given preferential treatment. You wait until this is all over . . . I'll ram his bloody whistle down his throat.'

'Our Paddy freed him,' I remarked quietly.

'Right. But I think Wells is scared his cover's going to be blown so he's overdoing it a bit. Honourable leader is more worried he's going to blow it for us, I reckon.'

'But he doesn't know who we are.'

'Right. So not too worried about getting the thumb screws out on a couple of drifters.'

The interminable day dragged on. Everyone ate and drank except for Terry and me. I tried to sleep as it got dark but the men were playing cards and making a lot of noise. Terry dozed and slowly slid off the pile of sacks on to the floor where people fell over him as they went out to the ruined cattle byre to relieve themselves.

The owner of the buildings must be aware that they're in use, I thought sleepily, when small butane camping lamps were lit. Still the men shouted, drank and swore. After another half an hour I went outside into the deep dusk, found the bike and discovered to my relief that the bar of soap I'd brought with me hadn't been taken along with everything else of even the smallest value. I washed as well as I could in a cattle drinking trough.

I was dressing again when Patrick came out of the barn, pausing for a moment in the doorway to look at Terry. Then he went into the byre. His bearing spoke of inebriation to a careful, finite degree.

'It was you who told me to slum it for a while,' he said when he reappeared.

When I went to him he leaned on me on the barn wall and nuzzled under my chin. He smelt of leather, whisky and sweat.

'I've thought about this long and hard,' he whispered. 'I can't carry on being angry if all you did with that randy young idiot was grope each other under a cold shower. And no one, not even you, could have made up such a daft story.' He laughed softly and kissed my throat. 'I'm a little drunk and about to get maudlin. There's no way — serving my country or no — that I'm going to besmirch my marriage vows by expecting you to perform filthy acts with me. But that means another way. Ingrid, I love you. Do you believe that?'

'Yes,' I said.

'Then hold me tight for I'm going to hurt you.'

I put my arms around him. He made a strange sound like a sob and then bit me so hard on the neck that I screamed. I carried on screaming and the blood ran and then he was towing me back into the barn, shoving me up the ladder to the hay-loft and throwing me down behind the bales.

I screamed again several times in the next few minutes in between holding his handkerchief to my neck, crying a little and at the same time ravenously eating a ham sandwich. A carton of milk and a fruit pie were to follow, also produced magically from his pockets. Patrick provided a few sound effects of his own, grunting graphically in case anyone below was taking the trouble to listen. After a while he fell very suddenly asleep.

Chapter Twenty

At a little before 3 a.m. I heard a car coming down the rough track that led to the farm buildings. Almost immediately Adam Wells ran lightly from where he had been keeping watch by the door, jumped over a few sleeping bodies and climbed the ladder to the loft. His head appeared on a level with mine.

'Wake him!' he hissed.

'What is it?' Patrick snapped, already awake because I had nudged him with a foot.

'It looks like the car O'Neill's using now.'

'Get the rest on their feet – just in case he's not alone.'

He wasn't. With him were a man I was sure was Alex Haywood and a woman with blonde hair. If the plan had been to catch us unawares it failed for by the time the trio came through the door Patrick and Wells had kicked, cajoled and thumped the men into a state of wakefulness. They were all too stupified with drink and sleep to notice that the process had a certain military efficiency about it.

'He came back,' Red announced. 'You wouldn't know it was him without the whiskers, would you? You know ... the guy who fancied the little red-head.'

Haywood appeared lost for words but O'Neill said, 'So you weren't the law.'

'The police aren't cowards,' Patrick murmured. 'But, no, you're right. I'm freelance.'

'What the hell do you want?' Haywood asked.

'To run this side of things a lot better than it has been up until now.'

Haywood gazed at Red in some desperation. 'Is this OK by you?'

Red shrugged. 'The men do as he says.'

O'Neill laughed. 'He's bigger than you are, you mean.'

'Ask him how it was that Des and Pete got picked up by the fuzz,' Red shouted.

'Ask me,' said another man, pushing his way in. After a moment or two I realized that it was Sunglasses. He looked quite different without them. He went on, 'Des and Pete got picked up because they were stupid. Red and I warned you that it was a bad move to rely on guys who were just bone-headed muscle. Not only that, thinking blokes like Paddy here don't take kindly to being lathered by a couple of thickoes.'

'Did you turn them in?' O'Neill asked Patrick.

Patrick nodded.

'I'm not sure I can work alongside a man who can't be trusted.'

'Then you'd better go back to shooting off-duty RUC men and blowing up women and children,' Patrick drawled.

'No one knows – ' Haywood started to say but was interrupted.

'I told you, I used to be in the SAS. I did a tour in Northern Ireland. His face was one of the two dozen or so that we had to memorize and were only allowed to forget when we'd put a bullet between their eyes.'

'But you haven't a gun now,' O'Neill asserted softly.

'No,' Patrick agreed. 'To my great regret.'

'Pack it in,' Haywood ordered. 'D'you hear me?' His voice rose to a bellow. 'O'Neill, if you kill him here – '

The gun was halfway out of O'Neill's pocket and then he froze. For Patrick had stepped forward and sprung the blade of the knife he had already in his hand. The tip of it and O'Neill's chin were perhaps an eighth of an inch apart.

'No killing,' said the blonde woman, speaking for the first time. Coolly she placed a hand on Patrick's wrist until he lowered the knife.

Wells said, 'I wouldn't have thought this outfit could afford to give refuge to terrorists.'

'I don't know you,' said the woman. She had a strong mid-European accent.

'Wells,' said Sunglasses. 'He's OK. We checked him out.'

'Oh sure,' Wells said. 'You checked me out all right. But please don't make it sound as though you ran my name through a computer. Even the London mobsters don't string you up and give you a going over for the best part of two days.'

'You have too many opinions,' said the woman. 'Alex, there are a lot of other strange faces here. I don't like that.'

Patrick said, 'There will be while you continue the policy of waylaying other bikers, stealing their money and persuading the criminal element to join you.'

'How else would you suggest we raise the money for day to day living?' Haywood enquired smoothly.

'It should be provided by you. After all, you keep the profits. Unless, of course, you can't make up your mind whether you're a petty hoodlum or something much bigger.'

'It's all right Lara, I'll handle this,' said Haywood when she looked at him in alarm. 'We'll have an executive meeting. O'Neill, Red, Billy . . .' here he pointed at Sunglasses '. . . and you, Paddy. There are a few things you need to know.'

Wells said, 'I demand you hear what I have to say first.'

'Want a place on the executive too?' O'Neill chided.

Wells dived into the assembled gathering, seized Terry and marched him back. 'This man is a plant. Him and the woman he was with. Someone knows of Paddy's liking for bent sex. Look at her neck. From the way she was screaming she has bites all over. But she's been paid. They both have. The law's after him and he's just as dangerous to keep around as O'Neill. Sooner or later the police'll come after them and then you'll be finished.'

I sat on my hands to stop them shaking. Wells, of course, was only doing his job. The art of infiltration is to create dissent and break up the command structure.

'I questioned both of them,' Patrick said quietly. 'I'm satisfied with their stories. Let him go.'

'You questioned him for five minutes,' Wells pronounced. 'I'd be interested to see what he's saying after a couple of days.'

Patrick swore under his breath. 'Look, I wasn't here when you were gone over and they peed all over your boots. Kindly allow me to use my intuition and know a little more about interrogation methods than you do.'

175

Terry broke the grip on his arm. 'No one's paid me. I seem to remember that I was cleaning a few oiled-up plugs at the side of the road when we were hijacked.'

I climbed down the ladder. 'No one's paid me either. I resent what you're saying ... that I'd go with him for money. I promised I would to stop him hurting Terry.'

Wells eyed me up and down. 'There *is* something about her that's not too awful. But that's all you thought of, wasn't it?' he said to Patrick. 'As soon as you saw her.'

'This is the most appalling waste of time,' Patrick said.

'I think he has a point,' Haywood said slowly.

'Easily resolved,' Lara snapped. She issued orders to Red and Billy.

Perhaps I lost my head. 'You wretched bitch!' I screamed at her. 'You're behind all the cruelty and the – ' At this point Patrick seized me roughly and hauled me outside.

'It doesn't help if you get hysterical,' he said when we were a short distance from the barn.

'It's her,' I raged, but quietly. 'She runs this. Haywood's just a figurehead. All the sickening, twisted things that happened to Prescott. ...' I choked back the rest of what I was going to say, Patrick knew already.

'The woman from Bude,' Patrick mused. 'I would imagine she has connections with East Germany or the Soviet Union.'

'You don't know half of it,' I said, and told him what Amanda Peterson had related to me.

'Well done,' Patrick murmured. 'What started as Haywood revenging himself on a group of people who crossed him has proved, no doubt, a lucrative hobby for this Lara. I wonder where they met each other.' He interpreted my silence with uncanny accuracy. 'It won't kill him, Ingrid.'

'Please don't do it.'

'I'll have to. You know as well as I do that if I refuse it'll look suspicious. And if I don't, Haywood will.'

The executive had their meeting, speaking quietly at one end of the building while everyone else dozed or drank the tea that Paula had been persuaded to make. It was getting light, the eastern sky a faint pearly pink. I stayed outside. I didn't want to see Terry strung up by his wrists to one of the roof beams, his whole weight on his arms, toes a good six inches from the floor. He probably didn't want to see me either.

Adam Wells was troubled. His bike and belongings had been returned to him – minus his wallet, for the time being – but this seemed to have done little to cure his unease. He looked up from repacking the panniers and saw me sitting on a broken down wall nearby.

'You've been crying.'

I blew my nose, ignoring him.

'I didn't think it would come to this,' he admitted.

'It's a bit late for regrets,' I replied.

'I just went and had a look at him. He seems to be bearing up quite well.'

'Who are you trying to cheer up?' I stormed. 'If he was what you're making out he would, wouldn't he? They'd choose someone who could bear up under all kinds of things. Not bleat like you have ever since we clapped eyes on you.'

'You're contradicting yourself. Just now you said – '

'It's too subtle for you,' I told him, getting off the wall.

'Then please explain.'

'There's nothing to explain.'

I went back into the barn for no other reason than to remove myself from the temptation to tell him everything. But what would that achieve now?

'No, that's no good,' Patrick was saying. 'I know I'm tall but I can't reach him up there. For God's sake cut him down and lie him on that pile of feed sacks. And go and fetch Wells.'

The instructions were duly carried out, Terry swearing fluently as he dropped to his feet.

Patrick unbuckled his belt. 'Four of you,' he ordered. 'Each to a hand or foot. Hold him tightly because he's going to thrash about. Ah, Wells. I would like you to adjudicate.'

'Adjudicate?' Wells echoed.

'This isn't punishment,' Patrick said with a trace of anger. 'So we're not going to flog him to death, are we? If he's telling the truth and I go too far then we're losing the use of a good man. I would like you to satisfy yourself that he's on the line and then tell me to stop. For pity's sake, man, *you* are accusing him of lying,' he added when Wells couldn't prevent his reluctance from showing.

The tapered end of the belt was tightly wrapped around a hand, swung and it cracked down. But on the feed sacks. The double thickness of brown paper slit as though it had been cut with a knife, calf nuts spilling out on to the floor.

'Too much wrap-around,' Patrick muttered absently, making adjustments. 'I'll try not to hit him too much over the kidneys. I passed blood for days afterwards.'

By now Wells was white.

'The real secret of extracting information without inflicting too much damage is hitting nerve centres,' Patrick continued, addressing the barn at large as though giving a lecture. 'Therefore you aim for the spine.' The belt swung again, the buckle glittering as it passed through a beam of sunlight shining through one of the narrow slitted windows.

Terry screamed hoarsely.

'One of the useful bits of knowledge I picked up in Northern Ireland,' Patrick elaborated. 'Hold him now – this really makes 'em kick.'

'No!' Wells shouted but was too late, the belt thudded down and again Terry cried out.

'So soon?' Patrick said.

'It's bestial,' Wells gasped.

'But is he telling the truth?'

'He must be. No one could hold out under that. And if you keep on he'll change his story just to get you to stop.'

'Enough,' said Lara in a disappointed but forced to agree tone.

Haywood said, 'We'll move out . . . just to be on the safe side. O'Neill, I'd like you to take care of the Peterson woman. You already have the address. Paddy, I've another job for you.'

There was a general scramble to depart.

I took a deep breath and released my hold on a section of birch trunk that was propping up one corner of the hay-loft floor where a beam had rotted. Just then Lara darted through the crowd, wrenched the belt from Patrick's hand and made for me, her face twisted with spite.

'The wretched bitch answers the little whore,' she said venomously.

Instinctively I curled away from her. Pain exploded across my back, the blow knocking me to my knees. I never found out who stopped her. She had lashed at me frenziedly and wildly several times before the buckle hit me on the back of the head and I fainted.

In a grey dreamworld I was placed behind Dirty Joe on his bike and we travelled what seemed a huge distance. Once we stopped and there was the smell of fish and chips but no one offered me any, and anyway I wasn't hungry. Just in pain.

Even though I was tied on the bike I was terrified of falling and my weight dragging it down on top of me. When we next stopped, and I couldn't understand why it was now night, my fingers had to be prised from wherever I'd been holding on, I didn't know where. Someone lifted me and I simply tumbled to what felt like turfy grass and stayed there. The world was peopled by shadowy figures with booming voices who slowly circled around me.

One of the shadowy figures picked me up and placed me in some kind of building, covering me with something warm. I was encouraged to drink a little water with what tasted like whisky in it. I opened my eyes into another dream where people settled down with bottles and packets of food. Dirty Joe appeared in my dream and offered me a piece of meat pie. When I turned my head away he jerked my face towards him and tried to kiss me. Someone shoved him away. Was it Terry or Patrick?

Later they settled down to sleep. Red's girl, Bett, went over to where he was organizing his sleeping bag in a corner and moved a lamp away so they were in darkness. Paula wasn't so fussy. She went first to whichever man had won her services at cards. Every time I opened my eyes there was a different male bottom humping up and down between her thighs.

'These people really are the pits,' I said into whatever was covering me. Then I became aware of Dirty Joe standing over me undoing his trousers.

During the next few minutes — it seemed like hours — I made the discovery that it is possible for a woman mentally to distance herself from the sight of two men fighting over her. Terry — yes it was him, I couldn't see Patrick anywhere — was of course not fighting for me in the same sense as the other man. But, said my small inner voice, it is only to be expected. If he can't have you, neither will any other man on this planet but Patrick.

No one tried to interfere, not even when Terry was sitting astride his adversary, banging his head on the floor of the building, yet another barn. When he finally rose, breathing hard and staggering, it was to raid several packs for provisions. He brought his booty over to where I lay.

'I've found out something,' he said when we were both quite replete and life was no longer hazy and dreamlike. 'Working under cover isn't really a matter of pretending to be someone else so much as surviving the consequences of doing so, smiling.' He settled down right beside me. 'I reckon I deserve a kiss.'

I gave him one.

'There's a nasty cut on the back of your head,' he told me. 'Try and sleep. I'll stay here.'

Despite hurting all over, I was half asleep already. 'Patrick hated having to do that to you.'

He shrugged but was smiling. 'I think he knew Wells would crack first. But there was an alternative plan. When I was strung up he came over and told me to yell twice and then pretend to pass out. I bet you didn't notice either that he turned the belt round in his hand and hit me with the smooth back of it.'

I hadn't 'Where *is* Patrick?'

'Haywood sent him to Hinton Littlemoor to finish off David Prescott.'

'Surely Prescott hasn't returned home.'

'Not to the bungalow apparently. He's staying with a friend in the village until it's sold. The Major's going to warn the local police that his life's still in danger.'

'Can't you two shut up whispering?' someone yelled.

'At least O'Neill won't find Amanda Peterson,' I said under my breath.

Chapter Twenty-One

In the morning we were given back the BMW, some breakfast and all of our possessions except money and Terry's camera. And also a warning. We would be closely watched, therefore escape was impossible.

'When do I get a job?' was Terry's response to this.

Billy, once again wearing his sunglasses even though the day was dull, said, 'You came too late, laddie. No more jobs. It's all going to be broken up.'

'Then why the hell don't you let us go?'

Billy's thin lips twitched into a smile. 'You can go after the pay-off . . . if the boss says so. Until then, you stay.'

Terry, not unnaturally, was keen to remove the pair of us from the immediate company and head off after Patrick. We had enough evidence. Without doubt Patrick would immediately report to Daws as well as to the police and at any time steps would be taken to round up the gang. Neither of us particularly wanted to be around when this happened for some of the gang we knew were armed, and the police without question would be too.

'We *must* be in Devon,' I observed, gazing around and trying to get my bearings.

'What makes you think so?' Terry enquired, busy checking over the bike. 'I love the way you never get lost, even without a map or compass.'

'Red earth,' I said. 'South Devon cattle. That light, bright look about the sky even when it's grey. Everything clean and shiny-looking. No, let me guess. We must be near the border with Cornwall — over in the west the ground rises. But it isn't

Dartmoor – there are no tors. I'd say that was Bodmin Moor over there. Which means we're somewhere near Launceston.'

'You're feeling better today,' Terry pronounced. 'Spot on ... it's another six miles from here down the road you can see behind those trees.'

'Not far from home,' I whispered. 'Oh God, I hope Amanda's all right.'

'She is if you weren't followed when you drove her down there.'

'O'Neill still only had the two addresses she'd given him.'

'That's what he *said.*'

OK, I thought, never take anything for granted. And I couldn't understand Haywood at all. Government scientist? He seemed no more than a mindless bully, swaggering about and running a pack of criminals for his own gain. The previous night, before he and Lara had departed, presumably for an hotel, I had heard him shouting that he would get even with Des for not realising that Alyssa was no ordinary girl and using her for his own pleasure instead of finding out if she could be ransomed. But for her one flash of temper with me, Lara remained aloof but I was sure that she controlled everything.

'Terry, you don't think that Haywood's somehow under Lara's influence?'

'Drugs, you mean?'

'Not in the sense that she supplies him when he does as he's told.'

'No, I'm with you. I'd thought myself that he was always slightly drunk ... loudmouthed, not all that steady on his feet.'

'And she usually drives the car,' I added.

'You said that you thought Alyssa might have been doped when she was with them.' Terry mounted the bike and put the keys in the ignition.

'There's no other explanation for her being so vague about the entire episode. Most girls would have had a nervous breakdown after what happened to her, but other than being in a state of shock for a few days she recovered completely.'

'If you stand the whole theory on its head then it fits in with a few ideas of my own.'

'Shoot,' I said.

182

'Idea one is that this guy isn't Haywood at all and the real one *is* in Bude but somehow a prisoner in the woman's house. The bloke here is just a petty thug and does drink too much. He might not even be *able* to drive for all we know.'

'But why the need to use a substitute?'

'Well, perhaps he gave Lara the names of the people he wanted to get even with and then got cold feet. The plan is that Haywood gets the blame. Perhaps they'll kill him, too, to cover their tracks.'

'It's pretty outlandish but let's leave that for now. What about Alyssa?'

'I don't think she's quite all there.'

'Rubbish! She seems all right to me.'

'I had more chance to watch her than you did when she came back with the Major. No, somehow she isn't quite right.'

Adam Wells pushed his bike over to where we were getting ready. 'No hard feelings?'

'Ingrid is the one who was really hurt,' said Terry shortly. 'Ask her.'

'That wasn't Adam's fault,' I hastened to say.

'Thinking about it though,' Wells continued, 'I'm just a little surprised. Apparently they gave him a hell of a hiding for trying to make off with Des's girl. You'd have thought he'd have been only too pleased to do the same to you. Only an idiot wouldn't realize that he was willing me to stop him. Now he's gone off to murder a man. Something's not quite right.'

'Don't think,' Terry growled. 'It's not healthy.'

'Are you threatening me?' Wells asked.

'No,' Terry said, or rather hissed. 'I'm trying to keep you alive.'

'Another thing . . .' Wells went on, ignoring this. 'I had a close look at his bike. The words "Brass Eagle" are actually painted on the handlebars. Why not "Golden Eagle"? A brass eagle is just another name for the lectern in churches. You know . . . the thing they rest the bible on. It's supposed to represent the – '

'Quite the little detective, aren't we?' Terry sneered. 'I expect his dad's a bishop and suggested the name because it sounded rather fetching.'

Wells gazed at us both for a moment and then went away.

'God, if he rats to Haywood in order to preserve his own cover, I'll throttle him with my bare hands,' Terry said.

I said, 'He can't have the first idea that Patrick's up to the same kind of thing as he is. Even if he suspects that we're plants, he might be worried that we'll get hurt when the police finally move in.'

'You're far too nice to be in this game.'

To keep my mind off my cuts and bruises I concentrated on Haywood. What had David Prescott said about him? Yes, that's right. Haywood never looked as though he had a brain but was clever all right. And, according to what Amanda Peterson had told me, he was a thoroughly unpleasant man. But it was possible that he had drawn back from actually taking savage revenge upon those who had brought the attention of quite a large part of the scientific world — at least in Great Britain — to an episode in his past life.

The pair had not put in an appearance before we left so I had not had a chance to compare in a good light the man with Lara and the picture I had in my mind's eye of the real Haywood. Or rather, pictures. For as well as the indistinct photograph that had appeared in the national newspapers at the time of Haywood's fake suicide, Daws had shown me a short clip of film when I had gone to his office for a final briefing. This had originally been part of a BBC news bulletin and featured Haywood arriving at a conference on the use of lasers in space.

They caught up with us at Holsworthy where the group had stopped at a café for breakfast — bacon rolls to eat on the road. I nudged Terry.

'You're right,' I said close to his right ear. 'Alex Haywood's taller than that. His legs are longer and he walks with big strides. Facially there's an uncanny resemblance, and our man's broad-shouldered like Haywood, but it definitely isn't him. Daws showed me a film.'

'It's an awful lot of trouble to go to,' Terry commented over his shoulder. He was still smiling gently after a confrontation with Red that could only be described as demanding money with menaces. Red had given him five pounds from his own wallet and we had eaten two bacon rolls each.

'Don't ditch the idea now. All the world knows Haywood as

184

a bit of a bad sort. If the entire blame for all these murders is laid on his shoulders and he's dead anyway no one will bat an eyelid.'

'What about Des and Pete? They aren't exactly blameless.'

'There's fifty thousand each for them in a Swiss bank to keep quiet and serve their prison terms. And when you really examine the evidence against them there isn't an awful lot. David Prescott couldn't positively identify them as the men who made him kill Leonard Crocker, and there's only Alyssa's rather hazy recollection of what happened to her. All they can be had up for is beating Patrick and anything else that can be pinned on them that they got up to with the gang.'

'Who told you about the money?'

'Patrick. Red had said to him that all the executive had been given promises of cash for their silence.'

'I don't like the sound of that as far as the others are concerned.'

Neither did I. Especially as Terry and I could be described as 'others'.

'No litter,' Red called out. 'This is a reputable bike club on an outing. I don't even want to see fag ends.' He turned back to hear what Lara was saying to him.

'Fifty thousand each,' Terry said thoughtfully. 'There isn't that kind of money in topping scientists.'

I hadn't really thought of it from that angle. 'So it really is financed by big crime?'

'There *was* that bullion robbery where the gang responsible vanished into thin air. And a diamonds snatch in Amsterdam last year where almost exactly the same method of attack was used. *And* a warehouse raid in Germany when half a million pounds worth of furs were stolen. Two security guards were killed at that one. I'm not being clever, clever, I get more involved with the international side of things than you do. Sometimes there's a tie-in between terrorism, spying and crime.'

There was no chance to discuss this further for at that point we left. Just after the village of Stratton we turned off the main road into a lane that headed, I guessed, in the direction of Hartland Point. This went uphill, gently at first, but after we passed a couple of farms the lane degenerated into no more

185

than a cart track and the going became steeper.

Soon we left trees and hedges behind and were riding across open countryside. Even with the stench of exhaust from the bikes I could smell the sea. And then we breasted a hill and the endless blue of the Atlantic was before us, Lundy Island a small blob on the horizon.

The track dropped suddenly and surprisingly into a tiny valley, one of hundreds that were carved by streams through the high Cornish coastline. Away from the lashing of sea gales were hedges of hawthorn, escallonia, blackthorn, beech and elder. As a child on holiday in such places I had counted the varieties, knowing that for each one the hedge was a hundred years old. As a child. . . .

No, don't think about it. Not now.

In almost the same kind of setting as those where we had stayed near Lyndhurst a group of stone buildings nestled in the bottom of the valley. The track ended by a five-bar gate and behind Haywood's car and two motor bikes was a notice that read: WHEAL LUCY ADVENTURE CENTRE.

Lara and the man I must continue to refer to as Haywood until it was proved otherwise had just arrived and were getting out of the car. Just then two men came out of a single-storey building next to the one that had originally been the engine house of a tin mine. They did not walk, they ran, with all the urgency of fugitives.

Des and Pete, unless my intuition was all wrong.

'They've never seen us,' said Terry quietly after I had wordlessly drawn his attention to them. 'The trouble'll start if the Major returns for any reason.'

Lara lost her temper. 'How dare you come back here when you've escaped!' she shrieked. 'Go on . . . get out! You know perfectly well that there are arrangements made for such emergencies.'

'Someone turned us in!' shouted Des.

'Paddy did,' Red was saying as we got nearer. 'He didn't take too kindly to you belting him like that.'

'And he's back,' chipped in Billy, obviously with an axe to grind. 'I wouldn't be surprised if he doesn't get *your* job, let alone Red's.'

Des looked as though he might contemplate murder but the

man called Pete laid a restraining hand on his arm as he went in Billy's direction.

'I told you, if you remember,' said Pete placidly. 'There was something about him. I couldn't put my finger on it but I had a feeling. Almost as if I'd seen him before.' His gaze drifted around the assembled group and came to rest on me. 'Who's that woman?'

'She's with him,' said Red, jerking a thumb at Terry. 'No one special,' he added, making my blood run cold.

For a long moment, Pete stared at me. Then he shrugged and walked away.

'I vote we make a break for it,' Terry said to me out of the corner of his mouth. 'When it's dark. If we push the bike up this hill we can ride down to the main road without using the engine.'

'Get away from here,' Lara urged Des. 'Both of you. You're risking us all by staying. I cannot imagine what possessed you to come.'

'While Paddy steps in,' Des grumbled.

Haywood said, 'The outfit's being folded. So clear out. If you don't, you won't get your money.'

Des started to shout but Haywood silenced him by sheer volume of voice and also by taking a big handful of the front of his jacket.

'It's your own damn fault for giving him such a hiding!'

'You ordered us to!' Des yelled. 'And took your turn.'

Pete turned from where he had been standing a short distance away, hands shoved into his pockets. He was smiling unpleasantly. 'Only because he wouldn't beg for mercy.' He caught sight of me again and stared hard. 'I know that woman from somewhere.'

'Understandable,' Billy smirked. 'She ain't too fussy who she goes with.'

Pete ignored him and made his way through the bikes towards me.

'You don't know me,' I said, praying that Adam Wells' silent partner had recognised the men too and was reporting over his radio.

'Take your helmet off,' he said. 'And you,' he told Terry.

When he had done so he looked at us again and I nearly screamed when his eyes blazed.

187

'Where did you get that scar on your head?' Terry was asked.

'Fell off the bike,' Terry grunted.

'Come here!' Pete shouted at Des.

Des came.

'Would you say,' Pete said to him, 'that that was the guy you hit with a spanner once upon a time?'

Des took a piece of chewing gum out of his mouth and threw it away. 'Nah.'

'Exercise that tiny brain of yours,' Pete said repressively. 'That village near Bath . . . remember? Where we dumped the redhead's boy. Where the boffin's bungalow was, dumbhead!'

'Where we had to leave the bike because some joker shot out the lights?' Des said uncertainly.

'Not me,' said Terry.

'The christening party,' Pete said, half to himself, disregarding him. 'And it was the same guy who checked up on Prescott's place later. There was a man and a woman with him.'

'Nah,' Des said again, unwrapping another piece of gum. 'Anyway, if I hit this geezer on the head it couldn't have been him in the bungalow, could it?'

'You'll have to lie down in a minute if you carry on with all this thinking,' Terry sneered.

Haywood said, 'You told me it was Prescott you hit.'

'We thought it was at the time,' Pete said. 'We'd followed him to this house and we thought it was him coming out again. But when we went back to where he lived some time later that night we saw him getting into a car. That's when I decided to arrange a little surprise for him when he came back.'

'Which went wrong,' Lara observed. 'Go.'

I had relaxed, Des and Pete on their way to their bikes, when Des turned and said, 'Anyway, why did Paddy come back if he got what he wanted — the girl?'

'Search me,' Pete grunted.

'She was hot property,' Haywood called to them. 'Paddy got ten thousand from her parents for taking her home. He reasoned that with such mutton-heads doing your jobs he could run things a lot better.'

'So how did her folks find *him?*' Pete asked.

'Will you get out of here!' Lara screamed.

Pete came back to the group. 'No. This is interesting. How *did* he get the job?'

'Ring them up and ask,' Des said triumphantly.

Pete opened his mouth to deride this suggestion, clapped Des on the back and went in the direction of the buildings instead. 'What was her name?' he said over his shoulder.

Red told him.

'People like that are bound to be ex-directory,' Terry muttered under his breath.

We had no choice but to dismount with all the others, stow our bike in a barn and follow the rest to another building obviously used as a canteen cum dormitory. Haywood, Lara and Des had gone into a small office and I could hear Lara ranting about the situation. But, oddly, Haywood seemed to have stuck his toes in and was insisting that Des had a point. They were still arguing, Pete continuing to dial numbers, when O'Neill arrived. He looked agitated and went straight into the office.

'D'you reckon he took the keys out of the ignition?' I said to Terry.

'Bound to have done. That one wouldn't trust his own mother.'

'I'm going to have a look,' I said, standing up. 'It's right outside the door.'

'Sit down,' Red ordered. I hadn't realised that he was watching us.

'Where's the loo?' I asked.

'Never mind. Just sit down and be quiet.'

I subsided. Out of the corner of my eye I saw that Pete had put the phone down. He stood up, looking through the door as if searching for someone. He came out and could not have made his findings known for the other three trailed after him questioningly.

'Where is she?'

I gripped Terry's arm. 'No,' I whispered. 'They'll kill you.'

'So I die,' Terry replied bleakly and stood up.

I got to my feet too and pushed myself in front of Terry as Pete reached us.

Just as bleakly, Pete said, 'I've just spoken to a bad-tempered cow who said she was Alyssa Goldberg's mother. She didn't pay anyone to find the kid. But she did have a visit from a couple who said they were man and wife. She can only remember the guy's first name — Patrick. The woman informed her that she was Ingrid Langley, a writer. She doesn't believe that now but I do. It was your baby that was being christened and your picture was in the paper along with that of your husband: Gillard. Patrick Gillard.' He turned to Haywood. 'Get it? Paddy. It was Gillard. He shot out the lights of the bike and arranged to have Prescott looked after. It was him in Prescott's place and him again who came after the girl only we didn't recognise him with the beard. Now you've given him all the evidence the police need to put us all away for a very long time.'

'We didn't recognise him with the beard,' Lara echoed disgustedly, her anger directed not at me but at the speaker. 'You utter fool. You and that other fool were the only ones to have seen him before. And you have the audacity not only to ...' She broke off and threw up her hands in despair. 'Enough. It is finished.'

Haywood moved to go to the door with her.

'I go alone,' she snapped.

'But you said — ' he began.

'Never mind what I said. See O'Neill. The plan's been changed.'

'What about me?' Pete enquired, shouting.

'You too. O'Neill will see to everything.'

'The money's in the car,' O'Neill said. 'I'll get it.'

'Wait!' Terry said and such was the utter authority with which the one word was spoken that O'Neill halted.

'There's no money in the car,' Terry continued calmly. 'Just some kind of powerful automatic weapon. You're all going to get paid off with death. This is a pretty remote spot and there's a JCB parked outside all ready to dig your graves. In that woman's eyes you're just lawless filth.'

'I'll check his motor,' said Pete grimly.

'You do it, Wells,' Terry ordered. 'Bring any weapons you find back with you.'

O'Neill made a rush for the door but Wells got there first. Wells didn't have to hit him. When he raised a fist the Irishman cowered away.

'You stay right there,' Terry said to Lara.

But the woman took a Beretta from her bag, pointed it indeterminately at Terry for a moment and then ran outside. There was the sound of a shot.

By the time Terry and I got outside Lara was behind the wheel of O'Neill's car and starting the engine. There was nothing we could do to prevent her driving away.

'She missed,' Wells panted, picking himself up off the ground. 'Surely you're not going after her yourself?'

'Too right,' Terry said, making for the bike shed.

'But what about this lot?'

Terry paused only long enough to exhibit pure Gillard scorn. 'Perhaps you'd better arrest them, officer.'

I cut in quickly. 'She'll make for White Lodge – her house in Bude. The police are already watching it. You'd be far better employed finding out if that man inside really is Haywood, and getting on the phone if he isn't.'

Terry carried on walking.

'It's an order,' I added.

He stopped and turned slowly.

'You can't leave Adam on his own with this crowd,' I told him. 'And please don't say that there's only three of us when you were prepared to leave him on his own.'

But by now everyone was outside. When they reached us it made no difference that I was a woman nor that neither of the men offered resistance. We were all knocked senseless.

Chapter Twenty-Two

Brass Eagle. What a bloody laugh! Riding away from Ingrid that night I felt more the yellow-bellied stinking rat. It took nearly twenty miles to convince myself that I wasn't *running* away and that it was vital to check up on David Prescott's safety and report to Daws and Brinkley. Yes, Brinkley. That was the price that he had demanded for letting me have the bike in the first place. He has his priorities too.

It was important that I actually went to Hinton Littlemoor. I wasn't sure if O'Neill would follow me to check up that I was obeying Haywood's order. He'd soon discover that Amanda Peterson wasn't where he thought she was but this would not necessarily make him suspicious as women change their minds all the time. If he did come after me, I'd make damn sure he ended up in the cells of Bath police station.

I don't know what prevented me from throttling that woman Lara when she went for Ingrid like that. But I've spent an awful lot of my life controlling my temper. Nevertheless if Terry hadn't moved faster than I've ever seen him and snatched the belt away from her, I don't know what would have happened.

Of course if I could have been aware that O'Neill, having found that Amanda Peterson wasn't at home and then heard that Des and Pete had escaped from police custody, would head straight for the head-quarters of the gang in Cornwall, I probably wouldn't have tarried so long in Somerset. In hindsight, Ingrid almost certainly saved Adam Wells' life by making Terry stay behind. Human nature being what it is, O'Neill would have taken out his fury on the man and made him scapegoat. They had always been suspicious about Wells, something to do with his darting eyes that always gave the impression that he was watching you *alone*. But three hostages made better sense than killing one man. So O'Neill took from Des the gun that he wasn't supposed to have and dared not use, piled them unconscious in Haywood's car with Pete to watch over them, added Des as an afterthought, probably as cannon fodder, and drove after Lara. At this stage it was likely that he was more interested in getting back his own car containing his clothes, money and what turned out to be a Heckler and Koch 9mm sub-machine gun. My guess is that, right then, more than anything, he wanted out.

I checked up on Prescott, indirectly, via Brinkley, I didn't want to ride up on the bike and risk resurrecting all his bad memories. Having been assured that two members of the Anti-Terrorist Branch were watching over him and his bank manager friend, I went on to tell Brinkley the latest manoeuvres and warned him about O'Neill. He was able to update me on most of this, concluding by saying that the gang were heading into Cornwall and giving me an OS reference of their latest position. It seemed to me that the man watching Wells and reporting in was doing a better job than anyone but I didn't say so.

Daws next. He sounded a bit resigned when he first came on the line, as though I was going to tell him the world was going to end in five minutes. He cheered up a bit when I told him the job was nearly over and that Lara was definitely a good catch even though terrorism might be the charge rather than anything D12 ought to be investigating. He ordered me to go to Cornwall, to observe — as he put it — the conclusion. But I would have gone anyway.

The Colonel has been very good to me and God knows I've probably provoked him until he would have happily put me in front of a firing squad. He breezed in when I was at the clinic in Kensington and required my thoughts on several relevant matters. I gave them and then he made it clear that as I was obviously suffering from some kind of middle-aged urge for excitement that entailed brawling with motor-bike thugs, I had better see it through. Ouch. But he was right, Terry should have gone and his boss stayed in the background. Daws

193

understood, I think, that I'd lost my bottle a bit and going back was the only way to cure the problem.

I'd made these phone calls from my parents' home. There was no one around so I had had to gain entrance in a way that I've never revealed to my mother in case she gets the horrors about burglars. As soon as Daws rang off I went back into the village again and loafed around invisibly for a while in the event of O'Neill showing up. There was no mistaking his car, it was a large red estate with 'go faster' stripes and fancy wire wheels. Perhaps his high profile was the reason for his being slung out of the IRA.

After an hour I went back to the Rectory. There was still no one in. I wheeled the bike into the old stable and left it there gladly. Daws had told me to drop my cover and get rid of the bike. I didn't need telling twice. I never want to ride one again. Sitting astride for hours on end puts such a strain on the weakest muscles of my legs that after a long journey I can hardly put one foot in front of the other.

Where on earth *was* everyone?

Use your loaf, Gillard. Saturday mornings involve shopping in Bath and then, if it is her turn, Elspeth does the church flowers.

They were all in the church. Mum, Dad, Justin, and Dawn, his nanny.

It was strange but up until that moment I hadn't realised that it was a beautiful summer's day. Beams of sunlight were shining through the stained glass windows and making coloured patterns on the stone floor. As they had done the day Ingrid and I were married. I had turned my head when the organ had struck up *Here Comes the Bride* and it had seemed that Ingrid's white dress had been spangled with brilliant jewels. Justin's pram was placed in one of these pools of colour and when I first saw him it looked as though he was trying to pick up the blobs of red and blue from his pram sheet. I had to stop for a moment and swallow hard.

He had grown and was sitting up and was as brown as one of those adverts for sun-tan lotion. As I watched he had another try at capturing one of the sun-beams and then smacked his hands down on the sheet, endeavouring to swat them. I suddenly became aware of my stupid get-up and the fact that I hadn't shaved for at least three days nor washed properly in seven. If I went any closer I'd frighten the living daylights out of him.

There were other people in the church. Several of the village ladies were on their knees arranging flowers along the altar rail and at the bottom of the rood screen. For a wedding by the look of it. A couple of them glanced up and saw me and there was a lot of nudging.

I went forward. Mainly because my father was just climbing up the side of the organ to hang up the board with the numbers of the hymns on it. He never will use the steps, preferring to struggle on to a window ledge. One of these days he's going to break his neck.

'Patrick!' my mother exclaimed when I was standing right behind him and I braced myself to catch him if he fell.

'Shall I do that?' I said.

Without saying anything he leaned over and rammed the board on to its hook. Then he climbed down. He didn't have to tell me how he loathed the way I looked, or smelled for that matter.

'Is Ingrid with you?'

'No. She's with Terry in Cornwall somewhere.'

'I see.'

He didn't see. 'Your little friend rang and wanted to speak to you.'

'Alyssa?'

'Yes, unless there are other young women in your life.'

'John –' my mother started to say but he interrupted, still speaking to me. 'I told her you were a married man and she wasn't to pester you. She asked me to give you her love.' He turned away from me to slam the lid on the box of wooden numbers, his face wearing what Lawrence and I used to call his white, tight look.

'Well, she would,' I murmured. 'She *does* love me.'

'You're in a house of God, Patrick!' he shouted.

'Her parents lied about the university place,' I said calmly. 'She did very badly at school. She spent most of the time shut away at home because they knew she wasn't quite normal.'

'Not quite normal?' he repeated.

'No. Deep down she's very disturbed. She doesn't know

195

what normal family life is like because she's never experienced it, and when it comes to human relationships is like someone from another planet. She loves me and tells the world because she doesn't know about a man loving the woman whom he marries. Her friend Deidre got her away as much as she could but the Goldbergs apparently had a most unpleasant chauffeur who used to be sent round for her.'

Elspeth said, '*That* would explain why she wasn't as upset as one would have expected after her terrible ordeal. Oh, poor girl. I wish I'd tried to help a bit more.'

'Being kidnapped and Leonard's death were just a continuation of the misery,' I said. 'She must have learned to switch off. The tragedy of it is that if she'd been brought up within a loving atmosphere and received treatment for what was probably only a minor behavioural problem when she was small this would never have happened. Now it's going to take a long time.'

'Running away from her parents shows that she can make the right decisions,' my mother decided firmly. 'We must have her to stay with us. While Justin's still here. Then she can help look after him.' She looked at me. 'Patrick, you should have mentioned this to Ingrid.'

'I hadn't worked it out then,' I replied, inwardly quailing as usual under the gaze that seems to be able to penetrate my soul. True, my conscience pointed out, but you didn't make much effort to communicate to your wife what were already strong suspicions about the girl. Too damaging to the male ego to have to admit that Alyssa went to all men initially for the affection given by most fathers and had learned to her cost what this entailed?

'I didn't take advantage of her,' I mumbled, the scent of the flowers unaccountably making me feel dizzy. 'Just cuddles and a few kisses so the others wouldn't begin to suspect.'

I went through the arch in the rood screen and knelt on the step by the altar rail. To pay my respects. You do, even when you know you're filthy within as well as without. You are quiet and open your mind with trepidation to what I had regarded at one time as a vast cosmic question mark. I know better now, needless to say, and also that He has His undercover agents working in the world. One of them was right behind me, her eyes drilling holes in the back of my neck. After a couple of minutes she came and sat beside me on the step.

'I've an hour,' I said. 'Daws is arranging a chopper to pick me up at noon.'

'Come and see your son.'

I waved to Dawn, who was looking a trifle left out of things. 'I'm such a mess he'll only cry.'

'He won't if you talk to him.'

I got to my feet, wished I hadn't and saw that I still wasn't in my father's favour. Sometimes he can be stubborn and rather baffling. I was damned if I could see why I should apologise so merely removed my leather jacket and draped it over the lectern, sleeves over the outstretched wings.

'Give it to Oxfam,' I said.

Justin gave me a big smile so I couldn't say anything for a moment, just carried him out into the sunshine. He grabbed hold of one of my earrings but I persuaded him to let go, parked him on the grass for a moment, took them out and threw them over the churchyard wall into a field. Elspeth found us sitting on Alice Tingle's grave, a favourite seat of the choirboys. She has been resting in peace since 1706.

'Your ear lobes are bright green!' she said, touching me to make sure she wasn't imagining things. The green came off on her hand.

'A brass brass eagle,' I explained, and she laughed.

Indoors, I drank a pint of milk, showered, shaved and changed into some old clothes I wear when I have to put slates back on the roof and things like that. Justin sat in his little chair, watching me and chewing on a rusk. Apparently his emergent teeth are still giving him occasional hell.

'If I'd known you were coming I'd have had something ready,' said Elspeth, placing a huge plate of bacon and scrambled eggs on the kitchen table.

'I don't think I can eat all that,' I said. 'The stomach shrinks with disuse.'

She gave me a teaspoon. 'Give some to Justin. It seems to be his favourite at the moment.'

'The man who comes home sometimes and feeds you bacon and eggs,' I said to him, tying on a bib.

Thinking about the little chap, I nearly walked into the tail rotor of the Gazelle when it collected me from the village recreation field.

I normally enjoy trips in helicopters but not this time. The pilot, a young bloke, must have been told I was a bigger brass hat that I actually am and went in for a lot of fancy flying to avoid some electricity pylons. There were no brown paper bags in sight so I just had to sit there with the saliva swilling icily around my back teeth.

So Alyssa had rung. . . . She had come to me on the first night I had joined the gang. Partly to get away from Des but mostly in her so far fruitless search to find a man who would love her without demanding sex. Predictably, Des had raised hell about it and I'd had to dredge up the strength to fend him off. That was all it had been, a fending off. He's a strong bastard and I still wasn't feeling too good after having to fight my way in on top of being taken ill after drinking polluted water. It was a bad mistake. I should have sorted him out for always and then I wouldn't have lost so much skin off my back a few days later.

It keeps coming back to me. I've never felt so helpless and vulnerable in my life as when I was tied to that damn gate. Even when the grenade exploded in the hills above Port Stanley and blew my legs to pieces, I hadn't thought I was going to *die*. No, perhaps there was the slightest premonition that I would. But people were all around me willing me to hang on, holding my hand, giving me first aid. It would have somehow been cheating them to give in and snuff it. But strung up to a gate, facing a wall. . . . Every time the belts hit me all the air had been bashed out of my lungs. I couldn't breathe. I really thought I was going to die from suffocation. I couldn't even cry out from the pain. All I had been able to do was concentrate on getting enough air and not losing control of my bladder and bowels. I can remember a kind of mist of blood droplets on each side of me on the barn wall. It's probably still there.

I'd heard a lot of shouting when Alyssa got away. Most of it's guesswork, of course, for I couldn't see what was happening behind me. And by this time I was almost beyond caring. It took me quite a while to realise that they'd stopped beating me. I'd turned my head as far as I could and couldn't see anyone. Then, all at once, Alyssa had been there, breaking her nails on the thin rope with which they'd tied me up. The next thing I'd known I was lying in the mud on my side with Alyssa bathing my face with water.

If it hadn't been for that girl I think I'd have died, never mind not got home. I would have just lain there until I'd faded away. She hugged, kissed and prodded me back to life. That was when I told her I'd been the guy she'd met in Prescott's bungalow. She said I'd been mumbling about someone called Justin. Looking back, she'd seemed to come alive then — perhaps we both had — as I'd told her about him.

I got home on whisky and Mars Bars. No, I didn't drink the former. God knows where Alyssa had found it but when I came over all sorry for myself nearly half way home and said I couldn't go any further, her streak of not quite normalness had driven her to pour some of the stuff down the back of my collar. The result probably did her more good than an hour on a shrink's couch and she cried, begging my forgiveness. She'd never heard a man scream before.

This had been when I'd realized how she'd switched off and just existed as a vegetable for most of her life. It was the reason why so much of what had happened to her when Leonard was killed and she was kidnapped had simply failed to register. The shame of it is that this will mean she won't be able to appear as a reliable witness for the prosecution.

The strange thing is that most of the time Alyssa gives the impression that she's all there. You have to watch her closely over a period of days for it to become apparent that there's an odd slant to her mind. Like looking at someone in a cracked mirror. I'm no expert on such matters but I'm convinced that if the girl spent time within a loving family atmosphere, it would do a lot for her. I'd like to have her with us in Devon for a while. But if I explained this to Ingrid, would she understand? It would be a lot for a wife to tolerate, having a lovely young woman in her house who adored her husband. No, perhaps it wouldn't be such a good idea.

I stopped daydreaming at this point, looked below and saw that we were flying over the eastern outskirts of Plymouth. We were actually right above Plymstock and not far away was the railway depot at Laira. In the distance was the thin silver strip

199

of the River Tamar with the two bridges spanning it – Brunel's iron railway bridge and the modern one right next to it for road traffic – looking just like models on a railway layout. We headed south, straight for the city centre, and I asked the pilot the reason for this. It was a good one, his radio was malfunctioning, Control couldn't hear him even though they were coming over loud and clear.

Contrary to my expectations we didn't head for the airport but continued south in the direction of the Barbican. We dropped low over the Citadel, a massive old fort that is nowadays – if my memory serves me aright – the head-quarters of 29 Commando Regiment, Royal Artillery, and landed. I prepared to lose my temper.

'Major Gillard?' enquired a smooth voice when I had disembarked.

I turned and confirmed this, adding that I didn't normally wear my rank on my gardening rig.

'Threlfall, sir. Only knew you were coming ten minutes ago. If you'd care to step into my office, I'll show you where your quarry's gone to ground.'

I had already decided that his first name was probably Rupert. I said, 'Thank you, Captain Threlfall, but it would be far more useful to be actually on the spot.'

'I know, sir. As soon as the pilot's been briefed you can take off again.'

'Is he going to be permitted to fly with a defective radio?'

Threlfall wriggled. 'It's not my decision sir. But if my opinion's worth a light, I'd guess they're stretching a point, seeing as it's a security job.' He had, I noticed, gone a trifle pink at the edges.

There was a chair in his office and I sat in it. An Ordnance Survey map lay spread out on the desk.

'There, sir.' A forefinger stabbed at the map. 'Just south of Hartland Point. There's a group of farm buildings that are used as some kind of adventure centre.'

I leaned over and had a look. Were they still alive? I said, 'You don't know any more about this than I do, do you?'

'As I said, sir, we only knew that your flight was being diverted ten minutes ago.'

All the anger ran out of me together with any remaining

200

strength and trickled through the gaps in the floorboards. My back hurt, especially across my shoulders. Since being beaten I just want to slouch; sitting or standing up straight for any length of time is purgatory.

'Can I get you a cup of tea, sir?'

'That would be ruddy marvellous,' I told him.

He was back remarkably quickly as though someone had put the kettle on as soon as the Gazelle had touched down on the parade ground. I folded the map so he could put down a tray with a large mug of tea on it and an iced bun with two cherries on the top. Poor Threlfall looked a bit offended when I laughed.

'Sorry.' I said. 'I had a sudden suspicion that officers get buns with two cherries, other ranks, one.'

He laughed as well, slightly forced. 'Oh no, sir. They all had two cherries today – I think it's the chef's birthday.'

The phone rang. It was Daws for me.

'The Anti-terrorist Branch have gone in,' he said, getting straight to the point.

'You didn't want me there,' I said, finding myself gripping the receiver so tightly that my hand ached.

'Meadows and your wife weren't there,' he went on, as usual ignoring childish remarks. 'Nor was the woman Lara Vogel, two other men who had already escaped police custody, or Sergeant Wells of Special Branch.'

'What about Haywood?' I asked.

'That's the strange part. There's a man with a beard who fits Haywood's description except that he's not tall enough but insists that his name's Bates. John Bates. The police are running it through their records now – he's of no interest to us.'

'Then Haywood's in Bude.' I said. 'At the woman's house, White Lodge. The police really have been watching him all this time.'

'Major, sometimes I think you tend to forget that I have a head on my shoulders.'

'Sorry, sir.'

'The place is being surrounded but with extreme care. The last thing we want is the media to get hold of it. I don't intend – and neither do the police – to have a shooting match. Get there.'

201

He then asked that the call be transferred so that he could speak with the commanding officer. I let Threlfall do that and then he was called back and left the room. When he reappeared he was carrying a Lee Enfield 7.62mm 'Enforcer' sniper's rifle. Gingerly, I thought.

'Ammunition?' I asked, checking it quickly after wiping sticky fingers down the sides of my trousers.

He emptied his pockets on to the desk and I filled my own with the ten round magazines.

'Is there anything else you need, sir?'

'Only something to wrap this in and a visit to your john.'

Outside, a few minutes later, when quite a few people had mustered, someone said, 'Er – sir, you don't fancy a little target practice before you go?'

'I need it but there isn't time,' I replied, preparing to take my seat in the chopper.

'It's just that there's this bird –'

'Shut up, Henderson!' said someone else in a loud whisper.

'Which bird?' I enquired.

'Just a bloody seagull caught in a tree,' said the man who had shushed him. 'Sorry, sir. Someone'll take care of it later.'

'That's what you said yesterday,' mumbled another voice anonymously from the back.

I looked at Henderson and he responded by pointing high in the air above our heads. 'There's some fishing line caught round its legs, sir, and that's got snarled in a branch. If you could just. . . .' He tailed off miserably.

Shit, I thought. But even when your wife is in the hands of desperate men there is such a thing as. . . . What on earth *do* you call putting a bird out of its misery so that a young squaddy doesn't get the wrong idea about the army, and a corporal gets put in the picture likewise?

I needed height before I could even get a look at what I was supposed to do. The whole lot trooped after me when I set off over the granite setts and climbed on to an old gun emplacement, the cannon still in situ. Lying down on the warm stone I squinted through the telescopic sights. Perfect. I loaded the weapon and then took another look.

It was a Greater Black-backed Gull. Not a fully grown bird, its plumage was still the juvenile brown mottled on white. As I looked at it it turned its head and seemed to gaze right back down the sights at me with its fierce golden eyes. As if knowing what I was about to do it flapped wildly, its wingspan all of a yard, and then hung resignedly, obviously near exhaustion. I could see the nylon line entangled around both its pink legs. This had caught in a bunch of twigs on the lower side of a thin branch of the tree, one of several huge chestnuts that had their roots on the steep embankment below the curtain walls of the fort. How it had got caught was anyone's guess, gulls don't usually land in trees.

I heard at least two sighs of disappointment when I retraced my steps to roughly the same spot as I had been standing before. From here I could hardly see the bird at all, it was obscured by leaves growing on the lower side of the branch it was caught in. It is very difficult to shoot almost straight up into the air but I took aim and all the muscles and tendons in my shoulders made their presence felt. Worse, I was shaking. I asked Henderson to come and stand by me so I could brace myself against him. Then I homed on the target and fired.

The bird flapped again and a feather drifted down. There was an extremely polite silence. Then, slowly, the branch began to dip under the bird's weight. I fired again and branch, bird, a lot of leaves and all fell.

'Catch it!' I yelled at the bemused men around me.

A red-headed bloke did and ended up on the ground with the bird walloping him with its wings. Henderson threw his jacket over it and everyone applauded.

Perhaps this small success went to my head.

Chapter Twenty-Three

The helicopter pilot had orders to land me somewhere on the beach at Bude. Which brilliant military strategist had thought this one up I didn't know but the instruction certainly hadn't come from Daws. The Colonel is sufficiently of this world to know that in summer, beaches tend to be full of holiday-makers. Thus it proved to be; we were still about a mile out to sea and approaching the town when I turned to the pilot and gave him the thumbs down.

Further along the coast in both directions were low cliffs, the waves breaking almost right up to the base of them as it was high tide. I intimated that I would prefer to be dropped further inland behind a hill above the town.

The decision was made very quickly when we saw a secluded little valley surrounded on all sides, except for the western one where it sloped to the sea, by trees. The drop was achieved quickly too. We hedge-hopped up the valley, surprising only a few sheep, and I got out fast in the middle of a small field. The chopper thrashed away, heading back out to sea. I made for the trees, a Roman-nosed bay horse watching me over a hedge.

'Where the hell d'you think you're going?' demanded a strident female voice.

But the pathetic one-man invasion force couldn't answer her, throwing up miserably into the grass. When I was able I straightened up and saw that the horse was now wearing a head-collar, its owner peering at me through the hawthorn.

'I'm sorry if I'm trespassing,' I said, going closer.

'Did you just come out of that helicopter?'

I nodded but was then forced to turn my back on her and recommence being ill.

'I suppose you're on some kind of initiative test.'

I suddenly realised that that's exactly what it was.

'Come over and up to the house. There's some ginger wine somewhere. Nothing like ginger for honking.'

'There isn't time,' I told her, or rather gasped.

'Please yourself. But you'll have to make an exit this way unless you want to get hung up on barbed wire — there's no gate up by the road. Here, give me that thing.'

'It's a gun,' I said.

'I'm not stupid,' the lady stormed. 'Of course it's a gun. A rifle by the look of it.'

I looked for a thin part of the hedge but ended up having to struggle over it, catching my right foot in a loop of bramble and nearly finishing up falling under the hooves of the horse.

'You don't seem very fit,' said my new friend, giving me back the Enfield.

'Tin right leg,' I admitted. 'Falklands.'

It seemed to make a lot of difference. When I showed her my ID card she barely glanced at it and I was chivvied up to a mind-blowingly untidy house, the horse plodding at the rear. There I was pressed to take half a tumbler full of ginger wine, at least two fingers of whisky sloshed in it for good measure.

'I'm Sheila,' said she, raising a glass of neat whisky. 'Here's to the damnation of the enemies of the Crown.' She threw a newspaper at the horse, Senator, who had been left to his own devices and was chewing at the wooden frame of an open window. He desisted, ears laid back, and began to eat the rambler roses instead.

'Are you allowed to scare the natives and their livestock silly by roaring all over the countryside like this?' was the next question.

'Yes,' I said. I never flannel.

'Where are you heading for?'

'The town. A house called White Lodge.'

'Oh, *her*. The peroxide bitch. Don't tell me she's got military connections.'

I gulped down the rest of a quite extraordinary drink, floating horse hairs and all. 'No. She's holding my wife prisoner.'

'Oh, it's only a mock-up,' sighed Sheila. 'How boring. I'd lend you the car if it wasn't in dock having the clutch done. But then again, if you've a tin leg that might not be a lot of use, might it?'

'Your grasp of practicalities is unnerving,' I told her, preparing to depart. 'Thanks for the drink.'

Sheila gazed at the horse wistfully. 'Now if you could ride, I'd let you have Senator. He'd love that. Used to be a police horse. Go anywhere, do anything. He was retired a bit early because he started to shift football yobs out of the way with his teeth.'

It took about thirty seconds to bundle Senator's saddle and bridle on him and he stood like the Rock of Ages while I fumbled with noseband and throat latch. But as soon as I mounted, it became apparent that he was quite keen to be on the move.

'There, look a man's riding you,' Sheila was burbling, yanking the girths tight. 'Just like old times. Be a good boy and don't tip him off.' Then to me, 'It's nearly ten years since he really worked so don't expect miracles.'

'Ten years!' I exclaimed. 'How old is he then?'

'Twenty-five on January the 1st. It's the official birthday of all thoroughbreds whenever they're foaled.' Sheila clapped him on the rump but he didn't need any urging. 'Take him to Hunt's garage when you've finished with him. That's where the car is. They know he's mine. Take the next turning left!' she shrieked after us. And then, almost lost on the wind roaring in my ears, 'Shorten your reins, Major! For God's sake shorten your reins!'

Of necessity I had been riding with the reins in my left hand but now held the rifle in thumb and three fingers and spared the index finger of my right hand to help gather up seemingly feet of leather. This was just as well for we were already at a businesslike trot and Senator espied the left turning into what turned out to be a bridle-path and veered on to it. Over the next fifty yards I re-discovered, thankfully, that you don't need the same muscles for riding horses as for motor-bikes. By this time Senator had come to the conclusion that full tilt was a little rash at his age so condescended to being pulled back to a fast trot. Even so, with his long stride — and he was a big horse, about

206

seventeen hands – we were covering the ground at an amazing speed, faster than a man with two good legs could have run.

It was then that the sheer stupidity of what I was doing occurred to me. A few ounces of whisky had addled my brain. Here was I, expensively trained to be invisible in the countryside, all set to clatter into a difficult and tense situation with as much subtlety as the Charge of the Light Brigade. My whole body must have gone taut for the horse stopped.

'Walk on,' I said through my teeth and then went on to call myself all the unprintable names I could think of. But before I had run out of ideas I urged Senator on, haunted by memories of a baby trying to catch multi-coloured sunbeams and his mother, who should have been helping to arrange those wedding flowers instead of being at the mercy of terrorists.

I had no plan and it was impossible to make one until I had assessed the situation. Protocol demanded that I make myself known to the senior officer in charge of whatever the police had set up around White Lodge.

But to drink when fine accuracy with a firearm might be required of me . . . I deserved to be slung out of the service.

The horse's breathing became laboured as we ascended a slight rise so I slowed him down slightly. No point in killing him. At the top of the rise the ground levelled off and it was only necessary to give with the reins for him to break into what I believe the equitation books call a hand-gallop, fast and yet not flat out. It took all my sense of balance and strength of thigh muscles to stay with him for he obviously hated getting his hooves wet and jumped all the puddles.

About half a mile further on the bridle path joined a road. Parked across it was a police car. I had by this time wound Senator in somewhat but we weren't exactly hanging around when he made straight for it and came to a dead stop. I pushed myself back into the saddle.

'Sorry,' I said, when the constable standing by the car had been forced to remove his glasses because the horse had steamed them up by breathing on them.

'I'm afraid this road's closed, sir.'

I gave him my ID card. After polishing his glasses and putting them back on he perused it carefully and then sat in the car to report over his radio, now eyeing me and the badly disguised rifle dubiously. Someone must have reassured him for when he next turned to me he was smiling just a little.

'If you carry on down this road, Major, you'll come to houses. Go straight on and Inspector Tidy will meet you at the next road junction.'

The aforementioned officer hove into sight on foot, insignia of rank hidden under what was probably someone else's rather dirty mackintosh. Although not wearing his hat either he gave me a polite salute and if I'd had a hand free I'd have given him a proper one back instead of just raising the business end of the rifle and inclining my head slightly. These things *are* important.

'I'm afraid we heard shooting inside the house a few minutes ago,' said Tidy in a soft Cornish burr, adding, 'impossible to tell what actually happened — the walls are too high to see over.'

I shut my mind to the possibilities and said, 'I'm actually here with orders only to observe so don't worry about the rifle. I'm not about to start a war.'

Tidy smiled sadly. 'There's bound to be trouble before this is over, I'm thinking. With a man like O'Neill it couldn't be any other way.'

'D'you mind telling me what you intend doing?'

'We wait. They don't know we're here, of course. We've surrounded the place but there's no one visible on the streets. Just a few plain-clothes officers going from door to door warning folk to stay indoors. We've closed all the roads off to traffic but you'd never be able to tell from inside the house as the grounds extend to about six acres and it's only light local traffic.'

'Is that the house down there?' I asked, pointing to where I could see the top of a chimney pot over a high wall.

'That's it. The house is nearer the wall on this side than at any other point. It's like an island in a way with roads all the way round. If you're going in I suggest you try from the eastern side roughly diametrically opposite to where we're standing. There are some quite large trees round there to give cover. But watch for the dogs.'

'You're positively egging me on, Inspector,' I murmured.

'I was ordered to give you *carte blanche,*' Tidy responded stiffly.

And I was one who might mop up a few of the ungodly and lessen the chance of police casualties, I thought. But I couldn't be angry with the man. I said, 'If you've members of the tactical firearms unit with you, then you can find me a silenced pistol.' I gave him what Ingrid always tells me is a horrible smile.

Tidy asked another question while he came to a decision. 'In your opinion will he wait until tonight and then make a break for it?'

'No, O'Neill will have had time to think by then and will kill the hostages before attempting to get away without being spotted. He's the only one you have to worry about. Without him the others would give themselves up.'

'Perhaps the shooting we heard was the hostages being killed.'

'Again, I doubt it,' I said. 'Shooting draws attention so I would imagine the three they're holding would be knifed or strangled. My guess is that what you heard was either my colleague or yours endeavouring to bring things to a conclusion.'

Tidy went white. 'One of ours is in there?'

'Adam Wells of Special Branch. And my wife. Didn't they tell you?'

'Stay there,' Tidy said and walked quickly to an unmarked car parked with its engine ticking over. It accelerated away. I followed in the direction that it had gone. Slowly, needing time to think. Far more people being held hostage have been killed or injured by the rash actions of their rescuers than by their captors, abroad at any rate. I had no wish for a first in this country.

The business of the shooting was sickeningly worrying. The break for freedom — if that's what it had been — would have emanated from Wells, not Terry. Or at least, if it *had* been Terry he would only have taken advantage of a dead cert situation which would have resulted in the whole business being over by now. In that kind of judgement Terry excels.

Tidy came back almost immediately. He didn't get out of the car this time, just handed me what I had asked for through the window. I slipped it into one of the large pockets of my trousers.

'Choose your spot carefully,' Tidy said. 'Everyone on this side of the wall knows what you're doing so you won't be challenged. I advise you to ride all the way round first.' He paused. 'It was admirable tactics to borrow the horse. Still, that's how you chaps work isn't it? Surveying a district in great detail and noticing things like the riding school just round the corner. If those indoors hear hooves they won't think anything of it and you've a perfect method of getting into the trees that hang over the wall.'

I suppose the kind of fixed feeling in my jaw was a smile.

'Good luck,' said Tidy, and the car purred away.

Why did I have a sudden feeling that Daws was watching me, laughing like hell?

I concentrated on the wall. It was about ten feet in height and had three strands of wire on the top, the two lower ones barbed, the upper a thin copper strand that was either live or connected to alarms. I didn't intend to touch it to find out which. The surface of the wall had been rendered and was perfectly smooth, painted to match the house. There was not so much as finger or toe holds which could be used to climb to the top. Then of course one would reach the wires.

As Tidy had said, all the roads had been closed. But as this part of the town seemed to have been laid out in squares, White Lodge taking up a whole square, this only affected the houses immediately facing the perimeter wall and from what I could see people were being permitted to reach these on foot and under escort. Now and then a helmeted head bobbed up from behind a hedge as I went past as members of the tactical firearms unit monitored my movements. A van drew up and from what I could see of the inside of it was not selling fish as the lettering on the side led one to believe but was crammed with blokes. A little further on an Alsatian dog had its nose pressed to the rear window of an estate car ostensibly used by a domestic appliance engineer. I peered in and there was the dog's handler crouching uncomfortably on a pile of washing machine hoses.

Passing the large double entrance gates I was very careful. The rifle, now stripped of its cover, I concealed by holding it along Senator's neck on the side away from the house in case anyone could see down the drive. More helmets appeared above garden hedges and although I knew them to be 'friendlies', the short hairs on the back of my neck prickled.

It was very quiet, only the horse's large hooves ringing on the road. To be honest I had almost forgotten about him, he was merely a form of transport. It was uncanny really, as though he could read my mind, for when I got back to the point where I had met Tidy he stopped before I asked him to.

The Inspector had been perfectly correct, it was the trees on the far side or nothing. There was no other way in and no other trees big enough to take my weight. I squeezed Senator with my knees and he went off at a slow trot, quite placidly on a loose rein now, my *alter ego*.

I rode him right on to the pavement beneath the largest tree, an oak, and told him to stand. One large ear did swivel questioningly in my direction when I stood up on the saddle but I repeated the order and he froze. My six foot two plus his seventeen hands meant that when I straightened I could see over the top of the wall. I ducked down slightly and took hold of the branch I'd had my eye on. It was roughly on a level with my hips so all I would have to do was put one foot up and sort of lie along it. Then I saw that it only cleared the top wire by about four inches. I leaned down on it slightly and the gap was narrowed by half. Damn.

The problem was that I didn't know whether the wire carried several hundred volts intended to electrocute anyone touching it or would merely trigger alarms within the house. I wasn't particularly worried about the former for if I took my left foot off the saddle at the same moment that I put all my weight on the branch then the current couldn't earth. But once I was lying on the branch I wouldn't be able to see if the branch touched the wire or not. There would be no going back either; if I put my foot back on the saddle both horse and I might be fried.

'Walk on,' I said, preferring a *fait accompli* to death by frizzling.

The branch dipped and creaked and I hung on, praying hard. Then, slowly, and trying not to make any jerky movements, I began to edge up the branch. For all I knew alarm bells could be deafening everyone indoors. I couldn't hear anything but my own heart beating, all mixed up with the sound of Senator's hooves as he walked away.

211

I carried on wriggling up the branch on my stomach. Just like you see in the recruiting films. But they don't show you guys of forty with one and a half legs more scared of making a fool of themselves than anything else. That's the trouble when you have a reputation as an achiever, it gets harder and harder to live up to it.

I was right over the wire now but dared not even lean down to see if the branch was touching it. Every inch forward towards the trunk of the tree meant that I was less likely to set off an alarm which – and this was quite possible – might involve no more than a flashing red light on a small control panel.

There was about a yard to go before I reached the main stem of the tree when a Dobermann came sniffing along at the base of the wall. I held my breath for it was more intent on smells than guard duty. Hardly moving, I edged the pistol from my jacket. When the dog paused to lift a leg, I shot it.

No sound, just the muted pop of the gun. The animal lay where it had dropped, killed instantly, the last thing I wanted was stricken yelping. I had no regrets, I had met dogs like this before. Trained to maul and tear anyone who wanders into their domain, they are worse than vermin. The thought that a child might take a wrong turning. . . .

I reached the trunk, swung my legs down and sat quietly for a moment. I was shaking all over now. But not from nerves, just the same weakness that had made life difficult at Plymouth. The trees' thick canopy of leaves hid me completely here, both from the house and also from those over the road.

Senator was still nearby for I heard him sigh heavily. This brought another dog to investigate. It went up to the dead one and sniffed it, ran away for a short distance and then returned, obviously puzzled. Then it scented the air as if it had detected me. I waited until it had walked a little bit closer to the base of the tree, presenting a better target, and then killed it. How many more were there?

Getting down to the ground was no real problem. There was another branch below the one I was on and another just below that. I'd only have a drop of a few feet to the grass. I went down, keeping the trunk between me and the house. It was a longer fall than I'd thought but I took all my weight on my

212

good leg, dropped right to the ground and then rolled beneath the cover of a rhododendron bush.

Turning over on to my stomach I parted the leaves a little in order to see. There was no sound or movement within the house. Perhaps they *had* killed the hostages and were waiting until dark to escape. I pictured walking into a room and finding Ingrid lying in a pool of blood. Of never seeing again those wonderful green eyes spark like they do when she gets mad with me. Of her wandering around the house smiling a little when she's deeply involved with her writing, or crying when she's just killed off one of her characters.

I crawled. There were shrubs and bushes all along the base of the wall towards the rear of the house. The ground beneath them was dry and covered with a thick carpet of dead leaves so moving silently was impossible. I had to keep stopping to listen. Another small problem was that although my artificial right ankle is articulated it doesn't move to the extent of allowing me to point my foot. This is to make tripping less likely. Therefore my foot caught in everything.

A row of four garages jutted from the house. Parked in front of them was O'Neill's estate car, one of those Japanese imitation Range-Rovers that I had always when I had seen it previously assumed to be Haywood's, and an old MG sports car. The distance from the end of the garages to the bushes below the boundary wall was about fifty yards at the narrowest point. I would have to make this completely open crossing of the lawn in one dash.

I was almost at the point where I would have to take to the open grass when two Dobermanns rushed me from behind. They didn't bark, just set about tearing me to pieces. One had hold of my right ankle, the other sank its teeth into my left thigh. The pain from the latter was excruciating but I managed to twist round and put the muzzle of the gun to its head. The other dog had let go by this time, having found its teeth grating on metal, and I didn't give it time to find another target.

A dark patch of blood was oozing through the cloth of my trousers but there was nothing I could do about it. I picked up the rifle from where I had dropped it and crawled on. There was a suspicion in my mind that someone indoors knew there

213

was an intruder in the grounds and was letting out the dogs two at a time.

Only two windows appeared to have a good viewpoint of where I would be most exposed, one which was obviously at one side of the kitchen and another on the first floor. This had frosted glass so was almost certainly a bathroom. It was, however, slightly open, a pink curtain billowing out.

I shoved the handgun into the belt of my trousers. With the silencer fitted it was really too big for my pocket and in danger of falling out. Daws having made his orders clear over shoot-outs, I still wasn't sure why he had requested that the rifle be given to me.

I stood up with difficulty for I was still inside a large lilac bush. Just then someone slammed the window I was assuming to be a bathroom, trapping some of the curtain in it. Purely on impulse I looked through the rifle sights at the small square of glass. Detail leapt at me. I could see the outlines of two people through the glass and then one went from sight and there was a movement that might have been a door swinging closed. For a minute or so nothing happened and I had to lower the weapon as my battered shoulder muscles got the shakes again. Then the window was opened again, wide.

It was Terry. He looked about him, leaning out, and spotted what I would have immediately made for, a cluster of the usual drainpipes below and to his right. One large pipe went all the way up to the eaves of the house but was, I guessed, just out of easy reach. He climbed on to the window ledge and prepared to do a fingers and toes operation, utilising an overflow pipe and the top of the window frame. He was just about to swing across to the pipe when someone re-entered the bathroom.

The man, Pete, threw himself towards the window and grabbed for Terry's leg. He caught him round the ankle and then swung a gun in his direction. Terry endeavoured to free himself by yanking his leg away, still holding on to the top of the window frame. I heard Pete shout that he'd shoot.

I had raised the rifle and was squeezing the trigger before I'd stopped to think, another split second and Terry would have had to surrender and go back into the bathroom. As it was he didn't. He fell off the window ledge and crashed to the ground. For I had missed Pete completely and hit Terry instead.

Chapter Twenty-Four

It was probably only the fact that I've spent half my life in the army that prevented me from going totally out of my head. Training alone made me stay where I was, quite still. Through the rifle sights I could see Pete aiming his gun in my direction, trying to locate where the shot had come from. He fired and just above my head some leaves were smashed into fragments, showering me. All at once I felt very calm, sighted him carefully and he toppled forward across the window ledge, his gun falling to the gravel below. Then I was running.

When the adrenalin's pumping I don't actually notice my man-made leg and had arrived in the lee of the end garage wall without being aware of having made the journey. I saw movement within the kitchen and threw myself back out of sight. O'Neill's car stood between where I was and the back door and I would be able to use it as cover for the final approach.

I did not imagine for one moment that O'Neill would come out. He called to me, his voice very clear and close by.

'I saw you, Gillard. Let's get one thing straight. I've got your wife with me here and if you don't do exactly as you're told, she dies.'

He was, at a guess, shouting from the back door.

'Throw down that rifle where I can see it. Right now ... I'll count to five.'

I threw it on to the grass. It wasn't an awful lot of use to me now anyway.

'Now any other weapons you might have.'

I pulled the handgun from my belt and tucked it back but

215

behind me, actually stuffing it into my underpants. 'That's all,' I called.

'What about that knife?'

'In the trousers of my leathers at home,' I told him. I can be very plausible.

'OK. Now walk out from where you are slowly and with your hands in the air.'

I went out and for one reason only.

They both left the house slowly, Ingrid in front, O'Neill prodding her forward with a Heckler and Koch sub-machine gun. Ingrid was avoiding my eye. She looked ghastly, in a state of deep shock and with her face bruised. O'Neill had probably told her about Terry being shot and who had done it.

The very last thing I wanted was for O'Neill to make a run for it in his car with Ingrid at his side. The men of the tactical firearms unit are fine shots, but even if she wasn't hit by accident the car was likely to crash after O'Neill had been filled full of lead. All this was buzzing through my mind when a man I hadn't seen before came round the corner of the house. Someone on Lara's staff presumably, he looked like a fairly mindless bruiser. He was carrying some kind of handgun, a Beretta by the look of it.

O'Neill fired a short burst into the ground at my feet. 'Your pockets are full,' he said when the echoes had died away.

'Ammunition,' I informed him.

'Let's have it.'

I lowered my arms slowly and threw the magazines one at a time on the grass. All eyes were on me, no one paying any attention to Terry who seemed mysteriously to have come back to life and was inching in the direction of Pete's gun.

'There's some more in my back pocket,' I said.

'Then put it with the rest,' O'Neill said, dangerously polite. 'I'm not fool enough to order Wilson to do it so you can grab him and use him for a shield.'

A pistol against a sub-machine gun is not my favourite odds but there was no choice. Without looking I knew that Terry had hold of the gun. He would have to take out Wilson as Ingrid was right in the line of fire between him and O'Neill. But I had overlooked the possibility of Ingrid contributing to the situation.

She dropped to the ground at the moment that I jumped to one side, pulled out the pistol and fired two-handed. O'Neill pitched forward, fell on the weapon he was holding and it fired several times into the gravelled drive. There were several more shots in quick succession, a couple near me as I rolled over on to my right shoulder and then up on to one knee. After this a slamming pain in my chest and suddenly all I could see was a lot of blue sky.

Three more shots in quick succession but I hardly noticed them, trying to breathe, what air there was in my lungs whistling out through my clenched teeth with the most peculiar sound. I could picture my chest filling with blood, and drowning in it. There was a roaring sound in my ears but I succeeded in rolling over and tried to cough. I retched instead with the nausea of the pain. If this was death, I thought, let it be quick.

But it wasn't death, not yet anyway. When I got to my feet everything seemed to be functioning normally. And while the action's happening you can ignore pain.

Terry was still lying on the ground but had Pete's gun in both hands and had obviously just shot the man Wilson several times for he was dying somewhat messily. I got up and checked but he was beyond help. After this everything became slightly surreal. Des burst out of the back door, was tripped by Terry and fell heavily. Seconds later Adam Wells hopped out after him on one leg, bleeding from the other, and hit Des over the head with what turned out to be a rolling pin. Then Wells collapsed.

Terry said, 'Excuse me, officer, do you have a whistle one might blow?'

The next few minutes were confused. I put my arms around Ingrid and kissed her and she clung on to me tightly. We were both too dead tired to feel any real emotion. Then we went to Terry and helped him up. He had a flesh wound in his arm and a badly sprained ankle. I just didn't know what to say to him, a state of affairs not helped by the fact that he seemed to be highly upset.

'I got the shakes, Chief,' he gasped. 'The first few shots went wide because I was shaking like a leaf. Where the hell did I hit you?'

'Are you?' Ingrid cried, perking up considerably, 'I was so busy getting out of the way that. . . .' She grabbed me and took a look. 'Oh God, you're bleeding.' My shirt was yanked out before I could stop her. 'Scored your ribs,' she announced. 'Right where you were shot last year in Canada.'

'Sorry, sir,' said Terry in a whisper.

'Terry,' I began. 'It was me who –'

'Oh no,' he interrupted. 'I heard you fire and the bullet hit the window frame near his head. I didn't know it was you of course and decided to bale out fast. At the same moment he fired and hit me. If I hadn't dropped down I'd be dead.'

The police were all over the house by this time. They found Lara dead in the hall and the real Alex Haywood hiding in the loft. The trouble had erupted just before the hostages had made a break for freedom. Lara had been furious with O'Neill for following her to the house and endangering her own safety. She had completely lost her head and had fired a shot at him. He'd killed her. Wells had then tried to hit him over the head with a chair but O'Neill had seen the movement behind him and turned to shoot Wells in the leg. Ingrid and Terry had sat tight at this moment, awaiting a chance. A while later, Terry had said that he wanted to use the bathroom, hoping that O'Neill would accompany him. But O'Neill sent Pete instead.

This account emerged when we all went into Lara's living room and sat down, most of us bleeding gently but persistently into the olive green velvet chairs. I had an elbow pressed to my ribs by this time and the blood had soaked right through the material of my shirt to the skin of my arm. Inspector Tidy came in to organise things and I got the impression he'd never seen so many walking wounded in his entire career. It was like one of those mock-ups the emergency services do of train crashes.

Ingrid said, 'I've a feeling that his case wasn't in D12's field of reference at all. That woman was just a cruel little crook, not bright enough to be recruited for espionage.'

'Daws has the gen on her,' I replied, feeling more than a little other-worldly from loss of blood what with the dog bite as well. 'But I tend to agree with you and at the moment it doesn't make a lot of sense.'

'The theory is that it was a rehearsal,' Adam Wells said from a few feet away where a constable was giving him first aid while

218

he waited for an ambulance. 'Sorry, I didn't mean to snoop on your conversation.'

'Thought you were out for the count with your eyes closed,' I told him. 'You mean a sort of practice run for one of those anarchist cum terrorist factions in Europe?'

Wells nodded weakly. 'Wrecking a democratic system. Taking out picked intellectuals. Penetrating a social structure with petty criminals. That kind of thing. An experiment to see if certain ideas would work. All aimed towards the success of some future revolution. It's only a theory. It was such a crazy theory that not a lot was said about it. It might still be crazy and with not a grain of truth. Perhaps we'll never know.'

'Nothing run by foreign governments then,' Terry murmured. 'Just screaming nutters.'

'Not necessarily,' I demurred. 'Nutters, I mean. If you think about it, it's rather a good scheme. They got away with quite a few killings before the law caught up with them.'

I had had my arm around Ingrid and she had been leaning against me in a kind of exhausted daze. But now she sat up. 'Am I seeing things or *is* there a horse in the garden eating the standard roses?'

'It's Senator,' I told her without looking. 'It's all right . . . he's with the Force.'

Just then, several ambulances arrived. Adam Wells was loaded into one of them and I unashamedly pulled rank on Terry to get him in it too so that his arm could be properly dressed and his ankle looked at. Given half a chance he'd have patched himself up with plasters and gone home.

O'Neill was dead. I regretted this for I hadn't meant to kill him. The bullet I had intended only to disable the arm holding the sub-machine gun had also entered his chest. So now a lot of questions would never be answered.

All this time Alex Haywood had been sitting huddled in a chair, alternately arguing with the constable watching over him or crying, screwing in his hands a large striped handkerchief. It would have been a waste of time questioning him right then as my anger would have got the better of me. It would take a few days' breathing space for me to be able to push to the back of my mind a picture of him sitting at home knowing that murder and mayhem were being perpetrated without trying to get a message past his guards and to the police. Right at the beginning, I guessed, when he had given the names of those against whom he held a grudge, his hatred had made him temporarily insane.

'Do you think you could drive a car?' I asked Ingrid in a whisper.

'I'm not sure,' she said. 'After a cup of tea perhaps.' Then she saw through my scheme. 'Patrick, you are going to hospital to have that wound dressed.'

'They'll keep us both in,' I told her. 'For observation and all that crap.'

'Right now I can't think of anything I'd like better,' she retorted. 'A bath, clean sheets and about a month's sleep.'

'But you can do all that at home,' I wheedled.

'Patrick. . . .' The green eyes sparked dangerously.

'I promise I'll go straight up to John Murray.' Murray was our local GP and lived only a matter of yards from the top of our drive.

She began to waver slightly.

'We'll go out for dinner,' I continued. 'And you can phone Elspeth, and she and Dad will drive down with Dawn and Justin when we've had a few days rest.'

But it was Tidy who took us home and we had, needless to say, forgotten all about Amanda Peterson. She was actually taking tea with Murray's wife, Lynne, the two ladies having met in the village post office two days previously and Lynne, typically, having taken her under her wing. Amanda swooped, aghast, on Ingrid and set about ministering to her every need while Lynne, tight-lipped, having intimated that her husband was a doctor not a vet for I needed shooting for travelling with such a wound, drove me to Stonehouse Hospital in Plymouth.

Chapter Twenty-Five

Someone was playing the guitar.

I got out of bed, put my dressing gown on and went to the top of the stairs. What time was it? Come to that, ye gods, what *day?*

Downstairs a soft arpeggio was plucked and then a chord and then silence, the music shivering into stillness. I sat on the top stair. I couldn't go down. It was Patrick playing the guitar.

An air and variations by Bach broke into the silence and I closed my eyes in an effort to stem the tears, and failed. I felt that I had been transported back in time. Perhaps six or seven years ago, during the ten years of our first marriage, I had sat and watched him learning to play. And in the course of that last dreadful row before we split up, I had thrown the instrument from the top of the stairs to the bottom and smashed it. From that day to this I had never seen him with a guitar in his hands and scalding shame poured over me every time I thought about it.

But here were not the fumblings and wrong notes of one seeking to carry on where he had been forced to desist. The playing was effortless and, to my ears, quite perfect. The air and variations concluded he played a scale, slowly, but cutting short the octave jarringly on a seventh, jabbing the string so that it buzzed.

Silence.

'I can see your shadow on the wall,' said he.

I went down the tiny winding staircase that led directly into the living room. But not right into the room. I sat on the bottom step and gazed at him.

'How long have you had the guitar?' I enquired lightly.

'From the morning after you busted the other. I keep it at the flat or the office.'

'It looks rather a good one,' I commented, observing mother-of-pearl inlay.

'A couple of hundred quid. It's worth a good bit more now.' He played the final note of his scale and smiled at me craftily. 'I think I needed to cheer myself up when I bought it.'

'Was there any insurance to come on the first one?' I felt that I had to know, I had been promising myself that I'd replace it one day.

He laughed. Yes, laughed. 'Bloody hell, no. I gave a bloke called Fred a tenner for it. I got it to learn on.'

'So all this time. ...' I couldn't go on for he was still laughing gently. Then I found my tongue. 'For all this time you've let me carry on thinking that I'd hurt you by destroying the music in your life.'

'I'm a real bastard, aren't I?' he murmured. 'No, perhaps not entirely. To be honest, I thought my strummings drove you up the wall.' His fingers drifted over the strings and melody ghosted into the room. Then he laid the instrument to one side. 'You look a lot better, Mrs G.'

I sat on the settee by his side. 'So do you. That tells me that I've been asleep a lot longer than I thought.'

Patrick gathered me in his long arms. 'Four days on and off. Murray made sure you got the rest you needed. Amanda Peterson insisted on looking after you for the first one while I was away having two units of someone's blood pumped into me and so forth. Larry's bringing Elspeth and Justin down tomorrow. Dad couldn't make it as he's Chairman at some Synod committee meeting.'

I said, 'Yes, I can remember Amanda being there and helping me drink mugs of soup. And I've a vague recollection of you giving me some of that yucky milky stuff they throw down the throats of invalids.'

'Never overestimate a husband's powers,' Patrick said sternly, grinning. 'I had to drink a bucket of the stuff myself before I had the energy to climb the stairs.'

Even his craziest statements always have a pinch of truth in them. 'What will Haywood be charged with?' I asked.

222

'Daws wouldn't say much on the phone,' Patrick replied. 'Don't worry about it. All he would tell me was that he was thinking of re-structuring the entire department. Perhaps in a day or so I'll feel a bit more interested.'

'Play the guitar,' I whispered.

A week later Daws came to us. It was the first time he had been to the cottage and it seemed to me that he was a little surprised at how small it was. He too had to duck as he stepped in to the living room to avoid hitting his head on a low beam. Any disapproval of us he might be harbouring did not, apparently, extend to Justin for a Harrods' carrier bag yielded a superb, plushy teddy bear. It was far too splendid to be given straight away to an infant who was still endeavouring to cram every object into his mouth. I sat it where he could see it from his playpen and gave him a rusk to chew on, praying that it would keep him reasonably quiet.

We had tea, cakes from the village shop, and still the Colonel talked about cricket, the impossibility of buying pyjamas that fitted, and a cousin of his who had been bitten by a rabid dog in China. By this time Patrick was frowning as though he had a monumental headache.

'Unpleasant fella, that Haywood,' Daws observed, accepting a second cup of tea and with scarcely a breath from commenting on Yorkshire's appalling bowling. 'There's no need for you to bother yourself with questioning him, Major. The entire story only took up a page and a half of the stenographer's notebook.'

'What of the woman — Lara Vogel?' Patrick prompted.

'Used to be part of a bunch of terrorists akin to the Red Brigade,' Daws said. 'She opted out and started up her own — mostly to make money. No political motives as far as Haywood knows. My opinion is that she had no politics at all, just hatred of stability and other people being happy. Absolutely off her head, if you ask me, the two of them made a good pair.'

'Where did he meet her?' I asked.

'In Germany. Haywood was over there for some symposium or other and went to a party with the couple he was staying with. He met Vogel and one must suppose they aired their

223

various pet hatreds. Haywood won't say a lot about that and I'm not sure that it matters. What I did lean on him over − I threatened to turn him over to you, Major, as a matter of fact − was exactly what they'd got up to next. He cracked up a bit, snivelled that she'd made him give her all the information and then locked him up in his own house when he said he didn't want her to go ahead with revenge.'

Patrick said, 'Wells intimated that someone on his side of things reckoned it was a rehearsal.'

'A dress rehearsal,' Daws said with a grim smile. 'I suppose that's not a bad term for it. Vogel already had criminal connections, both here and on the Continent, and it appears she wanted to put a few of her ideas to the test and make a lot of money on the side. She'd already masterminded a couple of big robberies in Germany. Haywood seems to think that through contacts she approached the security services of two or three countries behind the Iron Curtain for backing but was turned down flat by all of them. Thank God for *glasnost*.'

'D'you reckon she was hoping for help from subversives in this country?' Patrick asked.

'No doubt. Militants, Trotskyites − anyone, I suppose, who wants to see the end of democracy. Perhaps when no help was forthcoming from the Eastern Bloc she decided to turn her little organization into almost purely a criminal thing with the occasional project to further her own ideals.'

I said, 'I take it it was her idea to have a Haywood lookalike in the gang.'

'As insurance for this job,' Daws replied. 'That was when Haywood realized which way the wind was blowing. Wilson and another man watched him night and day, and once when he tried to escape over the wall they beat him up. Being a damn coward, he didn't try again.'

'And it was the lookalike who pushed Haywood's car over Beachy Head, one presumes,' Patrick mused. 'Vogel wanted him pictured in the press as a rat, living with another woman, then exposed as a weakling when he couldn't go through with the fake suicide. He would have been the scapegoat for all the killings while she sold her house and moved quietly away. How were they going to get rid of him, I wonder?'

'Haywood doesn't know,' Daws said. 'If, as Meadows

guessed, most of the gang were to be liquidated at the so-called adventure centre that they used as a front, and where they stored all the bikes when they weren't on the road, then it is likely that he would have been taken there either dead or alive and it would have been made to look as though he'd been killed in some kind of fight. The good Lord knows – we never will.'

'He must have loved Lara,' I said, half to myself. 'In the early days. There's nothing quite like meeting someone with whom you feel utterly in harmony. It goes to your head – makes you utterly irrational.'

Both men looked at me kindly and I knew they were thinking I was back in my romantic fiction. But one good thing had come of the past few days that certainly wasn't fiction – a reconciliation between Patrick and Larry. Elspeth must have had a lot to do with it, of course, but there was nothing phoney in the way Larry had carried in Justin then held out his hand to his brother in a token of peace. Seeing them together, the family likeness between baby and uncle had shaken Patrick not a little. How long it would last was another matter.

The Colonel was getting up to go, saying he had a train to catch, when Patrick said, 'What changes have you in mind, sir? For the department.'

'Oh,' said Daws. 'I'm resigning.'

'But D12 will cease to exist without you!' I protested.

He picked up his briefcase. 'Thought of going private. No nannying from on high and bleatings about the expense. Hire out experts and charge fees commensurate with what wants doing and who's doing the asking. It means I won't have to waste most of my time doing bloody stupid things and filling in bloody stupid forms.'

Patrick was struck dumb for the second time in two years.

'I can choose the jobs I want,' Daws continued with relish. 'If necessary work with the police in areas not open to them and when it needs insider knowledge. But not tilting at windmills,' he went on, wagging an admonitory finger at Patrick. 'None of your knight errantry and chasing after silly girls being chewed by dragons or whatever.'

'I don't believe I said a word, sir,' said Patrick faintly.

Daws moved to the door. 'Well, I can't give you too long to make up your mind whether to join me. Say, a week. There'll

be a lot more consultancy and considerably less action. ...
I've two jobs lined up already. Perhaps your good lady can
think up a name,' he concluded as if I wasn't sitting not two
yards from him.

I cleared my throat. 'I take it there'll be a number of
departments each with its own field of operations.'

'That's right,' he agreed.

'Then have twelve and call it D12 Security.'

He stared at me mutely for a moment or too, searchingly,
pondering on whether I might be pulling his leg, and then said,
'It's got a good ring ... businesslike. I'll think about it.'

He met Alyssa and Dawn — just back from a shopping
expedition to Plymouth — by the front door and there was an
exchange of pleasantries. Alyssa bounced in; new dress, shoes,
and lots of plastic jewellery to match, Deidre Crocker having
persuaded the Goldbergs to part with a generous monthly
allowance for their daughter's wellbeing — it was that or the
whole story of her neglect being released to the Press. She
hugged us both and behind her back Dawn gave a thumbs-up
sign.

Alyssa was coming along splendidly. A few days with
Elspeth and John had had a lot to do with it, and there had been
a very long telephone conversation between Elspeth and
myself. So I didn't mind when Alyssa kissed Patrick goodnight
or affectionately ruffled his hair at other times for she now had
a very clear idea that we were, in a way, her surrogate parents.

When Patrick arrived back from a trip to London several days
after this and had sunk a tin of beer with hardly a pause, he
said, 'It's all off. They've persuaded Daws to stay on.'

I wasn't sure whether I was pleased or sorry so said nothing
and waited for him to continue.

'He's screwed them down for everything he wanted,'
Patrick went on, throwing himself into an armchair. 'More
money for the department, more staff to do the dogsbody
jobs, another secretary for himself plus a personal assistant.
Better than all that, he's now accountable to the Prime
Minister's office only so there'll be just them breathing down
his neck in future.'

'Where does that leave us?' I enquired.

He chuckled. 'Nowhere really. Terry's come out of it very well and has been given a substantial rise. He deserves it, too. I thought he did a good job. Taking on new staff means I'll probably have to share an office with him — there's not enough space as it is.'

'That's not an ideal situation, is it?' I said warily.

Patrick shrugged and then, with a look of haunted guilt that I shall always remember, said, 'It was the only way I could get back on that bike and forget my fear ... allow myself to be eaten up with jealousy about you and Terry together. I thought of nothing else and it kept me going. I've apologised to him for going right over the top when we did meet up, but so far not to you.'

'None necessary,' I said. 'You thought we'd been to bed together.'

The camera never lies,' he observed with a grimace. 'What did the picture show? What did I see? Not a lot. I couldn't even be sure that it wasn't another couple whom Terry had asked to dinner.'

'It doesn't matter now,' I told him. 'The good that came of it was that you used what you thought you saw to make you angry enough to overcome your fear. You know what your father says — evil is goodness perverted and can create nothing of its own. You turned the evil back on itself.'

'Women's logic is utterly mindblowing,' Patrick said. 'Female novelist's ditto is not of this galaxy.' Then he roared with laughter.